Double Trouble

DOUBLE TROUBLE

All About Doubles

Sally Horton

faber and faber

LONDON · BOSTON

First published in 1993
by Faber and Faber Limited
3 Queen Square London WC1N 3AU

Photoset by Parker Typesetting Service, Leicester
Printed in England by Clays Ltd, St Ives plc

A CIP record for this book is available from the British
Library

ISBN 0-571-16859-0

Contents

Introduction

Once upon a time, when the world and the game of bridge were young, it was possible to double the stakes when you thought the opponents were not going to make their contract. If they were sufficiently confident, they could even double the stakes yet again with a call of redouble.

As the game developed it was found that, particularly at low levels, the opportunities to double the opponents profitably were few and far between, and it was thought that a better meaning might be ascribed to the call of *double* in certain situations. The first artificial double to be introduced was the simple take-out double of a one-level opening – your right-hand opponent opens the bidding with one of a suit and you double, not because you think he is going down but, on the contrary, because you wish your partner to bid his longest suit.

This was the beginning but, if our bridge ancestors knew what they were going to start, it is quite possible that they would have changed their minds about introducing the simple take-out double in the first place! In the hectic scramble of tournament bridge, it is quite rare that the meaning of the call of 'double' expresses an opinion about the success of an opponent's contract.

In any area of bidding the actual meaning of a bid is less important than that both sides of the partnership agree on its meaning. This is also true with doubles. In these pages I hope to explain the occasions when it is sensible for aspiring partnerships to have precise agreements about the nature of certain sequences of bids. In an area where there are countless possible sequences that might occur, it is better to develop some partnership rules that will cover all similar situations rather than try to remember all possible sequences parrot fashion. Even if a little efficiency is lost along the way, this will be more than compensated for by ease of memory and confidence at the table.

If a double is for take-out, when should you double and when should you bid a suit? What does it mean to double and then bid a suit? What does it mean to fail to make a take-out double on the first round of the bidding but double on the second round? When is a double still for penalty? These are just a few of the questions I have tackled.

Some of the answers are not black and white; much depends on the basic system structure and personal preference. There is often no 'right' answer. I have tried to present a comprehensive scheme which is consistent wherever possible.

In the area of doubles there is much scope for serious disaster – you make what you think is a clear penalty double and partner thinks it is for take-out, and instead of collecting 500 you perhaps lose 500; or you make what you think is a clear take-out double but partner thinks it is for penalty and instead of bidding your making contract you lose 670.

Even experts have these kinds of disaster on occasion. By the time you and your partner have reached the end of this book the danger of your having them will have receded considerably.

The Simple One-level Take-out Double

The simple one-level take-out double – i.e. our right-hand opponent opens a natural one-of-a-suit and we double – is one of the most basic conventions in the game. It is so basic that it is assumed that everyone plays it, and everyone does. In a simple rubber bridge game when we sit down with an unfamiliar partner, we will discuss our range of INT opening, our defence to three-level openings and whether or not we play Stayman and Blackwood, but it would be rare even to mention that we played a double of a one-level opening as take-out.

It is only in the beginners' arena where there is any question about this, but it is not a straightforward concept. The first and foremost use of 'double' is to double the stakes – i.e. to suggest that the opponents have overreached themselves and will not make the contract they have arrived in. Once a beginner has grasped this, it is not so easy to tell him that this does not apply directly over a one-of-a-suit opening. Indeed, my seven-year-old son was learning bridge on a cruise. One lesson they had been taught was that if their partner opened one heart and the next hand overcalled two diamonds, for example, they should not bid three diamonds if they held length in the suit. They were told that they should double instead, because three diamonds had quite a different meaning. The following day I arrived in the playing room to find my son involved in an unsupervised practice game with three other complete beginners. He was playing in a contract of two hearts. I asked what the bidding had been and was told: 'The hand on my right opened one heart and I had hearts as well so I doubled and everyone passed. But we didn't know what happened next. It seemed that I had made the final bid in the auction and so I should be declarer and presumably, because I had doubled one heart, that meant I should play in two hearts.'

Requirements for a take-out double

What, then, is the meaning of a double of our right-hand opponent's opening bid of one of a suit?
A double of an opening bid of one of a suit asks partner to bid his longest suit and to show some sign of strength if he has a good hand. The most common hand-type which might wish to contest an auction in this way is one with no good suit of its own.

How many points do I need to make a take-out double?
A take-out double shows approximately opening-bid values – a minimum of about 12 or 13 HCP but, as with an opening bid, if we have good distribution we do not need quite so many high cards.

What distribution do I need to make a minimum take-out double?
The perfect distribution would be 4–4–4–1 with a singleton in the suit opened. This is because then we would know that, if partner's best suit was four cards in length, our side would have an eight–card trump fit.

But we are not always dealt the perfect hand and, if we were to wait for it, we would find the take-out double to be of such infrequent use that it would hardly be worth playing. Opinions differ about what distributions are acceptable.

The prevailing British expert idea is that a minimum take-out double – i.e. a hand on which it is not intended to bid again unless partner forces us – should:

- contain at most a doubleton in the opponent's suit (this rule can be broken occasionally to allow three small cards if the rest of the hand is sufficiently strong to warrant a bid – if, say, 15 or so HCP are held and there is no alternative);
- contain at least three cards in all the other suits;
- also deny holding a five-card major that could have been bid at the one level.

Using this definition, the following hands would all be acceptable minimum take-out doubles of a one-heart opening:

(a) ♠ A 5 4 3 (b) ♠ K 8 7 4 (c) ♠ K 7 6
    ♡ 7 6   ♡ 8   ♡ J 8
    ◇ Q 7 5   ◇ A 7 6 2   ◇ A K 7 5
    ♣ A Q 4 2   ♣ K 10 5 4   ♣ K 10 6 4

(d) ♠ A 6 4   (e) ♠ Q 5 4 2
    ♡ 5   ♡ 7 6 2
    ◇ Q J 6 5 2 ◇ A K 4
    ♣ A Q 6 4   ♣ A Q 7

Note that hand (b), which has perfect distribution, has only 10 HCP, whereas hand (e), which is breaking the rules, has compensating extra values. In a perfect world, we should like to hold four spades for a take-out double of one heart. This is because, if the auction becomes competitive, partner is more likely to bid spades than any other suit as it is the only suit he can bid without raising the level. If four spades are not held, then there should be some compensation. Notice that hand (a), which holds four spades, has only 12 HCP, but hand (c), which has only three spades, has 14 HCP. Hand (d) has 13 HCP and only three spades, but has the extra advantage of a singleton heart.

Different partnerships specify different rules for their take-out doubles and many put a stronger emphasis on holding four cards in the other major. These players may well pass on hand (c), overcall two diamonds on hand (d) and double with hand (e) even if one of the queens were removed.

What if I have a five-card suit in a minor, as well as shortage in the suit opened? Is it better to bid my suit or double?

If the choice lies between a take-out double and a two-level overcall in a minor, modern expert opinion favours a take-out double provided at least three cards are held in the other unbid suits. One of the bidding panels in a British magazine posed the following two problems:

1 Love All. IMPs.

West	North	East	South
			1♠

West holds:

♠ A 5   ♡ Q 6 4   ◇ Q 7 2   ♣ A K 10 6 2

2 East/West Game. Pairs.

West	North	East	South
			1♡
?			

West holds:

♠ Q 3 2   ♡ —   ◇ A 7 6 5 3   ♣ A Q 8 7 3

On Problem 1, fifteen experts chose to double, while five preferred two clubs and two preferred one no-trump. On Problem 2, all but one of the panel chose to double rather than overcall in a minor.

Does it make any difference if the opening bid was in a minor?

When the opening bid is one of a minor, the standard British expert style remains unchanged. However, those players who put their emphasis on the majors would tend to double if they held both majors, regardless of their holding in the other minor. This is certainly a reasonable alternative style, but it must be borne in mind when choosing the response to partner's double.

I have heard people refer to Italian-style doubles, what does this mean?
The above was not the style used by the most successful bridge team of all time, the Italian Open team, who won the world championship ten times in succession back in the 1950s and 1960s. Their style was to double on nearly any hand with opening bid values that did not have too many of them in the opponents' suit and had no alternative action. They would undoubtedly have doubled on all the hands given above but they would also have doubled a one-heart opening bid with the following:

(f) ♠ A 5 4   (g) ♠ K 7 6 3   (h) ♠ K J 6 4
     ♡ 7 6 2   ♡ Q 7 5   ♡ Q 4
     ◇ A Q 6 4   ◇ K 7   ◇ A 8 7 4 3
     ♣ Q J 7   ♣ A J 8 5   ♣ K 7

What are the advantages and disadvantages of this style of double?
There are advantages and disadvantages to this style, which is still prevalent in mainland Europe. The main advantage is that whenever they have opening bid values (except with length in the opponents' suit) they take action on the first round. Therefore, if they take action on a later round of bidding, partner knows that they will not have the values for an opening bid. The main disadvantage of the Italian method seems to be that they have to do some good guessing about, first, how high to bid as responder when they cannot be sure that partner has a fit, and second, what to do on hand (h) above when they double one heart and partner responds two clubs. Should they pass or 'correct' to two diamonds (assuming their methods allow them to do so without overstating their values)?

Why did this style work so well for the Italians?
This style certainly did work for the Italians and the reason it worked so well has much to do with the well-known principle, 'When the opponents have a good fit, so do we.' Thus, if the

bidding proceeds 1♡ – Dble – 4♡, then the opponents obviously have a good heart fit and we will have a good fit as well. This means that the Italians did not need to worry too much about bidding and finding that partner did not have a fit with them; they just closed their eyes, bid and prayed, and their boldness was usually rewarded. Conversely, if the bidding simply proceeded 1♡ – Dble – Pass, they were inclined to underbid; the Italians would routinely respond, say, two clubs with 10 or 11 HCP and find that they did not have much of a fit but that they could make two clubs on sheer high cards. Occasionally they would miss game, but one does not make game very often without a fit when the opponents have opened the bidding. People said that they were lucky, but they were consistently lucky for a great number of years. What they did was to let the opponents tell them whether they had a fit or not, and it worked very well.

We have been talking about minimum doubles. Can my distribution be different if I have a better hand?

So far we have assumed that, having taken his initial action, the doubler does not intend to bid again. If the hand is strong enough to warrant another bid, then many of the rules stated above do not apply. The commonly played range of HCP for a simple overcall is about 9 to 16 and partner will bid on that assumption. It follows, then, that if we are dealt a stronger hand we have to do something different – i.e. we double first and then bid our suit to show a hand too good to overcall immediately. Similarly, the normal range for a 1NT overcall is somewhere between 15 and 18 HCP. If we are stronger than that, we double first and bid no-trumps on the next round.

The following are all hands which would be defined in the style mentioned above as 'too good to overcall' (over a one-heart opening bid):

(i) ♠ K J 5   (j) ♠ A K 5 4 3   (k) ♠ A K J 10 5 4
    ♡ A Q 6   ♡ 7   ♡ A 5 3
    ◇ K Q 6 3   ◇ A Q 7 5   ◇ A Q 6
    ♣ A J 10   ♣ A J 7   ♣ 5

(l) ♠ 6 4
    ♡ A 7
    ◇ A K 6
    ♣ A Q J 10 5 4

On hand (i) we would rebid in the lowest level of no-trumps, whatever partner responded. On hands (j) and (k) we would plan to rebid spades and on hand (l) we would rebid clubs.

Might I not find it difficult to show my suit if the opponents do more bidding?

In the 'good old days', the above was the common practice. However, it was found to be not always easy to express the hand later. If the opponents were kind enough to keep quiet, there were no problems, but these days there is much greater emphasis on active obstructive bidding. On hand (i), it is safe enough to double, intending to rebid no-trumps, because we have so many high-card points and such a balanced hand that it is unlikely that the opponents will get in our way. However, consider hands (j) and (k). If the opponents keep quiet and partner responds, say, two clubs to our take-out double, we would rebid two spades with either hand, trusting partner to bid again whenever he has a few values. After his rebid, we would bid three diamonds on hand (j) and three spades on hand (k) and would stand every chance of arriving in the right contract. However, suppose our unkind left-hand opponent raises to four hearts over the double. Let us first take the case where this is passed back to us, if we bid four spades now on both hands (j) and (k), what is poor partner supposed to do if he holds, say:

(m) ♠ 6 2
♡ 4 2
♢ K 3 2
♣ Q 9 8 6 3 2

If we hold hand (j), he should convert to five clubs, which is virtually laydown, whereas four spades may be in extreme difficulty if trumps are 4–2, since we will be forced at trick two and still have to set up the clubs. However, if we hold hand (k), it would be clearly ludicrous to want to play in five clubs rather than four spades.

So, perhaps we say we would only bid four spades over four hearts if we held hand (k), and if we held hand (j) we would make a second take-out double. That is all very well, but what is partner supposed to do if he holds, say:

(n) ♠ Q 5 4
♡ 8 7
♢ J 5 4
♣ 1 0 9 6 5 4

How is he to know that we hold five spades? Here four spades is a fair contract which stands some chance of success, whereas five clubs is very much against the odds. He can't guess to bid four spades, since we may just have a 4–1–4–4 distribution with significant extra values and four spades could be a silly contract with five clubs laydown.

All this supposes that partner passed four hearts in the first place. It will be seen when comparing hand (m) with hand (b), when partner had as little as:

♠ K 8 7 4
♡ 8
♢ A 7 6 2
♣ K 1 0 5 4

that the opposition are certainly going to make four hearts, whereas five clubs will usually go only two down (assuming the opening bidder has the ace of spades), making it a good sacrifice at all but unfavourable vulnerability. Partner may choose to bid five clubs directly over the four-heart bid – not a very clever thing to do if we hold hand (k).

Hand (l) is even worse. Our spade shortness suggests that partner will probably hold reasonable length in the suit. If the opponents bid four hearts he is very likely to try four spades on some such hand as:

(o) ♠ Q J 7 5 3
    ♡ 6 4
    ◇ Q 7 5 3 2
    ♣ 3

After all, if we hold hand (b) shown, this is only likely to go one or two down. However, he has done very much the wrong thing when we hold hand (l). Our side will probably end up losing a penalty when we could have beaten four hearts.

What is the solution to this problem?
The latest idea is that the most important thing to do with a distributional hand is to start bidding suits. The arguments are as follows:

1 We will not normally have a game on after the opponents have opened the bidding unless we have a fit.
2 The most likely place to have a fit is in our longest suit.
3 If we have a fit in our longest suit, then if we simply bid it, partner will raise and then we can investigate game later.
4 Even if partner passes our strong overcall, the modern practice of negative doubles (see Chapter 5), means that very often the opener will reopen the bidding and give us a second chance.

The modernists would prefer an initial simple overcall to a take-out double on hands (j), (k) and (l). The hand would have to be strong enough to be close to making game on its own before they would feel that they had to start with double.

A simple response to a take-out double

When should I pass my partner's take-out double?
The most common mistake beginners make when responding to a take-out double is to pass when they have a very weak hand. They have learned that they need a few values to respond to an opening bid and when they have nothing they should pass. This is not the case when responding to a take-out double. A double asks us to bid our best suit, and bid our best suit is what we should do, unless we have so many cards in the opponents' suit that we have a realistic chance of beating their contract. The following is an example of a hand where we should pass part-ner's take-out double of one heart:

(a) ♠ 6 5
   ♡ J 10 9 7 5 4
   ◇ Q 6 5
   ♣ 8 4

Although we have only 3 HCP, we can reasonably expect to take three tricks against one heart and perhaps the queen of diamonds may be useful as well. Partner has announced at least minimum opening bid values (and, given our left-hand opponent's silence, may well have more) and so is quite likely to contribute another four defensive tricks.

Expert practice in this area is quite strict, perhaps too strict. A panel of experts were asked what they would respond to a take-out double of one spade at Game All, playing Pairs, when they held:

♠ Q 10 9 8 2
♡ J 7 4
◇ K 9 4 3
♣ 7

Only one panellist (out of twenty-three) chose to pass – the winning action.

What should I do with a weak hand which does not have enough trumps to pass?
OK, so our trumps are not good enough to pass the take-out double, but we have a very weak hand. We simply do what has been asked of us, bid our longest suit at minimum level. Here are some example hands (after a take-out double of one heart):

(b) ♠ 8 6 5 4   (c) ♠ K 6 4   (d) ♠ 6 4
    ♡ 8 7 5   ♡ 5 4 2   ♡ 9 6 3 2
    ◇ 9 3 2   ◇ Q J 8   ◇ 7
    ♣ 10 4 3   ♣ 5 4 3 2   ♣ K 10 7 6 3 2

(e) ♠ 6 4 3   (f) ♠ 6 4 3
    ♡ 9 6 3 2   ♡ Q 10 9 5
    ◇ 5 4 2   ◇ 5 4 2
    ♣ 6 5 2   ♣ 6 5 2

Hand (b) is a truly dreadful hand, but still we have to bid, and should simply respond one spade. Hand (c) is quite a fair hand by comparison, but we still do not have sufficient values to do other than make a simple response in our longest suit – clubs. Even though our points are in the other suits, partner will expect to hear of our longest suit – remember that ideally partner's distribution will be 4–1–4–4 and we want to find an eight-card fit.

Hand (d) is potentially very powerful – the heart length makes it more likely that partner has a singleton and as weak a hand as:

♠ A 7 5 3
♡ 5
♢ A 8 5 4
♣ A J 8 4

would make game a fair proposition. However, we still do not have enough to do more than bid two clubs – remember, if we have a very good fit, so will the opponents, in which case there will be more bidding.

Hand (e) is everybody's nightmare – not only do we have a complete Yarborough but our only four-card suit is the opponent's! The normal practice with such a dire hand is to bid one's lowest three-card suit, but it is usually unwise to bid a three-card major. This is because partner is more likely to raise us enthusiastically when we bid a major – a ten-trick game is much easier than an eleven-trick one, so if he holds, say, a 4–1–4–4 16-count, he is more likely to think of inviting game if we respond in a major than if we respond in a minor. If we hold no four-card suit other than the one opened, it is safer to respond in our lowest three-card minor.

Hand (f) is the same as hand (e), except that the heart suit is better. It seems attractive at first glance to respond one no-trump, but partner will surely expect us to have a better hand. Unless there is a specific agreement to the contrary, he is likely to expect the same values to respond one no-trump to a take-out double as to an opening bid, perhaps even a little stronger – say 7–10 HCP. Here, again, we should respond two clubs.

Whereas it can be dangerous to respond in a three-card major to a take-out double, many experts prefer to keep the bidding low when they have a near-Yarborough. A panel of experts was asked what they would respond when partner made a take-out double of a one-diamond opening, vulnerable against not, playing IMPs, holding:

♠ 7
♡ 10 6 3
◇ Q 9 6 5 2
♣ J 8 3 2

The panel of twenty-two was evenly divided between one heart and two clubs. One of the reasons for the popularity of the former was that it was felt to be likely that partner had a hand too good to overcall one spade and it was better to allow him to express this at the one level rather than have to rebid two spades over two clubs.

What should I respond when I have two suits?
So far, we have held (at most) only one suit in which to respond. Let us consider the following hands where we hold two suits (again after a double of one heart):

(g) ♠ 7 6 4 3
    ♡ 5 4 2
    ◇ 5 2
    ♣ K Q J 6

(h) ♠ Q J 4 2
    ♡ 9 6 4
    ◇ 8
    ♣ J 10 7 5 3

(i) ♠ 6
    ♡ 8 7 4 3
    ◇ Q J 6 4
    ♣ K 7 6 3

(j) ♠ 6
    ♡ 8 7 4 3
    ◇ 9 7 6 4
    ♣ 8 7 6 3

With two four-card suits, one of which is a major, we should always respond in the major. This is because partner is more likely to hold four cards in the other major than in an unbid minor (remember, we needed more HCP for the initial double when only three cards were held in the other major). Hence, on hand (g), we should respond one spade. Partner is also more likely to bid further if we bid one spade and, with our nice club suit, we would be pleased if he did so.

Hand (h) is interesting and would probably divide a panel of experts. Were we to play the double to guarantee four cards in the other major, we would clearly respond one spade; were we to play the Italian style of take-out double, we would clearly respond two clubs; however, playing 'modern British' there are arguments both ways. We have quite a suitable hand, so could argue that by bidding one spade we would encourage partner to bid again: on the other hand, if the bidding progresses quietly (say the opener rebids two hearts which is passed back to us), we would like to make another bid ourselves, in which case we can describe our hand much more accurately if we start with two clubs and then bid two spades when the opponents bid two of a red suit.

On hand (i) we should respond two diamonds. Partner is just as likely to hold diamonds as clubs and two diamonds prepares us better for any subsequent auction. If partner bids again – say he has a good hand and bids two spades or cue-bids two hearts – it is much more comfortable to rebid three clubs, rather than to have to bid three diamonds, having bid two clubs the first time. In fact, if we do start with two clubs and subsequently rebid three diamonds, he will surely think we have five clubs and four diamonds.

In some ways, the same things could be said about hand (j), if we absolutely have to bid again, we would rather bid diamonds and then clubs, at least offering two suits. The difference is that this time we will not bid again unless he forces us to do so. Also, he knows that if we have nothing, including no four-card suit other than opener's, we would respond two clubs. Conse-quently he is more likely to make a pushy try for game if we respond two diamonds (which does usually show length in the suit) than if we bid two clubs.

Suppose they open a minor and I hold both majors?

Let us now suppose that the bidding starts with a take-out double of one of a minor – say 1◇ – Dble – and we hold:

(k) ♠ Q J 7 6 (l) ♠ 6 5 4 3
♡ Q J 4 2 ♡ 8 7 5 3
◇ 6 5 4 ◇ 6 5 4
♣ 5 4 ♣ 5 4

What should we respond now? The classic argument is that we should respond one spade with hand (k) and one heart with hand (l). The reasons usually propounded are similar to those given above. On hand (k) we would be delighted to make another bid if partner suggests we do so or if the opponents compete further, so we bid one spade, thus preparing the ground for bidding both our suits naturally. On hand (l), however, we do not want to bid again and therefore we bid our lowest suit, which is consistent (barely) with having nothing and perhaps even only a three-card heart suit.

There is a flaw in this argument. Partner is equally likely to hold either major; if we bid a major at all and partner has a fit for us he is equally likely to hope we have more than this whichever major we bid; if he allows us to, we will pass whatever strong action he makes; however, if he forces us to bid (by cue-bidding the opponents' suit or perhaps making a further take-out double at a higher level), we would still prefer to have bid spades first, so that we can bid hearts the next time, thus offering a choice.

What if I have four hearts and he has doubled a one-spade opening?

We have mentioned earlier that, generally, bidding majors tends to interest the doubler more than bidding minors, because it is easier for us to visualize the possibilities of a ten-trick game rather than an eleven-trick one. This is something to bear in mind when considering our response after partner has doubled a one-spade opening. Holding a completely worthless hand with four hearts, it may be more advisable to respond in a four-card (or even a three-card) minor. There is little room to investigate game after the sequence: 1♠ – Dble – Pass – 2♡ and he will tend to assume we have a little something – if we don't, he is going to be disappointed.

I have heard people mention Herbert negatives. What are they?
One method of solving some of these problems is to use Herbert negatives in response to a take-out double. Thus the next step up (usually two clubs over a take-out double of one spade) is not natural and shows a very weak hand – say a maximum of 4 HCP (excluding the odd stray queen in the opponents' suit). This certainly solves some of the problems, because it is possible to differentiate immediately between varying strengths of minimum response. But there is an obvious drawback to losing a natural response.

Suppose our left-hand opponent opens one diamond, partner doubles, the next hand passes, and we hold:

♠ K 5 4
♡ Q J 7 6
◇ 8 7 4 3
♣ 7 6

What should we bid? If we respond one heart, partner will think we have less than this unless we bid again. If we respond two hearts, what do we bid when we have a 'real' two-heart bid?

Looking at it from the other side of the table, suppose our left-hand opponent opens one diamond, partner doubles, the next hand passes and we respond one heart. What should he bid holding, say:

♠ A Q 6 5
♡ A Q 6 5
◇ 7
♣ K J 7 6

This sort of hand ought to be the one when the system works best for us – partner knows immediately that there is no game on, whereas he might have made a small try had we responded one heart under normal methods. However, he has no idea what suit to play in. If he passes he may find we have shortage in hearts and length in either (or both) black suits; if he bids one spade he might find that our only suit is hearts. This drawback seems to have been found insurmountable by most top partnerships, and Herbert negatives are not widely employed.

How many points do I need to respond one no-trump to partner's take-out double?

As mentioned earlier, a one no–trump response to a take–out double is generally played as showing a little more than a normal one no–trump response to an opening bid – say 7–10 HCP. One reason why it needs to be a little stronger is that we already know that the hand on our left probably has a long suit which he is likely to lead, something that is not the case when making a normal one no–trump response. Another reason why the one no–trump response is used to show a better hand is that we can bid a suit at the two level with very few values, which is not the case over an opening bid.

Why don't I respond one no-trump whenever I have a balanced hand of 7–10 HCP?

Other than the necessary HCP, the other requirement for a one no–trump response is a strong holding in the opponents' suit. Partner will not expect us to have stops in any other particular suit, indeed we may even have a singleton. This is because he has implied length in the other suits, so has less need of our help there; but because he has shown shortage in the opponents' suit we are going to have to stop the run of that suit all on our own. For example, after 1♡ – Dble, the following are some typical one no–trump responses:

(m) ♠ 5 4
♡ Q J 10 8
♢ K 10 5
♣ Q 10 3 2

(n) ♠ Q
♡ J 9 8 4 3
♢ K Q 7
♣ Q 6 5 3

(o) ♠ 8 7 4 3
♡ K J 10 6
♢ A 6 5
♣ J 5

(p) ♠ 7 6
♡ A K 10 9
♢ Q 7 6 3 2
♣ 6 5

However, if we alter the position of the high cards, generally removing the intermediate cards in hearts, they become more suitable for a response in a suit. For example:

(q) ♠ 5 4
♡ Q 7 4 3
♢ K 10 5
♣ Q J 10 9

(r) ♠ 2
♡ J 5 4 3 2
♢ A K Q 7
♣ 6 5 3

(s) ♠ K 7 4 3
♡ J 10 3 2
♢ A 6 5
♣ J 5

(t) ♠ 7 6
♡ A 6 5 3
♢ K Q 10 3 2
♣ 6 5

With hand (q) we should content ourselves with a simple two clubs. Hands (r) and (t) are well worth a jump to three diamonds and hand (s) is worth a jump to two spades.

Can't I respond one no-trump with less than 7 HCP when I have very good stops in their suit?
Some expert partnerships allow a one no-trump response to be made on a much weaker hand than the above, provided that the main feature of the hand is the heart strength. For example:

♠ 6 5 4
♡ K J 10 9
♢ 5 4 3
♣ 7 6 5

If this is the partnership agreement, obviously much care has to be exercised in the subsequent auction in order to avoid getting too high. This will be covered later on in this section.

A jump response to a take-out double

What do I need to make a jump response?
A jump in a new suit in response to a take-out double generally shows in the region of 7–10 HCP. However, more is known about the take-out doubler's hand (especially if playing the modern British style) than after an opening bid, so the high-card requirements can be viewed a little more flexibly since the degree of fit is also important. Consider the following hands in response to a take-out double of one heart:

(a) ♠ Q J 10 5	(b) ♠ K Q 4 3	(c) ♠ Q 6 5 4 3
♡ 8 7 6	♡ Q J 5	♡ 7 6 3
◇ K 10 6 4 3	◇ J 5 4	◇ K Q 3
♣ 5	♣ J 7 3	♣ 7 6

Hands (a), (b) and (c) are all suitable for a jump to two spades. Although hand (b) is the strongest in terms of HCP, it is much less attractive in terms of distribution and its three points in hearts are likely to be wasted values. One useful test to determine whether or not we should make a try for game or slam in any situation is to see if we can think of a suitable minimum hand for partner to hold which will make game (or slam) a good contract. If we can think of one quickly, then we should make our try. Here, we should imagine we are facing a 4–4–4–1 distribution with two aces and a king; if game is good facing such a hand, then we should make a jump response. By this reckoning, hand (a), despite only having 6 HCP, is nearly worth four spades. It is the double fit which makes the playing strength of the combined hands so powerful. Hand (b), by contrast, would expect to make only eight tricks. Hand (c), would also give fair play for ten tricks. This shows the power of the nine-card trump fit – not only because of the extra likelihood of only one trump loser, but also because there is one less small 'non-trump' to dispose of.

Does it make any difference whether our single jump is at the two or three level?
There is a significant difference between jumping to the two level and jumping to the three level, partly because we simply need more values to make a three-level contract but also because there is little room for partner to co-operate by making a further try – he will have to make a final decision. If we jump to two spades on any of the above hands, partner can make a further try; if the opening bid had been one spade and we were considering jumping to three hearts, he would have to make a final decision as to whether or not to play in game. Consequently we should have a little more to jump to three hearts over a double of one spade than we need to jump to two spades over a double of one heart.

Is there any difference between a jump in a major and a jump in a minor?
If we jump in a major, more often than not partner will simply consider whether or not he likes the idea of playing in game in that major. If we jump in a minor, his first thoughts are likely to be concerned with playing in no-trumps, simply because eleven tricks are a lot to make. Consider the following hands in response to a take-out double of one heart:

(d) ♠ 5
    ♡ 8 7 6
    ♢ Q J 10 5
    ♣ K 10 6 4 3

(e) ♠ 7
    ♡ K 10 5
    ♢ 6 5 4
    ♣ K J 10 6 5 3

(f) ♠ 7 6
    ♡ 7 6 3
    ♢ Q 6 5 4 3
    ♣ K Q 3

With hands (d) and (f) we should content ourselves with merely bidding two of our best minor. We will certainly bid more if given a chance, but the hands are not very suitable for playing in no-trumps and the playing strength is insufficient to suggest that five of a minor is likely if partner does not bid on. Hand (e) by contrast, is potentially very suitable for playing in no-trumps. If partner has extra values and a club fit sufficient to hope that the suit will run, he can cue-bid three hearts and we will gladly bid three no-trumps.

What does a double jump response mean?
The most sensible meaning of a double jump response – say a jump to three spades in response to a take-out double of one heart – is just to show a stronger hand than a single jump response. It says, 'Please bid game with good controls even if you are minimum.' This can certainly be useful, since, although we established that game was a good contract with our hands (a) and (c), facing our 4–1–4–4 with two aces and a king, it is by no means clear that partner should proceed over a single jump response. Thus, the double jump response bridges the gap between the two-spade response, which, as we have seen, can be made on as little as a shapely six-count, and a full-weight game force.

Is a double jump response to the four level in a minor any different?
A jump to four of a minor obviously precludes playing in three no-trumps, so should show no bolster in the opponents' suit and a very suit-oriented hand – after 1♡ – Dble, a jump to four clubs might be made on:

    ♠ A 4
    ♡ 7 6 3
    ◇ 5
    ♣ Q 10 8 7 4 3 2

A cue-bid response to a take-out double

What does a bid of the opponents' suit mean in response to a take-out double?
The cue-bid response to a take-out doubie traditionally shows a
good hand, forcing to two no-trumps or suit agreement. However, modern-day thought suggests that there should be a weaker
hand-type included. Suppose we hold the following hand, which
we have seen already on page 18:

♠ K 7 4 3
♡ J 10 3 2
♢ A 6 5
♣ J 5

We have established that after a double of an opening bid of one
heart, this hand is worth a jump to two spades. However,
suppose partner has doubled an opening bid of one diamond?
Presumably, the hand is still worth a jump response as it has not
become any worse. Our problem is how to guess which major
partner holds as it would be silly to jump to two of one major,
find him passing and only discover when he put dummy down
that we are playing in a 4–3 fit when there was a perfectly
respectable 4–4 fit available elsewhere.

We would have the same problem with a slightly better hand
with the minors. Say partner doubles an opening bid of one spade
and we hold:

♠ 8 7 6
♡ A 6
♢ K 10 7 6
♣ K 9 8 7

With 10 working HCP, we are clearly worth a jump response,
but to which suit? At the three level, it could be even more costly
to play in the wrong suit.

It is to solve problems such as these that the cue-bid response has been amended. It may still be as strong a hand as it always was, but its first meaning – i.e. the meaning we should first assume – is that it shows the values for a jump response with either both majors (if a minor has been opened) or both minors (if a major has been opened) and it does not promise another bid.

The subsequent auction

What does it mean if partner makes a simple response to my take-out double and then I bid on?

We have already established that a simple response to a take-out double may be made on a Yarborough: it may also be made on up to a poor 9 HCP (particularly when made in a minor). It follows that any further bid by the doubler after a simple response in a suit shows a strong hand – even a simple raise. Let us suppose that the bidding has started: 1♡ – Dble – Pass – 1♠ – Pass. What are the doubler's possible courses of positive action?

1   One no-trump would show a stronger hand than an initial one no-trump overcall. If an immediate one no-trump over-call showed 16–18, then double followed by one no-trump would show about 19–21 HCP.

2   Two clubs or two diamonds would show a five-card suit and significant extra values, say 17–21 HCP. However, given that we have seen what possible future problems may occur if we decide to double in the first instance with an off-centre distribution, these bids are also likely to have tolerance for the other suits, perhaps a 3–1–4–5/3–1–5–4 distribution. Although these bids are not forcing, partner should try to bid over them if he has anything useful – he can infer from the bidding so far that if we need to take any finesses they are very likely to be right, therefore an ace is likely to be worth

two tricks, one in its own right and one as an entry to take a finesse. A fairly typical hand for a two-club rebid by the doubler would be:

♠ A K 5
♡ 6
♢ A Q 4 3
♣ A K 8 5 4

From this it can be seen that the following responding hands would all give reasonable play for game:

(a) ♠ Q 6 4 2   (b) ♠ Q J 6 4 2   (c) ♠ J 7 4 3
    ♡ 8 7 4 2   ♡ 8 7 4   ♡ Q J 9 2
    ♢ K 5   ♢ 5 2   ♢ 6 5 2
    ♣ 9 3 2   ♣ 9 3 2   ♣ Q 3

(d) ♠ 9 7 4 2   (e) ♠ Q 7 3 2
    ♡ 8 7 4 2   ♡ 8 7 4 2
    ♢ 6   ♢ K 5 2
    ♣ Q J 3 2   ♣ Q 3

With hand (a) he has a working 5 HCP and a possible ruffing value, but still eleven tricks is a lot to make, so a quiet raise to three clubs is best. With hand (b), he does not have enough for great enthusiasm for clubs but he does have a good five-card spade suit which is well worth rebidding – four spades could easily be very good. With hand (c) he has hearts very well guarded, plus a useful queen of clubs, which should make three no-trumps a good contract, so he should just bid it – if he had any more he would either have bid one no-trump or two spades on the last round. Hand (d) is very minimum in terms of high cards, but has an excellent club fit. With this distribution it is very unlikely that three no-trumps would be the right contract, so he should show his enthusiasm for clubs by raising to the four level. Hand (e) is a little more tricky – he has a very good hand but no clear direction. He should cue-bid the opponent's suit, two hearts, to show that he is good for his one-spade bid but he doesn't have five spades, three clubs or a heart stop.

3 A raise to two spades would show a good take-out double with at least four-card spade support, but he would need to be close to maximum for his one-spade response to proceed. A typical two-spade raise might be a 4–1–4–4 16-count, say:

    ♠ A K 8 5
    ♡ 6
    ♢ A J 4 3
    ♣ A 8 5 4

If that is our hand, it can be seen that only hands (a) and (e) give fair play for game. Hand (e) is good enough to raise straight to four spades, but with hand (a) he should content himself with a return game try, either bidding his values or where he needs help, according to partnership agreement.

4 A jump raise to three spades would show roughly a king more than a single raise – say the above hand with the king of clubs instead of the eight. It can be seen this would make game a good contract facing all our hands (a) to (e), and certainly he should bid it with all of them, although with hand (c) he should try three no-trumps to offer us a choice of games.

5 A jump to two no-trumps would show a stronger hand than one no-trump – say 22–24 HCP.

6 A jump in a new suit, three clubs or three diamonds, is a very strong bid. Classically it was played as forcing, but modern-day tendencies are to play it as showing about an Acol two bid. Again, it really should have tolerance for the other suits, so a 3–1–3–6 or 3–1–6–3 distribution is very likely. For example:

♠ A K 5
♡ 6
♢ A Q 4
♣ A K 10 9 5 4

Whenever we are considering what a particular bid should show, we must always bear in mind what alternatives we had available. Many players nowadays play an immediate jump cue-bid as asking partner to bid three no-trumps with a stop in the opponents' suit – e.g. 1♡ – 3♡ would ask for a heart stop. If we play this then partner would know that when we doubled and then made a jump to three of a minor, the one thing we wouldn't have is a solid minor suit with no heart guard, for with a hand like that we would have bid three hearts in the first place. Therefore a single heart stop and no club fit is not sufficient to bid three no-trumps – he would either need a second heart stop or a club honour or, say, three small clubs to make three no-trumps a good contract opposite the above hand. If we use an immediate jump cue-bid to express a different hand, then this would not apply.

7 A cue-bid of two hearts would show a strong hand that could not be shown in any other way (a catch-all bid) – it asks for further information. It could be a strong balanced hand without a heart guard; it could be a hand with four-card spade support but also a heart stop which wishes to consider playing in three no-trumps rather than four spades; it could be any strong hand which is too strong for a non-forcing bid. In response to this cue-bid, partner should bid:

- two spades with any completely worthless hand – this certainly does not show any extra spade length. If we bid a new suit after this, that is forcing and partner must bid again.

- a new suit to show four cards and a few values – say 4 or more working HCP. Again if we bid a new suit after this, that is forcing.
- no-trumps to show a heart stop – two no-trumps with 3–5 HCP and three no-trumps with more.
- a return cue-bid, three hearts, with none of the above but too much to sign off – say 5 or more HCP.

8 A jump cue-bid of three hearts is played in different ways by different partnerships. Alternative meanings are:

- asking partner to bid three no-trumps with a heart stop (only if you don't play an immediate jump cue-bid to mean this).
- showing a very strong raise to three spades, asking partner to bid game unless he has an absolute bust.
- as a slam try agreeing spades, perhaps specifically showing a singleton or void (splinter bid) according to partnership agreement.

Does it make any difference if the simple response was made at the two level – say after a start to the auction of 1♠ – Dble – Pass – 2♡?
Most of the above is applicable, but because there is less room there are some modifications:

1 We now have only one rebid in no-trumps below game, therefore a two no-trump rebid shows 19–21 HCP and with more we have just to close our eyes and bid three no-trumps.
2 We no longer have the luxury of a simple and a double raise of partner's suit, therefore we need to use the cue-bid to show the values for a double raise. Earlier we considered the sequence 1♡ – Dble – Pass – 1♠; Pass – 2♡ – Pass, when we bid two spades to show a very bad hand. This is sensible because it is economical and allows the partnership to stop at a low level. However, the sequence we are discussing now,

1♠ – Dble – Pass – 2♡; Pass – 2♠, is rather different. Here there is a strong case to use two no-trumps as an artificial negative, denying a five-card heart suit; three hearts would be a negative with a five-card heart suit and all other bids would show some enthusiasm.

How do we rebid if partner has responded one no-trump to our take-out double?

If the one no-trump response is played as 7–10 HCP, it makes sense that all subsequent rebids in suits should be forcing for one round. After all, we have established that to make a take-out double with the intention of bidding again shows a strong hand, and therefore the combined hands should have sufficient values to be able to proceed safely at least a little higher. In this instance a raise to two no-trumps would be natural and invitational; a simple bid in a new suit would show at least five cards and would be a suggestion that no-trumps might not be the best denomination; a jump bid in a new suit would show a good six-card suit and be a slam try; a cue-bid would show a good 4–4–4–1 hand and ask partner to value his hand in the light of that information. In response to any of the above the one no-trump bidder should raise or bid a suit if he has one, provided that all his values are not in the opponents' suit, when he should rebid no-trumps, jumping to three no-trumps with a maximum.

What if we allow the one no-trump response to be made on a much weaker hand with good stops in the opponents' suit?

If we allow the one no-trump response to be made on significantly weaker hands we need some way to stay low. Consequently most of the above would apply, with the exception that a bid in a new suit by the doubler would be non-forcing. If he has the expected 7–10 HCP he should bid as above, but if has only, say, 3–5 HCP, he is allowed to pass. The corollary of this is that the cue-bid becomes less specific, since if the doubler had a very strong hand he would have to start with a cue-bid rather than a non-forcing bid in a suit.

What do rebids mean if partner has made a jump response?
Here the position is straightforward – all bids other than a raise are forcing. This is because the jump response shows about 8 HCP, and if the doubler was minimum he would have at least three-card support, in which case he would not need to try to improve the contract unless he was interested in game.

One could argue that, if the doubler bids a new suit, the auction should be forcing to game because the hand that intended to double and then bid a new suit would have 17+ HCP and the jump response shows in the region of 8 HCP. However, just because the doubler has bid a new suit over a jump response it does not necessarily mean he would have done so over a simple response. Suppose we hold:

♠ A 65
♡ 7
♢ K Q 76
♣ A Q 763

We start by doubling our right-hand opponent's one-heart opening bid, intending to pass partner's simple response, but when he responds two spades we are too strong to pass. The most natural thing to do is to introduce our club suit, since we do not yet know whether spades, diamonds, clubs or even no-trumps are the right final denomination.

Similarly, a two no-trump response must be forcing, since it must show a hand too strong for a one no-trump overcall (although it may be more usefully employed by expert partnerships, on frequency grounds, as some sort of artificial game try). Although we could rebid three no-trumps to show a hand too strong to overcall one no-trump, a forcing two no-trumps is much more flexible as it allows partner to rebid his own suit or perhaps rebid a second suit. Thus it should show a strong, balanced hand but not so no-trump-oriented that it wishes to rule out other possibilities. Hence, a three no-trump rebid is very much to play and partner should nearly always pass.

A cue-bid after a two-spade response to a double of one heart would usually show a strong raise, quite possibly with only three-card spade support, whereas a cue-bid after a response of three of a minor would ask for a stopper for no-trump purposes.

How should I rebid if partner cue-bids the opponents' suit?

We established earlier that modern-day usage allows a cue-bid response to a take-out double to be made on a limited (7–10 HCP) hand with either both majors if a minor has been opened, or both minors if a major has been opened. Over this cue-bid response, if we just have a normal minimum take-out double we simply rebid in our best major or minor as appropriate; if we have extra values we can jump in our best major or minor to invite game; and if we want to make a forcing bid we can bid either two no-trumps, cue-bid or bid a suit partner has not shown. For example:

West	North	East	South
1 ♢	Double	Pass	2 ♢
Pass	?		

2 ♡/♠   best major in a minimum hand
2NT   forcing for one round, asking for further information
3 ♣   natural, forcing
3 ♢   asking South to bid his best major
3 ♡/♠   non-forcing, but invitational

If South actually has the stronger variety of cue-bid, he can show this by bidding on when North simply chooses two of a major. For example:

West	North	East	South
1 ◇	Double	Pass	2 ◇
Pass	2 ♡	Pass	?

2 ♠ a hand too good to bid two spades immediately, forcing for one round, suggesting only four spades

2NT natural, non-forcing, but showing a less good heart stop than an immediate 2NT response

3 ♣ natural, forcing

3 ◇ game-forcing, asking for half a stop in diamonds

3 ♡ natural, invitational

3 ♠ natural, forcing, setting trumps and asking for a cue-bid

3NT natural, but suggesting alternative contracts, if North is very unsuitable

Note that we can use the cue-bid followed by two no-trumps or three no-trumps to imply doubt about our choice. This is a theme that crops up in many sequences, whether uninterrupted or competitive: when there are two ways to arrive in no-trumps, one immediate and one more 'slow', the 'slower' route always implies doubt.

A take-out double in the protective position

Is there any difference in the meaning of a take-out double in the protective position?
This is a very difficult area of the game. Suppose that we hold:

♠ 6
♡ A Q J 10 6
◇ A 5 4
♣ A K J 7

and our right-hand opponent opens one heart. We have very little alternative but to pass and hope that we will be allowed to show our hand later. The corollary of this is that if the one-heart opening bid is passed round to partner and he holds very little in the way of high cards but also very little in the way of hearts as well, say:

♠ K752
♡ 5
♢ K962
♣ 9852

he can pretty sure that we have a hand such as the above. What is he to do about it? He has two choices: he can either pass or he can double. If he passes there is a risk of missing a substantial penalty, or even a game (one would expect to make three no-trumps with these combined hands); if he doubles and we do not have quite such a good hand as this he risks us leaping to three no-trumps or trying for a penalty because we think he has rather more than he has. All very tricky!

Is there is a solution to this problem?
The best (although not foolproof) way to cope with this sort of problem is to use the principle of 'transferring an ace'. What this means is that the hand in the protective position mentally adds an ace to his hand and bids accordingly; correspondingly, the responder to the protective double mentally deducts an ace from his hand and he also bids accordingly.

This means that the values needed for a protective take-out double start at about 8 HCP, or a little less, as here, with perfect distribution. It also means that the values needed for a jump response start at about 11 or 12 HCP.

For example, after a one-club opening bid, a suitable scheme of bidding would be:

West	North	East	South
1 ♣	Pass	Pass	Dble
Pass	?		

1 ◇/♡/♠	0–10 HCP, natural
1NT	11–13 HCP, natural
2 ♣	cue-bid, as we saw previously, but a little stronger, say 11+ HCP with both majors, or any distribution with a stronger hand (15+)
2 ◇/♡/♠	11–14 HCP, natural, but remember that North did not overcall immediately, so his suit quality will not be very good (depending on your overcall style)
2NT	14–15 HCP, natural

If I make a protective double, are my rebids then affected by the changes in the range of responses?

If we bid a new suit after hearing partner's simple response, we will be showing only about 14 or so HCP and must cue-bid first with a really strong hand (say 19+). Also, the values needed for a one no-trump overcall in the protective position are less than in second seat, say 11–15. It follows, then, that to double and then rebid in no-trumps at minimum level shows in the region of 16–18 HCP. We are helped a little in this in that a two no-trump overcall in the protective position is usually played as natural (rather than 'unusual', which is more common in second seat). Therefore, with 19–21 HCP we can bid two no-trumps immediately, and with more than that we double and jump rebid in no-trumps.

If partner makes a simple response, say one heart, we would rebid along these lines:

West	North	East	South
1 ♣	Pass	Pass	Dble
Pass	1 ♡	Pass	?

1 ♠	14–18 HCP, five-card suit
1NT	16–18 HCP, natural
2 ♣	'catch-all' as described above
2 ◇	14–18 HCP, five-card suit
2 ♡	minimum raise, say at least 12 HCP with good distribution, and up to 16 if balanced
2 ♠	Acol two type, as before
2NT	22–24 HCP, natural
3 ♣	as in the direct position, whatever your partnership decided
3 ◇	Acol two type
3 ♡	strong raise, say 16–18 with good distribution, up to 20 if balanced – with a stronger hand start with a cue-bid

Because the cue-bid is at such a low level, there is room to follow it up with a strong raise, a strong bid in a new suit or even a two no-trump rebid to show the same strength as an immediate two no-trumps but with less strength in hearts. However, if the auction starts with a one-spade opening, it all gets much more awkward:

West	North	East	South
1 ♠	Pass	Pass	Dble
Pass	2 ♡	Pass	?

2 ♠	'catch-all' as before
2NT	16–18 but clearly this is less attractive than rebidding 1NT since partner may have very little. Some partnerships get round this problem by changing the range of their 1NT overcall in fourth position according to the denomination of the suit opened
3 ♣/◇	natural, non-forcing, say 14–18, as before
3 ♡	minimum raise, with more start with a cue-bid

It can be seen that there is much less room for accurate investigation. We just have to do the best we can, employing such well-tried principles as 'overbid when you have a fit, underbid without', 'overbid at teams and underbid at pairs'.

Points to remember

1   We must respond to a take-out double unless we have sufficient length in the opponents' suit that we can hope to beat their contract.

2   We need about 7 or 8 HCP to make a jump response to the two level, and about 9 or 10 HCP to jump to the three level. However, distribution is often more important than high-card points, so we should jump with less if we have good shape.

3   We can make a cue-bid response on the same values as a jump response provided we have at least four cards in both majors (when a minor has been opened) or both minors (when a major has been opened).

4   A one no-trump response shows about 7–10 HCP (unless we have a specific agreement to the contrary).

5   If we make a take-out double and then bid on we have shown a good hand, one that was too good for any other action on the first round. If the doubler rebids in a new suit, this is forcing after a jump response.

6   A take-out double in the protective position can be much weaker than in direct position. When bidding over such a double, both partners should mentally 'transfer an ace' from the responding hand to the doubler's hand.

7   When we have two ways to bid no-trumps, one directly and one via an alternative action, such as a cue-bid, the direct route shows the more no-trump-oriented hand.

2

Doubles of Higher-level Natural Opening Bids

In Chapter 1 we discussed how much more difficult it is to bid accurately over an opening bid of one spade than it is over an opening bid of one club. This is because the one-club opening only took one of our possible bids away (and gave us one back – double) whereas the one-spade opening took away three bids. It is even more difficult to bid accurately over an opening bid at the two level – which is one of the reasons that people open with weak twos, pre-emptive threes and other such bids.

Doubles of weak two openings

Is a double of a weak two opening any different to a double of a one-level opening? Can we not just bid in the same way as we have seen previously?

If we agreed to treat weak twos exactly as one-level openings, which is a commonly used method at club level, we have one serious problem. Suppose we hold a hand such as:

♠ Q 5 4
♡ 8 4
♢ A 6 2
♣ K J 6 5 2

Our left-hand opponent opens with a weak two spades and partner doubles for take-out. What are we supposed to do? We have to choose between three clubs, which is consistent with no values at all, two no-trumps, which rather overstates our spade stop, and four clubs, which goes past three no-trumps.

How can we overcome this problem?
It is because of problems such as these that various methods of defending against weak twos have been developed. In order to begin to surmount some of these problems one of the following is necessary.

1   The initial bidder has a choice of take-out options, depending on the strength of his hand. For example, in the Hackett defence, three clubs is used as a weak take-out and three diamonds is used as a strong take-out, which leaves the responding hand in a better position to guess.
2   The responding hand has some way to distinguish between when he has nothing at all and when he has invitational values.

It is beyond the range of this book to go into full details about various defences to weak two bids; we are merely here to discuss doubles. A double of a weak two bid can be played in one of three ways: penalty, take-out or optional.

There is little to be said if the double is played as penalty: partner usually passes unless he has extreme distribution when he bids whatever seems appropriate. There would be quite a strong argument for using a two no-trump response to a penalty (or optional) double of a weak two bid as artificial (after all it could hardly be much use in its natural sense), showing a hand which has removed the double because of weakness; then the corollary would be that to remove the penalty double to a suit would be constructive. The same can be said for an optional double (a true optional double would mean that the hand was something like a strong no-trump with, say, A-x-x in trumps).

The problems associated with choosing to play double as penalty or 'optional' as a defence to weak two bids lie not so much in the use of double but in finding some other bid to use for take-out. As mentioned above, if we use only one bid for take-out, then there are problems because responder has to do a lot of lucky guesswork. If we choose to use, say, the Hackett defence, we have two take-out bids, thus reducing that problem, but we have lost two very valuable natural bids.

For reasons such as these, most of the world's tournament players use a take-out double. Another advantage of this is that, perhaps surprisingly, the penalty can be picked up *more* frequently. If another bid is used for take-out, the penalty is lost when the other hand has the trumps and wished to take a penalty. Using take-out doubles, we double with short trumps and partner can pass or bid as he pleases; much of the time when we would like to make a penalty double, we can pass and wait for partner to reopen with a double.

However, if a take-out double is used, some structure needs to be developed, in order to satisfy the second condition above. Here we will concern ourselves with bidding over a take-out double (which is by far the most commonly employed).

Is the strength and distribution needed for a double of a weak two bid the same as for a one-level bid?
Certainly it would be possible to put the same restrictions on a take-out double of a weak two bid as we did to a take-out double of a one-level opening. However, suppose we hold:

♠ 5 4
♡ A K 6 2
♢ Q 8 7 3 2
♣ A 6

If our right-hand opponent opened one spade, we would have had a tricky bid playing 'expert British' take-out doubles and may well have decided to pass for the time being. We would be unlikely to miss a game unless partner could venture something;

if one spade were passed round to partner he would protect with one no-trump on as little as a balanced 11-count; if the next hand raised to two spades we could bid on the next round; if partner had some distribution he would bid on many different hands where game would be good for our side. However, over an opening bid of two spades we are much less likely to get a second chance. The opening bid is so limited that our left-hand opponent is unlikely to bid over it, unless it is to make our life even more difficult by raising spades; and if our left-hand opponent passes, partner can hardly be expected to protect with two no-trumps on as little as 11 or 12 HCP. So, we have little option but to double two spades and hope for the best (we could hardly bid three diamonds on such a poor suit). Partner needs to keep in mind that we might be stuck for a bid and that the double might not have ideal distribution.

How should I respond to partner's take-out double?
Whatever our compromises as to the distribution needed for the double, it is important, as stated above, that in response we have one bid to show extreme weakness; if we can achieve this then all our other bids will show some values (one could use one bid to show values and then all the rest would show weakness, but it is usually better to have greater definition when game is more likely to be in the picture). The next thing to decide is which natural bid we would least dislike to give up to serve this purpose, and the one that immediately springs to mind is two no-trumps.

But what if I want to bid a natural two no-trumps?
Even if two no-trumps is natural, it is difficult to decide how many points it should show. If we say 10–12, then when we have 8 or 9 we have to make some other inappropriate bid. So, general opinion seems to be that if we want to bid no-trumps, we have to bid three no-trumps; otherwise we bid in a suit.

How, then, does this two no-trump response work?

The following scheme of responses has been developed (and is widely used by top partnerships) after a take-out double of a weak two bid:

1 Two spades (over two hearts) shows 0–7 HCP and a four-card or longer spade suit.
2 Two no-trumps is an artificial negative, showing 0–7 HCP and any distribution (except a spade suit over a double of two hearts); the bid can also be used as the starting point on a number of stronger hands.
3 A simple bid in a suit at the three level is natural and shows in the region of 8–11 HCP.
4 All jumps in new suits (below game) are natural and forcing.
5 A cue-bid is game-forcing, showing four cards in the other major and no stop in the opponents' suit.

How do we find a suit to play in once I have responded two no-trumps?

In response to our two no-trumps, partner should bid his lowest four-card suit, unless he has significant extra values, when he can either jump or cue-bid the opponents' suit. We can then either pass partner's rebid or introduce a suit of our own.

The following are some possible responding hands to a take-out double of a weak two hearts:

(a) ♠ Q 5 4 3
♡ J 6 5 4
◇ Q 5
♣ 7 6 5

(b) ♠ 6 5 4
♡ J 6 5 4
◇ Q 5 3
♣ K 7 6

(c) ♠ 7 6
♡ J 6 5 4
◇ Q J 10 4 3
♣ 6 5

(d) ♠ 6 5
♡ Q 6 5 4
◇ Q 6
♣ K Q J 6 5

(e) ♠ K Q 10 6 5
♡ A 4 3
◇ K 6
♣ J 6 5

With hand (a), a simple two-spade response is plenty. Hands (b) and (c) should both start with a two no-trump response. On hand (b), we should pass three of either minor should partner bid it – it may well be a 4–3 fit, but is probably the best we can hope for. On hand (c) we should convert partner's three clubs to three diamonds. Hand (d) is well expressed by an immediate three-club response, non-forcing but showing constructive values. Remember that if we held the same hand with a five-card spade suit we would start with a two no-trump response and then bid three spades, as an immediate three spades would be forcing and is what we would bid with hand (e).

Why would we start by bidding two no-trumps when we have a strong hand?

It was mentioned above that two no-trumps could be the starting point with some strong hands. Its main use (apart from being used to show an invitational hand with spades over a weak two hearts) is to differentiate between various types of balanced hands, with and without guards in the opponents' suit and with and without four cards in the other major. Consider the following strong responding hands (after partner has doubled a weak two-heart opening):

(f) ♠ Q J 5   (g) ♠ K 5 4   (h) ♠ K J 5 4
    ♡ A Q 9 4   ♡ A 10 4   ♡ Q J 4
    ♢ K 6 5   ♢ Q J 6 5   ♢ A 6 5
    ♣ 7 6 5   ♣ K 10 5   ♣ Q 6 5

(i) ♠ K J 5 4   (j) ♠ K 5
    ♡ J 5 4   ♡ 7 5 4
    ♢ A Q 10 6   ♢ A K 10 6 5
    ♣ Q 5   ♣ Q J 5

Hand (f) is balanced with two good heart stops and is strong enough to insist on game. We can express all this in straightforward fashion by bidding three no-trumps. Hand (g) is also balanced, and of more or less the same strength, but is much less suitable for no-trump play. We can express this by first bidding two no-trumps and following it up with three no-trumps when partner rebids three of a minor. Hand (h) is similar, but here the difference is that it contains four spades. Now we should also start with two no-trumps, but when partner rebids three of a minor we cue-bid three hearts to show both a heart stop and a four-card spade suit; if we held the same strength and distribution of hand without a heart stop, we would make an immediate cue-bid, which would be our action on hand (i). With hand (j) we should make an immediate response of four diamonds, natural and forcing, with some slam prospects.

When the opening bid has been two hearts, there is arguably no real need to be so strict about needing four cards in the other major for an initial cue-bid. After all, if partner bid three spades over our three-heart cue-bid, we could always bid three no-trumps, denying four spades and showing a single heart stop in a hand which would be suitable for suit play should he wish to try another suit. However, when the opening bid has been two spades, there is no space for such luxuries after a cue-bid, so in that instance, it is important that the three-spade cue-bid is very specific. For simplicity's sake it is better to play the same thing over both opening bids.

Is the double any different in the protective position?
The same rules that applied for balancing doubles over one-level openings apply over two-level openings, but slightly more care has to be exercised because of the higher level. In the same way that the hand in fourth position needed to protect with a double on a weak hand with shortage in the suit opened, so do they over a two-level opening, but because the level is higher, it is probably better to operate around a 'transfer a queen' principle rather

than 'transfer an ace'. Therefore it should be assumed that the protective doubler has a minimum of 10 HCP; responder should bid the two no-trump 'negative' with 0–9 HCP and make a semi-positive response with 10–12. Sometimes we will get too high, but the reason they pre-empt is to make life difficult for us.

Doubles of strong two openings

Is there any special way of defending against a strong two opening?
Our defensive style when considering bidding over a strong two opening is very different to when the two bid is weak. We bid over a weak two bid primarily for constructive reasons. Over a strong two opening it is also true that we may have a strong hand which we wish to bid constructively and, indeed, some partnerships bid the same way, just using a double as take-out. However, once our right-hand opponent has announced a strong hand with substantial playing strength, we are more likely to want to bid for obstructive and sacrificial reasons.

By definition, a normal take-out double implies a semi-three-suited hand, which tends to be more suitable for defensive purposes than playing the hand. There is a strong case for playing a double of a strong two bid as two-suited rather than three-suited, since this hand-type inherently has more playing strength and is more likely to lead to our side bidding a making game or sacrifice. Using this method, a double of a strong opening would show a Michaels cue-bid type hand – i.e. five cards in the other major and five cards in an unspecified minor (with both minors overcall two no-trumps).

Doubles of weak three openings

What happens if the opponents open at the three level?
If a weak two bid made life difficult for us, then a weak three opening makes it even more so – inevitably a lot of guesswork

will be involved. The basic requirements for a take-out double of a weak three opening are the same as for a one-level or weak two opening. However, in the same way that we had to double on hands with less than perfect distribution over weak twos, so do we, even more so, over weak threes.

What do I do with a balanced hand with a stopper in their suit? It seems very dangerous to bid three no-trumps on my own with as little as, say, 16 HCP.

If we play that a double of a weak three bid is for take-out and a three no-trump bid is to play, then when we hold a balanced hand which is worth a bid we should bid three no-trumps. It may be dangerous but it is a lot less dangerous than doing anything else. A common mistake is to double on a balanced hand with a guard in the opponents' suit on, say, 14–16 HCP. The normal result of bidding like this is that partner bypasses three no-trumps when it is our best spot, thinking that we have more distribution.

Isn't it very dangerous to bid at all when my opponents force me to bid at the three level on a hand that I would have only chosen to bid at the one level?

Yes, it is, but it is even more dangerous to pass and miss our own game. They have forced us to guess at a high level. The best thing to do is hope that partner holds an averagely weak hand – say 7–9 HCP – and bid accordingly. If he has less than that, then the pre-empt has worked and we were unlucky. We should bid over a three-level opening if 8 HCP or so would be sufficient for us to make a contract at that level.

How should I respond to a take-out double of a three-level opening bid?

Partner will be assuming that we hold about 7–9 HCP when he decided to double in the first place, so we do not need to make a jump response unless we hold more than that or compensating distribution. It follows from this that if we make a simple response to a take-out double, he should bid on if an average hand with 8 HCP or so would be sufficient for game. Let us consider the following hands in response to a take-out double of an opening three hearts:

(a) ♠ K 6 5 3   (b) ♠ 7 5 3   (c) ♠ K J 10 6
    ♡ Q 7 5   ♡ A Q 6   ♡ 8 7 3
    ♢ A 5 3   ♢ J 5 3   ♢ A 5 3
    ♣ 9 6 5   ♣ J 9 6 5   ♣ Q 6 5

(d) ♠ A 5 3   (e) ♠ A 6 5
    ♡ 8 7 3   ♡ 7 6 3
    ♢ K J 10 6   ♢ Q 5
    ♣ Q 6 5   ♣ K Q J 6 2

On hand (a), we have only 7 useful HCP since it is extremely unlikely that the queen of hearts is worth anything at all – we should just respond with a simple three spades. Hand (b) is even weaker in terms of HCP. However, there is no guarantee that four clubs will be a good contract: we might as well bid three no-trumps with our double heart stop and hope for the best – it may well be a better contract than four clubs and at least if we make it we will score a game bonus. Hand (c) contains 10 working HCP – more than partner could hope for if we responded a simple three spades – so here we should jump to four spades. Hand (d) is identical, except our spades and diamonds are swapped round, which makes a great deal of difference. Not only is there less guarantee that he holds diamonds with us, but also game in diamonds requires us to make eleven tricks rather than the ten we would need in spades – we should settle for a quiet four diamonds and hope for a plus score. Hand (e) is significantly stronger and our club suit is sufficiently strong even if there is not much of a fit, so here we should jump to five clubs.

There are no guarantees on any of the above hands – where he errs on the cautious side we may well miss game; where he has bid more aggressively we may well end up too high, and may be doubled. All we can do is play the percentages.

How should I respond if I have two suits?
So far, we have only been concerned with what level we should bid at. Often we are dealt hands which have two suits and we would like to play in the best fit. If we are weak, without the values to make a jump response, we just have to pick a suit (a major if we have one) and hope, but if we have the values to bid game, then we also have the option of cue-bidding the opponents' suit. For example, suppose we hold:

(f) ♠ K J 6 4   (g) ♠ K Q 6 4
    ♡ 6 5 4   ♡ A J 6 5
    ♢ A Q 5 3 2   ♢ 7 6 4
    ♣ 7   ♣ 7 6

With hand (f), if partner had doubled three-club or three-heart opening, we would certainly consider that we had enough values to make a jump response. If we jump in diamonds, we may well miss the spade fit; if we jump to four spades, we may end up in a silly 4–3 fit, when we would have been much better in diamonds. The answer is to cue-bid in the opponents' suit. If the opening bid has been three hearts and we cue-bid four hearts, partner will bid four spades if he has four spades and there we will play; if he doesn't have four spades he is likely to bid five clubs, which we will convert to five diamonds. If the opening bid was three clubs and we cue-bid four clubs, he is likely to respond four diamonds or four hearts. If he bids four hearts, there is no problem – we simply bid four spades and he will know we also have diamonds. If partner bids four diamonds, we should still bid four spades since he may also have four spades – he will know we don't have hearts because we didn't bid them.

It should be noted that if we changed our spade and diamond holdings around, we should simply bid four spades over partner's double of three clubs or three hearts. Whatever concessions may have to be made on distribution for a take-out double of a pre-emptive opening, partner should always be prepared for us to jump to game in a five-card major. Unless we have such a good hand that we are seriously interested in a slam, we should never have a five-card major when we cue-bid in response to a take-out double of a pre-empt – the only exception to this is when the opening bid has been in a minor and we hold both majors.

On hand (g), if partner doubles an opening bid of three of either minor, it would be silly to guess which major to play in. Again, we should cue-bid the opponents' suit and let partner choose.

Is a double any different in the protective position?

Again, a double in fourth seat may be very much weaker and once more a lot of guesswork must be done. However, partner will only be very weak when he is very short in the opponents' suit and thinks we are going to pass his balancing double. Much of the time that he reopens with a double we will find that we have length in the opponents' suit and our best action is to pass – even if the contract makes, we may find that it would have been more expensive to bid and go several down doubled. If our trump holding is inadequate for a pass, then we just do the best we can.

Here are some example hands (after the sequence 3♡ – Pass – Pass – Dble; Pass):

(h) ♠ 6 4
♡ Q 9 6 4
♢ A 7 5
♣ Q 7 6 2

(i) ♠ J 5 3
♡ K 10 6
♢ A 7 5
♣ J 7 6 2

(j) ♠ 6 5 2
♡ K 10 7
♢ A Q 5 4 3
♣ 7 5

(k) ♠ K Q J 7   (l) ♠ 7
     ♡ 8 7 2   ♡ 8 7 3 2
     ♢ A 7 5   ♢ A 5
     ♣ 6 5 2   ♣ K J 10 9 4 3

On hand (h), we have one certain trump trick with fair prospects of a second, perhaps via a trump promotion – pass and hope for the best. Hand (i) is more difficult and would probably divide an expert panel. The choice is between pass and three no-trumps – either could be right, but the balanced distribution and lack of trick source suggest that pass may well be the winner. On hand (j), conversely, we have a good source of tricks in diamonds so should plump for the no-trump game. On hand (k) we are clearly in no position to pass the double and really have to guess how many spades to bid – of course we may go down, but we are really too good for a simple three spades and should bid the game. We should also bid game on hand (l) – again we have no guarantee that it will be a good contract, but we have too much distribution to try to land on a pinhead in four clubs.

Doubles of higher openings

How should we try to cope when they open at the four level against us?
Doubles of opening bids of four of a minor are usually played in a very similar way to doubles of three-level opening bids – i.e. for take-out. There is a tendency for them to be made more freely when both majors are held – this is particularly the case when the opening bid has been made in diamonds. After all, suppose we are dealt:

     ♠ K Q 6 5 4
     ♡ A K 8 7 3
     ♢ 5
     ♣ 6 5

When our right-hand opponent has opened four diamonds, we have to take some action or we would often miss our major-suit game. Other than guessing which major to bid, our only sensible course of action is to double and hope that partner bids a major. If we held the same hand over a three-diamond opening, we also had the option of cue-bidding four diamonds, best played as asking partner, in the first instance, to choose between the majors and not necessarily showing a particularly strong hand.

What about doubles of four of a major?
Doubles of opening bids of four of a major, on the other hand, are a different matter. Our right-hand opponent has taken up all the bidding space by simply bidding game straightaway and, unless we are dealt a straightforward single-suited hand, our only possible take-out devices are double, four no-trumps and possibly a cue-bid of the opponents' suit. Since the cue-bid of the opponents' suit would, in most instances, force us to slam, it is rare that such a good hand is held and we have to choose between double and four no-trumps.

There are two schools of thought about the best use of these bids:

1 Double is for take-out; four no-trumps shows a two-suiter.
2 Double is optional (i.e. about strong no-trump values with honour to three in the opponents' suit); four no-trumps is for take-out.

In practice these two styles overlap. Also, in practice, because we have so little choice, we just have to do the best we can with what we are dealt. The main reason for defining what we are supposed to hold for a particular action is not to reject all hands which fall outside our definition, but rather to give partner some basis for making a decision in response to our double.

What is the best way to play our bids of double and four no-trumps?
The situation is different when the opponents open four hearts
to when they open four spades. When they open four hearts they
have left us with the possibility of playing in a four-level contract – namely four spades. When they open four spades this
possibility no longer exists. Having studied the expert views of
many a bridge magazine bidding panel, I feel current main-
stream expert practise seems to be as follows:

1   A double of a four-heart opening bid is for take-out (a
    4–1–4–4 14-count would perhaps be the perfect minimum
    hand). Partner is expected to remove to four spades when-
    ever he has five or more spades and usually when he has only
    four spades. Of course, the doubler may not have been dealt
    four spades, but he will not pass a four-spade response if he
    has less than three. If responder does not have four spades, he
    may bid a six-card minor; bid four no-trumps with two
    five-card suits (and a very strong hand if one of them is
    spades); but otherwise, with a more balanced hand, he
    should pass and hope for the best.

2   A double of a four-spade opening bid is optional (a balanced
    16-count with little wastage in spades – say x-x-x or A-x-x,
    but not K-J-x – would be a perfect minimum). Partner will
    more often pass a double of four spades, but may remove
    with good distribution, as above. This is not to say that one
    should not double a four-spade opening on a 1–4–4–4 14-
    count as well – after all, that would not be sufficient reason to
    attempt to bid to the five level. We want to double four
    spades with both hands, but partner does need to make some
    assumptions.

It should be borne in mind that since the opponents have
actually bid game, the penalty for choosing to defend and then
finding that it is impossible to defeat their contract is substan-

tially less than it would be if we had doubled a lower opening bid. The general rule is to choose to defend with a balanced hand and remove when unbalanced.

When the opponents open four of a major against us, or even five of a minor, they will generally have a long, strong trump suit. The higher they bid, the more true this will be. Therefore we are rarely going to have sufficient trumps, in terms of strength or length, to double them with any certainty. Also, as the bidding gets higher, everybody is likely to have much more distribution, which means two things: first, our defensive tricks may not stand up, and, second, if we do buy the hand, our suits are less likely to break well. Generally it is best to defend when our side has no guarantee of a fit, and bid when we either know of a fit (because we have a long suit) or can offer a choice of fit (because we are two-suited and can respond four no-trumps, or perhaps even five no-trumps over a double of a five-level opening).

Here are some examples of how modern-day experts bid after doubles of opening bids of four of a major:

1 North/South Game. Pairs.

West	North	East	South
	4 ♠	Dble	Pass
?			

West holds:

♠ 4   ♡ Q 6 5 3 2   ◇ 3   ♣ 10 9 8 4 3 2

2 Game All. IMPs.

West	North	East	South
			4 ♡
Pass	Pass	Dble	Pass
?			

West holds:

♠ K 10 7 4   ♡ Q 6   ◇ 9   ♣ A 10 8 7 4 2

3   Game All. Pairs.

West	North	East	South
			4 ♡
Pass	Pass	Dble	Pass
?			

West holds:

♠ J 10 9 6 5 2   ♡ Q 10 8 5   ◇ 6   ♣ Q 3

On Problem 1, fourteen experts (out of seventeen) felt they had so much distribution that they should remove the double of four spades, even with so few high cards. Of those fourteen, eight chose four no-trumps to offer partner a choice of contract, intending to remove five diamonds to five hearts. Five panellists chose to bid five clubs because they thought that if partner had equal length in clubs and hearts, they would prefer to play in clubs. They expected partner to remove five clubs on a singleton anyway.

On Problem 2, nineteen experts (out of twenty-four) removed partner's double to four spades, despite their good six-card club suit. This was because they knew partner was prepared for them to respond four spades, whereas the same was not true of five clubs. Three panellists chose five clubs and two chose to pass.

On Problem 3, seventeen experts (out of twenty-four) removed the double to four spades. Despite their likely trump tricks in defence of four hearts, they expected to score better by playing the hand.

What does a double of a five-of-a-minor opening bid show?
Again, there are two schools of thought but the most common expert treatment is to play a double as take-out. When an opponent opens with five of a minor he is going to hold a long good suit and he is unlikely to be frightened of being doubled for penalty. Since he has shown a lot of distribution, it is likely that

our side also has distribution, so we will more often hold a hand where we wish to make a take-out double.

Points to remember

1   Doubles of all pre-emptive bids are for take-out, but they should be left in more frequently as the level advances.

2   We have chosen to give up a natural two no-trump response to a double of a weak two bid, in order to use it as a negative response.

3   When partner chooses to bid over a weak three or four opening, he is already playing you for some values, so don't punish him for his enterprise by overbidding.

4   Opponents pre-empt to cause you problems, and some of them are insoluble. Try to take your plus score whenever possible rather than be too optimistic about getting a bigger plus score by bidding on.

5   When partner doubles an opening bid of four of a major (or higher) we should generally remove when we have a distri-butional hand (say a six-card suit or two five-card suits), but pass when we are more balanced (unless we have spades and partner has doubled four hearts).

3

Doubles of One No-trump

So far we have looked at take-out doubles of opening bids in suits, at various levels. We will now turn to one of the most frequent uses of the penalty double – when an opponent has opened one no-trump against us. However, as we will see, this Section will not be confined exclusively to the realm of the penalty double.

Requirements for a double of one no-trump

What does a double of a one no-trump opening bid mean?
A double of a one no-trump opening is for penalty, either a strong balanced hand or a hand with a long, good suit which expects to beat one no-trump. After all, how could it be for take-out as you can't have a take-out of all four suits!

How strong a hand do I need to double?
The normal requirement for a penalty double of a one no-trump opening in second position is to hold about 16 HCP. This can be reduced slightly if the hand has a good opening lead, and can be reduced considerably if the hand contains a long running suit.

Is it the same in the protective position?
In fourth position, the strength can be lowered a little but here the opening lead element is not so relevant since we will not be the one to make the opening lead. Consider the following two hands:

(a) ♠ K 6 5   (b) ♠ K J 7
    ♡ A 4 3   ♡ A J 6
    ◇ K Q J 10 5 4   ◇ A J 4 3
    ♣ 7   ♣ Q 4 3

With hand (a) we would be delighted to double a 12–14 no-trump in second seat. We would lead a diamond, thus establishing six certain defensive tricks, and would be unlucky if partner could not contribute a little to beat the contract. If we held the hand in fourth seat, however, double becomes less attractive. Partner may well lead a club which would probably not be good for our side; our king of spades is less likely to make a trick; and if partner does not lead a diamond (and why should he?) we may well find that declarer makes seven or more tricks before we get a chance to cash ours.

As for hand (b), it has its full complement of 16 HCP, but all opening leads look fraught with danger, so much so that some would choose not to double one no-trump in second seat. However, if we held the hand in fourth seat we would be delighted. Here we positively want partner to lead his best suit, for we know that, whatever it is, we have useful cards which will help to establish some tricks.

Removing partner's double of one no-trump

Should I remove partner's double of one no-trump when I have a weak hand?
If we are very weak (say 4 HCP or less), we should generally only remove the double when we have some distribution – at least a five-card suit. The exception to this is when the opponents are vulnerable and we are not. At most vulnerabilities, when we have a weak balanced hand, even if one no-trump makes, if we were to remove it, it is likely we would be doubled in turn and find that

we lost a large penalty. At favourable vulnerability, if they are going to make one no-trump, it is likely to be cheaper to remove it, even if we lose a penalty ourselves.

Should I ever remove the double when I have a good hand?
We should remove the double when we are strong in playing strength, so suspect that game is quite likely, but are afraid that partner may make an unsuccessful opening lead against one no-trump.

In this case we will presumably be either one-suited (when we can simply jump to an appropriate level in our long suit) or two-suited. If we are two-suited, then we should respond two no-trumps to partner's double. This cannot be natural, for if we had a natural two no-trump bid we would surely prefer to defend against one no-trump doubled. This two no-trump response is forcing to suit agreement (i.e. we can stop in four of a minor if necessary). We bid suits in which we are prepared to play, up-the-line, until a fit is found. For example:

	N		
♠ A 7 5			♠ K 10 8 6 2
♡ K Q 5 4			♡ A J 8 7 3
◇ A J 5 3	W	E	◇ 8
♣ K 6			♣ 9 2
	S		

West	North	East	South
			1NT
Dble	Pass	2NT	Pass
3◇	Pass	3♡	Pass
4♡	All Pass		

	N	
♠ K Q 4 2		♠ 6
♡ Q 6	W E	♡ 7 3
◇ A 7 6 3		◇ K Q 8 4 2
♣ A Q 6	S	♣ K J 7 5 2

West	North	East	South
			1NT
Dble	Pass	2NT	Pass
3♣	Pass	3◇	Pass
3♠	Pass	4♣	Pass
4◇	All Pass		

Note that, in our second example, East continues to show his hand even though his partner has bid one of his suits straight-away. This is because, first, it still might not be the best fit (as here), and second, his partner may have diamond weakness but an otherwise suitable hand for three no-trumps.

What should I do if the next hand redoubles?
It is important for partnerships to discuss what to do if the next hand redoubles (for penalty). It is obviously possible to bid just as we would have done without the redouble, as described above. However, many pairs have found that the time the next hand redoubles is when there is a really juicy penalty to be had. This is because, if responder has the values to redouble, it likely that the double was of the playing strength, rather than the HCP, variety. There is little more frustrating than to sit there holding, say:

♠ A K Q J 10 9 6
♡ A 4
◇ 7 6
♣ 3 2

and to hear the bidding proceed: 1NT – Dble – Rdble, and then to hear partner bid two clubs, for example. For this reason, many partnerships have the agreement that if responder redoubles, the next hand *must* pass, whatever his hand. Then if the doubler can beat one no-trump in his own hand, he passes; if he is more balanced, then he is the one to remove himself.

What about if the redouble is weak and is part of an escape mechanism that many pairs seem to play these days?

If the redouble is weak then we should pass unless we also have a weak hand with a long suit. Then, when the opponents remove to a suit, either of us can double for penalty. If we pass the redouble and later remove partner's penalty double, then we have also shown some constructive values.

How should I bid if responder passes, but the pass forces the one no-trump opener to redouble?

Many pairs nowadays play an artificial escape mechanism if one no-trump is doubled. Often an integral part of this mechanism is that with a hand of classic redouble strength, a pass is called for, whereupon the opener redoubles, and responder either passes with strength or bids something to show some type of weak hand. If we are playing against a pair using such a method, we cannot have the luxury of perhaps playing in one no-trump redoubled when the doubler has a long suit, since when partner passes the redouble he does not know whether it is also going to be passed by the next hand. It would be patently absurd when holding, say, a balanced 16-count after the bidding:

West	North	East	South
			1NT
Dble	Pass	Pass	Rdble
?			

to be forced to remove oneself, when the responder to one no-trump might have been weak all along. On this sequence it has to be the partner of the doubler who is the one to remove.

However, waiting until this round is perhaps not the best way to remove oneself with a very weak hand. We are now in a very exposed position, because the one no-trump opener knows that his partner has a good hand, so he can double himself if he has good trumps. The following is a better scheme (we assume that the pass of one no-trump doubled forces, or at least invites, the opener to redouble):

1   With a very weak balanced hand, we remove ourselves to two clubs immediately. This tells partner that we have at least some support (perhaps only a doubleton) for any suit that he may care to bid. In this way it is not so easy for the opponents to double – if opener has the clubs he does not yet know that his partner has any values; and if his partner, who does have values, does not have clubs it is difficult for him to double also.

2   With a very weak hand with a long suit (other than clubs) we should bid immediately – again this may make it difficult for the opponents to double when we are in trouble.

3   With a very weak hand with long clubs, or with a long suit which is not clubs but contains some potential, we should wait until the second round before removing.

The opponents run from one no-trump doubled

What should we do when the opponents run to a suit after the double of one no-trump?

When the opponents run from a double of one no-trump, it is important that we are in a reasonable position to double them when we can take a substantial penalty, or bid our own hand when we can't. There several schemes currently in use.

Scheme 1

All doubles by either side are take-out. Pass is forcing on the doubler if the removal has been to a minor, but only forcing on him if he is short in the opponents' suit if the removal has been to a major.

Thus a sequence such as: 1NT – Dble – 2♣ – Dble is take-out. If we wish to make a penalty double of two clubs, then we must pass and wait for partner to make a take-out double which we will pass.

There are two main problems with this method:

1 How take-out is take-out? Can this take-out double be made on a void? A singleton? Or does it have to contain a doubleton in the opponents' suit? There has to be some agreement or the other hand doesn't know when he should be passing. Whatever the agreement is, there will be hands where it is unsatisfactory – i.e. if it can be made on a void, the other hand will remove much of the time when a substantial penalty is available; if it promises a doubleton, then the hand may not have a satisfactory bid when it has less length than that.

2 Opponents often run from one no-trump doubled into a minor that they do not actually possess. They are intending to redouble when they are doubled. This means that we may pass two clubs, say, and wait for partner to make a take-out double, but when the auction reaches him, he also has length in the opponents' suit. If he does make a take-out double, we may later have difficulty in playing him for such strength/length in their suit; if he doesn't we may miss a substantial penalty.

If the opponents remove themselves in an artificial way – i.e. they use a redouble or a pass to show some weak hand-types, as mentioned above – the first double made by the defending side should be for take-out. As a take-out double implies support for all unbid suits, subsequent doubles should be for penalty.

Scheme 2

This is simplicity itself. Our treatment of the opponents' removal of 1NT is exactly the same as if they had overcalled our 1NT instead – i.e. whatever we are used to playing when they come in over our one no-trump opening (with a natural overcall) we play here: Lebensohl, transfers, etc. A double of 1NT – Dble – 2♡ would be exactly the same as if the bidding had gone 1NT – 2♡ – Dble. This is not perfect because the doubler of one no-trump does not promise a balanced hand in the same way that he does when he opens one no-trump, but the double is usually balanced and the method won't go far wrong. It has the merit of applying a situation we are comfortably familiar with to another area, thus easing up problems of memory strain.

Scheme 3

1 When the opponents remove themselves to two of a minor, double is penalty and pass is forcing.

2 When the opponents remove themselves to two of a major, everything is played as in Scheme 2 – however we would play if they intervened with two of a major over our 1NT opening.

3 A double by the original doubler – i.e. the hand under the trumps – shows, typically, honour to three trumps (with extra values if the removal has been to two of a major).

The reason that minors and majors are treated differently is that removal to two of a minor is often used as a 'wriggle' on a weak, semi-balanced hand, not necessarily including the minor, whereas removal to two of a major is usually made on a five-card suit. Another reason for treating majors and minors differently is that it is less of a disaster if we choose to defend two of a minor doubled and find that it makes.

Because the pass of a removal to two of a minor is forcing, it allows us to define our hands quite accurately if we are not going to defend.

1. Pass either shows values or a hand so weak and balanced that we are prepared to pass out a second double should that be partner's choice of action.
2. Double is penalty, usually a four-card holding.
3. An immediate bid shows a long suit but very little in the way of values.
4. Pass followed by a bid (including a removal of partner's double) shows a few scattered values – say 5–7 HCP.
5. An immediate jump bid shows a six-card suit with a weakish hand – say 5 or 6 HCP.
6. Pass followed by a jump bid shows a stronger hand with a six-card suit.
7. An immediate cue-bid shows a three-suiter with shortage in their suit – say a 4–4–4–1 5- or 6-count; we are likely to pass partner's simple response.
8. Pass followed by a cue-bid shows a three-suiter, but is game-forcing.
9. An immediate two no-trumps is a weak two-suiter.
10. Pass followed by two no-trumps is a stronger two-suiter.

The principle is straightforward – bid immediately with weak hands; with stronger hands pass first and bid on the next round.

If the opponents remove the double of two of a minor to something else, it is best to play penalty doubles immediately over the bid suit (usually four trumps) and optional doubles under the bid suit (usually three trumps). For example:

West	North	East	South
			1NT
Dble	2♣	Pass	Pass
Dble	Rdble	Pass	2♡
Dble			

should be penalty but

West	North	East	South
			1NT
Dble	2♣	Pass	Pass
Dble	Rdble	Pass	2♡
Pass	Pass	Dble	

should be optional.

The sequence should be forcing: we either double them or bid on ourselves.

If the opponents remove themselves from one no-trump in some other systemic way – for example, if the bidding goes:

West	North	East	South
			1NT
Dble	Pass	Pass	Rdble
Pass	2♣		

the simplest agreement to have is that if they begin by removing themselves to two of a minor, however they do it, the above principles apply and the auction is forcing – i.e. we either double them or bid on ourselves.

Non-penalty doubles of one no-trump

What does a double of one no-trump by a passed hand show? Obviously it can't show 16 HCP.

Whatever our chosen defence to a one no-trump opening, it is probably not ideal. We will find that some hands are difficult to deal with. Unfortunately, this is an unavoidable problem. We only have four bids available at the two level with which to describe an enormous number of different hand-types – one-suiters, two-suiters, three-suiters, etc. Nobody has a method that enables them to bid on all the hands on which they would like to bid. However, if double is assigned a conventional mean-ing, it can be used to describe some hands which otherwise would be difficult.

The best meaning for a passed-hand double depends to a large extent on what defence to one no-trump is used in the first place. Here is an example. Suppose our basic system includes weak two openings (or a Multi two diamonds) and that our normal defence to one no-trump is an Astro variant whereby a two-club overcall shows hearts and another suit and a two-diamond over-call shows spades and another suit. This is a common defence to one no-trump and generally works well, but there are often some problems in responding to it because we do not know which second suit partner holds. For example, suppose we hold:

♠ 6
♡ A 6 5 4 2
◇ Q 4 3
♣ Q 6 5 3

and we hear partner bid two diamonds (spades and another) over an opposing one no-trump. If we knew he had diamonds for sure, we would pass two diamonds, but we could look silly if he held a different second suit. So, we bid two hearts, denying spade support. Now if he bids two spades, what do we do? Do we stay in what is surely a 5–1 fit, or do we bid ever upwards to try to find somewhere better – after all, he could still have clubs. All very difficult.

One common way to use a passed-hand double to help with this type of problem is the following:

1   Double shows either both majors or both minors.
2   Two of a minor shows that minor + one major suit (some insist that the minor is a five-card suit and the major a four-card suit).
3   Two of a major is natural (but this depends a little on your style of opening bid – if you open all sub-opening-strength hands with weak twos, then you could agree that two of a major by a passed hand shows that five-card major plus a four-card minor, so that partner knows to remove if he has only a singleton in the major).

There are many ways in which the passed-hand double could be used and it is beyond the scope of this book to discuss the various defences to one no-trump in detail. The above is merely an example of what is possible.

Is it right to play a double of a strong no-trump as penalty? It seems that they have shown a good hand and it would not be very likely that we would hold a penalty double.

Some expert pairs play a conventional double when the one no-trump opening is strong – say 15–17 or stronger – for they feel that the chance of getting a penalty from such a strong opening is unlikely. However, other equally expert pairs do not agree with this and prefer to play the double as normal penalty.

If we do not wish to play a penalty double here, then the most sensible treatment is to play it in the same way as a passed-hand double of a weak no-trump.

One idea that is widely played in the United States is that a double immediately over a strong no-trump is conventional, as above, but that a double in the protective position shows about 10–13 HCP and a balanced hand. These players argue that the time when a strong no-trump will play badly is when the defensive high-card strength is evenly divided, thus this is the time when they can defend doubled. This is true, but we may also have a true penalty double of a strong no-trump in second seat, when we are basing it on the suit that we are about to lead.

Points to remember

1 A double of a one no-trump opening is for penalty, not take-out. It shows about 16+ HCP, but may be less when there is a good suit to lead.

2 When considering a close decision between doubling one no-trump and passing, we should take into account whose lead it is. If we have a good suit to lead, the double is more attractive when we are on lead; if we have tenaces in every suit it is better if partner is to be on lead.

3 We should not remove partner's double of one no-trump with a weak hand unless we have some distribution or are non-vulnerable against vulnerable opponents.

4 Many tournament players who play a weak no-trump use a conventional escape mechanism. Be sure to discuss with your partner how you are going to cope with this.

5 A double of one no-trump by a passed hand is best used to show a hand that your normal defence to one no-trump finds difficult.

4

Other Doubles in Auctions Where the
Opponents Have Opened the Bidding

Everything that we have covered so far has been reasonably straightforward, but now things begin to get rather more involved. In this chapter we are going to look at a number of different sorts of double in many different situations, but what they all have in common is that they occur after the opponents have opened, and after there has been more bidding, either by our side or by an opponent.

Doubles in fourth seat

If one opponent has opened the bidding and the other has responded, what does a double show?
Doubles in fourth seat when both the opponents have bid should be subdivided into three categories:

1   The opponents have raised.
2   An opponent has responded 1NT.
3   An opponent has responded in a new suit.

Suppose the opponent has raised 1♡ – Pass – 2♡ – Dble?
A double after the opponents have bid and raised a suit is essentially the same as any other take-out double and would ideally hold support for all other three suits. However, we do not live in a perfect world. If we hold reasonable values with shortage in the opponents' suit and we do not take action over the raise, we will probably find that in a few moments partner

will be choosing his opening lead against two hearts. Any of the following hands would be reasonable doubles after the sequence $1\heartsuit - \text{Pass} - 2\heartsuit$:

♠ K 7 6 5	♠ K 7 6	♠ K J 6 5	♠ A Q 4 3
♡ 5 4	♡ 7	♡ 8 3	♡ A 3
◇ A Q 6	◇ K J 10 8 3	◇ A Q 10 6 5	◇ J 5
♣ K 10 5 4	♣ A K J 5	♣ A 5	♣ K 10 6 5 4

Note that the strength increases as the shape suitability decreases.

How should I respond to my partner's take-out double?
In response to a take-out double of a sequence such as $1\heartsuit - \text{Pass} - 2\heartsuit - \text{Dble}$, we have two problems. First, we may have game on our way and need to be able to differentiate between weak and invitational responding hands. We have also seen that partner may not have perfect distribution for his take-out double and therefore we would also benefit from having some way of distinguishing between real suit length and more balanced hands.

We can use a response of two no-trumps to help us. As we saw in the section on responding to take-out doubles of weak two bids, to give up the ability to play in two no-trumps is no great loss – most of the time, with a hand which would like to bid two no-trumps naturally we can either pass the double or bid three no-trumps.

So, do we treat this take-out double in the same way as a double of a weak two bid?
This is a difficult decision to make. We cannot use a two no-trump bid both to help define hand strength *and* to help define suit strength. We have to make a choice. When we were defending against weak two bids we chose to come down on the side of defining strength, because it was quite likely that our side would

have a game on. Here it is less likely but quite possible and for that reason, it is best to treat this sequence in the same way.

Suppose the opponent has responded one no-trump: for example, 1♡ – Pass – 1NT – Dble?

The tried and tested meaning of a double in the above sequence is to play it as a hand that would have made a take-out double of a one-heart opening – i.e. around opening-bid values with heart shortage and support for all the other suits. The responses are just as they would have been to a double of an opening bid, but the double is more likely to be passed for penalty with heart length and strength. This is because the heart strength now lies over opener's hearts rather than under them. In fact, this is quite a frequent source of a good penalty. After the sequence:

West	North	East	South
			1 ♡
Pass	1NT	Dble	Pass
?			

partner is quite likely to have a smattering of values with heart length and strength. After all, we are short in hearts; the one no-trump bidder won't have too many of them; opener has neither chosen to rebid a long heart suit nor redouble to show extra values. A typical hand for partner to hold in this position would be:

♠ Q 6 5
♡ K Q 10 8
♢ J 5 4
♣ J 6 5

This hand would be quite suitable for passing the double of one no-trump. He has good chances of making three heart tricks; he has a little help in any other suit we may lead; and he has sufficient high cards to suggest that our side holds the balance of strength. Also, especially playing Teams, it is not the end of the world if one no-trump makes anyway – it is worth risking losing 180 to gain perhaps 500.

If a double is take-out, what do I do when I have a strong balanced hand?

One of the problems of choosing to play a double as a take-out of the suit that was opened is that you are left without a bid when you hold a strong no-trump type of hand – say a balanced 17-count. For this reason, some pairs choose to play a double of a one no-trump response as showing a strong hand, usually balanced, similar to a hand that would have doubled a one no-trump opening bid. These pairs then use a two-club bid in this position as showing a take-out double of the suit opened – 1♡ – Pass – 1NT – 2♣ shows a take-out double of hearts.

This seems a good idea. What are the problems with it?

The drawback is that you can often give up your best chance of a penalty. When the bidding proceeds, say, 1♡ – Pass – 1NT – Dble; Pass, the chances are that our side has roughly the same number of high-card points and the same number of cards in any particular suit, whatever the nature of the double – in this instance we are likely to hold between 18 and 22 HCP, and approximately seven spades (neither opponent has bid them), six hearts and thirteen cards in the minors, probably divided fairly evenly – say no worse than eight cards in one minor and five in the other. Thus, would we not rather defend one no-trump doubled when our hands were:

	N	
♠ Q 6 5		♠ K J 7 2
♡ K Q 10 8	W E	♡ 5 4
◇ J 5 4		◇ A Q 7 2
♣ J 6 5	S	♣ Q 8 2

than when they were:

```
♠ Q 6 5 2        N          ♠ K J 7
♡ 10 8 5                     ♡ K Q 4
◇ J 5 4 2    W       E       ◇ A Q 7
♣ J 6            S          ♣ Q 8 5 2
```

On the first pair of hands we have the potential to take three spades, three hearts, two diamonds and a club (nine tricks), while they are only likely to take one spade, one heart, perhaps a diamond, and three clubs (five or six tricks). On the second pair of hands, assuming (which is unlikely) that we find the best lead of a spade, we can only expect to take two spades (no entry to the long spade), one heart, two diamonds and a club (six tricks), while they have prospects of making one spade, four hearts, perhaps a diamond, and three clubs (eight or nine tricks). This is obviously only a rough guide as we do not know where their high cards are, but it does illustrate the point. We would rather defend one no-trump when their long suit is breaking badly for them and when our high-card points are divided more evenly. It is better for us to have 12 HCP facing 8 than it is to have 18 HCP facing 2, especially when the strong hand is under the stronger of the opposing hands.

So, is it better to play double as take out?
The tried and tested method of playing a double of a one no-trump response as a double of the suit opened is probably best. If we have a strong, balanced hand we have two alternatives. First, we can just pass. After all, we are unlikely to have game on when the opponents open the bidding and choose to play in one no-trump. Our failure to bid anything with all our values may encourage declarer to go wrong in the play and we may find that he goes two or three down in one no-trump when we couldn't make anything anyway. If we really can't bear to pass such a good hand, we could agree that a two-club bid in this position showed a strong balanced hand.

What do I need to double when an opponent has responded in a new suit: for example, 1♡ – Pass – 1♠ – Dble?

The normal meaning of a double in fourth seat after the opponents have bid two suits, is take-out – showing at least four cards in both the remaining suits. This should show a reasonable hand since we are entering an auction in a dangerous position: both the opponents have shown some values and because they have not yet located a fit, it is quite likely that we do not have a fit either.

We are in the fortunate position of having a multitude of bids available, some of which we can use to show the other two suits. One no-trump would normally be played as natural here, unless by a passed hand. But what would two hearts mean? Or two spades? Or two no-trumps? Some people like to play bids in the opponents' suits here as natural, but it seems unlikely that we would want to bid hearts naturally when the announced strength is over us, and if we wanted to bid spades naturally it may well be profitable to wait until the next round – perhaps opener will rebid one no-trump and then we can double to show a good hand with spades. If we wish to use such bids artificially, this would be a reasonable scheme:

1 Double shows fair values, with at least four cards in both of the unbid suits, but may occasionally be the first move on a strong hand with only one of the unbid suits.

2 Two no-trumps shows at least five cards in each of the unbid suits, just like an immediate unusual two no-trump overcall – partnerships should define the strength needed for this in the same way as in direct position.

3 The lowest cue-bid (here two hearts) shows six cards in the lowest unbid suit (clubs here) and four cards in the other (diamonds). Because of the implicit playing strength shown by such a hand, it does not need very much in the way of

high cards, certainly K-J-10-9-x-x and A-J-10-x would be acceptable.

4 The highest cue-bid (here two spades) shows six cards in the highest unbid suit (diamonds) and four cards in the other (clubs).

When we are a passed hand we can choose between double and one no-trump, using double to show a more balanced hand with more defensive strength.

Does the same thing apply when the new-suit response is made at the two level?

So far we have been concerned with a situation when not only are we doubling a one-level contract, but we are also doubling when both of the unbid suits are of the same rank, and therefore of the same importance. The situation is slightly different when the bidding starts, for example, 1♡ – Pass – 2♣. Here we are in a much more dangerous position, since our right-hand opponent has shown significant values. A double here needs to be much more sound, and would normally contain a five-card diamond suit and four spades. It is dangerous to choose a take-out double with five spades and four diamonds, since partner will tend to choose to bid the lowest suit when he has equal, say three-card, length, so we are likely to end up in the wrong suit. Also, in this position, when we have six diamonds and four spades this may well be worth showing via a two-heart cue-bid, but there is much less point in playing the higher cue-bid, three clubs, to show six spades and four diamonds as the diamonds will be much less significant. If we are worth bidding at the three level, we will usually do better to make the more pre-emptive three-spade bid immediately.

When the opponents bid two suits of the same rank, the scheme detailed above applies, but when they bid two suits of different rank, the following is suggested:

1 Double is take-out, but needs sound playing strength if the response has been at the two level.
2 The lowest cue-bid shows six cards in the unbid minor and four cards in the unbid major.
3 Two no-trumps shows at least five cards in each of the unbid suits, and is accurately defined as to strength and suit quality in the same way as any two-suited overcall should be.
4 The higher cue-bid shows at least five cards in each of the unbid suits but is less accurately defined.

Responding to a take-out double when the next hand has raised

In Chapter 1 we covered responding to a take-out double, but what happens if the next hand bids before I have had a chance to respond: for example, after 1♡ – Dble – 2♡?

Sometimes we will hold a hand with a respectable suit which we are happy to bid even though at a higher level; sometimes we will pass, knowing we have insufficient values to bid at the higher level; sometimes we will have values with no good suit and then we can make a responsive double.

What is a responsive double?

When partner has made a take-out double of an opening bid of one of a suit and the next hand has raised, it is possible that we will find that we hold a hand on which we would like to make a penalty double. However, over the years it has been found that this is not often a very profitable approach. More frequently we hold a hand with some values on which we would like to enter the auction, but with no good suit of our own. Rather than guess a suit, usually at the three level, we would prefer simply to show a few values and invite *partner* to bid a suit. So . . . we double, a responsive double.

74

When should I double and when should I bid a suit?

Different players have different ideas concerning whether the double should promise or deny holding four cards in any unbid majors, but the majority consensus seems to be that, since partner is more likely to hold four cards in the other major than in any other suit, when we hold a major in response to a take-out double we should bid it. The exception to this is when we hold a good hand (i.e. intend to do more than just pass partner's response to our double), and the major suit is of poor quality.

Let us suppose the bidding proceeds 1 ♡ – Dble – 2 ♡ and we hold:

(a) ♠ J 6 5 4　　(b) ♠ J 6 5 4　　(c) ♠ 6 5
　　♡ A 4 3　　　　♡ A 4 3　　　　♡ 4 3 2
　　♢ Q 7 6　　　　♢ A Q 7 6　　　♢ A J 7 6
　　♣ 9 6 3　　　　♣ 10 6　　　　　♣ K J 6 3

(d) ♠ 6 5 4　　(e) ♠ 6 5
　　♡ 4 3 2　　　　♡ K Q J 10 3
　　♢ A Q J 7　　　♢ Q 7 6
　　♣ K 6 3　　　　♣ 9 6 3

With hand (a), we would only have responded one spade had our right-hand opponent passed one heart, but we would have been conscious that we had a lot more than we might have had for that action. Here we bid two spades. Partner should not expect us to hold a hand that would have jumped to two spades.

On hand (b), we have significant extra values and are worth inviting game. We could just bid three spades, but this would lead to a silly contract if partner held, for example:

♠ Q 7 2
♡ 7
♢ K J 4 3 2
♣ A K 8 5

It is more flexible to start with a responsive double. With this hand partner would then bid three diamonds, we would show our spade suit (we have to bid it straightaway, otherwise partner will not believe we hold four) and, without four-card support, he will rebid four clubs, which we will convert to four diamonds. Partner will now know that we have a good hand (otherwise we would have responded two spades in the first place) and is in a good position to judge whether to raise to game. On this hand, with a very minimum double, he will surely pass.

Hand (c) is a perfect responsive double, four cards in each minor and just the right values to want to bid. If we did not have a responsive double available we would have to guess a minor, which would risk playing in a 4–3 fit unnecessarily.

Hand (d) contains only one suit and, although it is only four cards in length, it is sufficiently robust not to be afraid of risking a 4–3 fit, especially since it is unlikely that any other fit would be better. In three diamonds, even if it is a 4–3 fit, at least we will be taking any ruffs with the short trump hand.

With hand (e) it is important not to make a mistake which is common to many players who are just beginning to learn about conventional bids. They often hope that they can use the bid both in its natural and in its conventional sense and that partner will be sufficiently psychic to work this out. This is not a good idea because partners are not telepathic. With this hand we have to pass two hearts. On a good day partner may have sufficient extra values to double again, when we will be delighted to pass; on an ordinary day everybody will pass and we will defend undoubled.

Does it make any difference when the opponents are bidding spades rather than hearts?
The situation when the opponents are bidding spades is slightly different. When the opponents were bidding hearts, we could

easily bid spades at the same level, and tried to do so whenever possible. However, when they are bidding the highest-ranking suit, we have to go to the next level to bid any suit, including the other major.

Let us assume the bidding has started 1♠ – Dble – 2♠.

(f) ♠ 6 5 4	(g) ♠ 6 5 4	(h) ♠ A 6 5
♡ K Q J 3	♡ Q 7 3 2	♡ Q 7 3
♢ 7 3	♢ 7 3	♢ J 7 3 2
♣ Q 9 5 3	♣ K Q J 9	♣ K 9 5

(i) ♠ A J 10	(j) ♠ 6 5 4
♡ Q 7 3 2	♡ 4
♢ K J 10 7	♢ A K 7 3 2
♣ Q 9	♣ A Q 5 3

On hand (f) we have a very good heart suit and would not be afraid of playing in a 4–3 fit. It is best to bid three hearts straightaway. On hand (g), with good clubs and poor hearts, it is best to start with a double. If partner bids three clubs we will pass, and if he bids three diamonds we will convert to three hearts. On hand (h), although we only have one suit, it is of such poor quality that we would not welcome the prospect of playing in a 4–3 fit. It is better to start with a double and hope that partner has a five-card suit to bid; if not, his best four-card suit will probably play better than our ropey diamonds.

On hand (i) we hold a different type of hand altogether (and the same principles would apply if the opponents had been bidding hearts). We have the values for game but don't know whether to play in three no-trumps or four hearts. It seems a little rash to jump to four hearts when three no-trumps could easily be better, especially when partner holds only three hearts. With this hand we should double first and then bid three no-trumps over part-ner's response. This should alert him to the fact that we are worth bidding three no-trumps, but that our hand is suitable for playing elsewhere should he feel so inclined. If we held a hand that wished to insist on three no-trumps we would have bid it straightaway.

On hand (j) we have the values for game in a minor suit and, indeed, it is reasonably likely that there might be a slam on. Six clubs could be virtually laydown if partner holds as little as:

♠ 2
♡ A J 6 3
♢ Q J 4
♣ K J 10 6 4

Without a responsive double we would have to start with a cue-bid of three spades, then bid our diamonds and the club fit might be lost altogether. Now we can start with a responsive double (the same would be true if the opponents had been bidding hearts). When partner responds in a minor we can now cue-bid to show our good hand (or perhaps cue-bid the other minor at the four level, according to partnership agreement) and then start cue-bidding controls. These two hands are never going to be easy to bid to slam, but a possible sequence might be:

West	North	East	South
1♠	Dble	2♠	Dble
Pass	3♣	Pass	3♠
Pass	4♣	Pass	4♢
Pass	4♡	Pass	4NT
Pass	6♣		

After the three-spade cue-bid, partner rebids his clubs as he has five of them and a minimum take-out double. We cue-bid four diamonds and he co-operates by cue-bidding his ace of hearts. Now we have a difficult bid because we do not have a spade control but would like to make one further slam try.

Many expert pairs have decided that when both sides are cue-bidding and a minor suit has been agreed, Blackwood is not the most useful meaning for four no-trumps – after all, often the response will force us to slam anyway. They use a bid of four no-trumps to distinguish between a hand that wishes to sign off and a hand that wishes to make a further slam try. Here, had we held two doubletons in the majors, we would have been content to sign off (after all, we have already made a slam try when he had shown nothing more than a minimum double), but here we would like him to bid a slam if he has a spade control, so we make the stronger bid of four no-trumps. He should see that, although minimum, he has a very useful hand – a singleton spade, a five-card club suit and useful diamond fillers (likely to be more useful than heart cards since we expressed no interest in playing in hearts).

Does it make any difference if the suit the opponents are bidding is a minor?

When the opponents are bidding minor suits, the rules are similar to when they are bidding hearts, but over a minor suit we can bid either major suit at the same level. Thus a responsive double tends to imply both or neither major. Again, there would be an exception to this when the hand contained good values but a poor four-card major. Let us suppose the bidding started 1♦ – Dble – 2♦:

(k) ♠ K J 6 5
    ♡ Q J 4 2
    ♦ 7 5 2
    ♣ 9 5

(l) ♠ K J 6 5
    ♡ 4 2
    ♦ A 7 5
    ♣ 9 5 3 2

(m) ♠ Q 6 5
    ♡ K J 10 4
    ♦ A 7 5
    ♣ 9 5 3

(n) ♠ Q 6 5 3
    ♡ A 4
    ♦ A 7
    ♣ J 10 9 5 3

With hand (k), it is well worth bidding a major, but we would have to guess which one if we did not have a responsive double available. Here we are delighted to be able to double. On hand (l), although we have four clubs as well as four spades, we are only worth one bid, so should content ourselves with a simple two spades. On hand (m), even though we only have a four-card heart suit, it is quite robust and offers the most likely prospect of game – we should jump to three hearts. Hand (n) is a different matter. We have good values and would be justified in inviting game, but our spade suit is poor. We have no reason to assume that partner has four spades and the best game could well be in clubs, or even no-trumps. We should start with a double. If partner holds, say:

♠ K J 2
♡ K Q 3 2
♢ 8 6
♣ K Q 6 2

he will bid two hearts. We will now bid two spades to show our extra values and four-card spade suit, and he will bid his clubs. We must now try for game, but at this stage we do not know whether to try three no-trumps or five clubs. We can persuade him to help us in making this decision by cue-bidding three diamonds to see if he has a diamond stop. On the hand he has, with above minimum values, even without a diamond stop he should cooperate by showing his K-J-x in spades. This would be enough for us to try five clubs. Had he held K-x in diamonds and J-x-x in spades, he would have bid three no-trumps and that would have become the final contract.

If my partner makes a responsive double should I always just bid my longest suit (lowest suit with two of equal length)?
On all the above hands, we have assumed that the initial take-out double was of the common minimum variety. But what are we to

do when we have game interest, even if he is minimum, and do not want to make a simple bid in a suit for fear that he will pass?

Let us suppose the bidding has begun 1 ♡ – Dble – 2 ♡ – Dble; Pass and we hold:

(o) ♠ K J 10 4   (p) ♠ J 6 5 3   (q) ♠ K 6 5
    ♡ 6 4   ♡ 6 4   ♡ 6 4
    ♢ A Q 4 2   ♢ A K 4   ♢ A Q 4 2
    ♣ Q 6 3   ♣ A 10 9 6   ♣ A K 6 3

(r) ♠ K 6   (s) ♠ K 6
    ♡ A 10 4   ♡ A Q J 6
    ♢ A K 4 2   ♢ K Q 10 4
    ♣ A Q 6 3   ♣ A 6 3

When confronted by a responsive double of one heart, in particular, the first thing to decide is what to respond when we hold four spades. Should we bid them even when partner has denied holding four spades (unless he is going to bid them on the next round)? The best approach is to bid only a four-card spade suit when it is sufficiently robust to have no fear of playing in a 4–3 fit. Remember that occasionally partner will have 4–3–3–3 distribution with a poor four-card minor and if that is the case we are better off playing at as low a level as possible. Consequently we should respond two spades with hand (o) but not with hand (p).

OK, so presumably we respond three clubs with hand (p)?
There is a problem in responding three clubs with hand (p). If we compare hands (p) and (q), we can see that we have something of a problem in differentiating between them. Hand (p) is a completely minimum take-out double with no game interest, whereas hand (q) has substantial extra values and we may well wish to play in game.

What is the solution to this problem?

The way to get around this is to use a bid of two no-trumps in this sequence artificially. We established in an earlier section that a take-out double followed by a bid of no-trumps shows a hand too good to overcall one no-trump in the first place, so even if two no-trumps were played naturally in this sequence, it would show at least 19 HCP and thus would have to be forcing.

So, in order to differentiate between hands (p) and (q), on one of them we will bid two no-trumps and on the other we will bid three clubs.

Which way round should we choose?

There are arguments for both ways, but one of the important things to bear in mind when agreeing a system with partner is that we are only human. If we devise a fiendishly complicated system where different bids mean different things in different sequences, one of two things is likely to happen: either one of us will forget or we will expend so much energy in remembering our system that we will make more errors than usual in other areas. In Chapter 2 we saw that in response to a take-out double of a weak two opening, a bid of two no-trumps showed a poor hand and a simple response in a suit showed positive values. Consequently, we should have a general rule that whenever a bid of two no-trumps is used to help define the strength of hand in response to any double of any bid of two of a major, the two no-trump bid always shows the *weaker* hand-type.

On hand (p) partner should bid two no-trumps and pass our response. On hand (q) partner should bid three clubs immediately to show his game interest.

Can we sometimes use two no-trumps as the first move on a strong hand, like we did over a double of a weak two bid?

Yes, it is still possible also to use the weak two no-trump response as the first move on some stronger hands. With both hands (r) and (s) we do indeed hold balanced hands that were too strong to overcall one no-trump in the first instance. On hand (r) we are very suitable for playing in a minor suit if he is distributional, so we should start by bidding two no-trumps. When he responds in a minor, we can show our hand-type accurately by rebidding three no-trumps, suggesting a strong balanced hand with only one heart stop which is suitable for playing elsewhere. With hand (s), however, we are not interested in alternative contracts and should just jump to three no-trumps.

What happens if opener reraises after partner has made a responsive double: for example, 1♡ – Dble – 2♡ – Dble – 3♡?
After the bidding has started, say 1♡ – Dble – 2♡ – Dble, the opening bidder is quite likely to try to disrupt us further by continuing with three hearts. This is another situation where we can use a responsive double: if we have a clear-cut bid to make, we make it, but if we wish to bid further but would rather partner choose a suit, we can double. A certain amount of care should be exercised in this area. The opponents are at the three level and it may well be that they have overstretched and we should be taking a penalty. Although this double may be defined as responsive, it should contain significant extra values and also show a balanced hand so that partner can pass with some frequency when he also holds a balanced hand.

OK, we've covered what I need to make a responsive double, but what about other bids – say two no-trumps: for example, 1♡ – Dble – 2♡ – 2NT?
The subject of artificial two no-trump bids in competitive auctions is large enough to occupy a whole book (and indeed has done so) and is outside my scope here. However, it is difficult to cover the subject of doubles without going into some detail about all the possible responses to them. The book would be incomplete if it did not touch upon artificial two no-trump

responses, as indeed we have already done in different sequences.

In this particular sequence, it is perfectly sensible to play a two no-trump response as natural. After all it is moderately likely that we hold 10 or 11 HCP with a good heart stop and just wish to express this naturally.

However, it would also be useful to have a way of differentiating between the following hands after the sequence, say, $1\heartsuit$ – Dble – $2\heartsuit$:

(t)	♠ 6 5 4	(u)	♠ 6 5 4
	♡ 7 5 3		♡ 7 5 3
	◇ Q J 8 7 4 3		◇ A Q J 4
	♣ 7		♣ K 9 3

On both these hands we would like to bid three diamonds. On hand (t) it might lead to a good sacrifice or a very thin game when partner is distributionally suitable. On hand (u) we have a fair number of high cards but no distribution, so we may wish to compete for the part-score, suggest a lead, possibly bid a game constructively, but have no interest in suggesting a sacrifice. Many pairs feel that to be able to distinguish between these two hands is more useful than having a natural two no-trump bid. Consequently, they would respond two no-trumps with hand (t) and three diamonds with hand (u).

There is a fundamental problem with this idea. If everybody round the table has a lot of distribution, as hand (t) would tend to suggest, then what is likely to happen is that the next hand will bid four hearts. Now partner will have no idea whether to sacrifice because he does not know which minor we hold.

What does it mean if I cue-bid the opponents' suit after they have raised, for example, $1\heartsuit$ – Dble – $2\heartsuit$ – $3\heartsuit$?
The responsive double has taken away the traditional need of the cue-bid to show nearly any strong hand as with many strong

hands we can start with a double and cue-bid on the next round. There are two sensible ways to use the cue-bid.

1   It simply asks partner to bid three no-trumps with a guard in the opponents' suit. On occasion this could be useful, but first, partner is unlikely to have much of a guard in their suit when he has chosen to double in the first place, and second, we are unlikely to have enough running tricks to be sure that three no-trumps is where we want to play, even if partner can oblige.

2   It shows a very good hand for bidding to that level in the other major – i.e. the above sequence would show a very strong three-spade bid (partner should only sign off in three spades when his hand is totally unsuitable). The sequence 1♠ – Dble – 2♠ – 3♠ would show a better hand than an immediate four-heart bid; the sequence 1♡ – Dble – 2♡ – 4♡ would show a better hand than an immediate four-spade bid. When we are dealt a full opening bid with five cards or more in the other major and little wastage in the opponents' suit, it is difficult to express this over partner's take-out double. We cannot start with a responsive double for he will never believe we hold five cards in the major, therefore we have either to underbid by jumping to game in our major or to risk the five level by bidding higher, neither of which are satisfactory. This use of the cue-bid neatly avoids the problem.

How should I bid when my right-hand opponent makes a jump raise: for example, 1♡ – Dble – 3♡?
A double is still best played as responsive provided that the opponents have not pre-empted as far as game (1♢ – Dble – 4♢ – Dble would be responsive, but 1♡ – Dble – 4♡ – Dble would not). Because the opponents have stolen all the bidding space, it is more important that partnerships should have an agreement

about the expected length in the other major. The usual agreement in Great Britain is that a responsive double of a jump raise denies four cards in the other major. As soon as the bidding proceeds as high as it has here, it is likely that opener will raise the ante still further by bidding four hearts. If we have doubled three hearts and partner does not know how many spades we hold, it will be very difficult for him to make the right decision.

What if my right-hand opponent responds 2NT, showing a good raise: for example, 1♡ – Dble – 2NT?

A double of two no-trumps is best played as a normal responsive double, just as if our right-hand opponent had actually bid three hearts. However, because partner is forced to respond at the three level, it can be lighter in terms of high cards, but should contain good distribution as we are encouraging partner to bid further at a high level.

A cue-bid of three hearts would show a good three-spade bid, as before. A cue-bid of three spades (after 1♠ – Dble – 2NT) would show a good four-heart bid.

Responding to a take-out double when the next hand has bid one no-trump

What if my right-hand opponent responds one no-trump: for example, 1♡ – Dble – 1NT?

A double in this position is usually played as penalty, but as well as a fair number of values, say 9+ HCP, a good holding in the opponents' suit is necessary. This is because partner has announced shortage in the opponents' suit and unless we can stop the run of the suit, we may find that we do not make the best opening lead and the opponents may be able to run off a lot of tricks against us. The following hands would be suitable for a double after the sequence 1 ♡ – Dble – 1NT:

(a) ♠ Q J 6   (b) ♠ Q J 6   (c) ♠ J 10 6
    ♡ A J 10 5   ♡ J 10 9 8 4   ♡ Q J 10 5
    ◇ 7 6 2   ◇ A 7   ◇ A 7 6
    ♣ 8 5 3   ♣ 8 5 3   ♣ Q 8 3

(d) ♠ 6 5 2
    ♡ A 6 4
    ◇ K Q J 7 6
    ♣ 8 3

Hands (a) and (b) are both just worth a double because we have a very good holding in the opponents' suit and because, in the queen of spades, we have an attractive opening lead. Hand (c) is a little stronger, because the jack of spades is less likely to be as effective an opening lead and because the heart holding is less strong – don't forget that declarer is likely to play us for heart length. With hand (d) we have broken the rules about strength in the opponents' suit, but this is because we have such a good opening lead that we can expect to establish five defensive tricks at Trick 1, without any help from partner at all.

What other options do I have if I am not suitable to double one no-trump?
If our hand is unsuitable for a double, one of our alternatives is obviously to respond in a suit as before. We also have a cue-bid of their suit available and a bid of two no-trumps (which cannot possibly be natural here as we have not doubled one no-trump). There are alternative ways to play these bids but a sensible scheme is:

1   When the opponents open a minor – e.g. 1◇ – Dble – 1NT:

- a cue-bid (here two diamonds) shows both majors;
- two no-trumps shows at least five clubs (often six) and four cards in one of the majors – partner can cue-bid three diamonds to discover the major.

2   When the opponents open a major – e.g. 1♡ – Dble – 1NT:

- a cue-bid (here two hearts) shows four cards in the other major (spades) and five or more cards in one of the minors – partner can bid two no trumps to find out the minor;
- two no-trumps shows both minors.

It may seem slightly confusing that the one no-trump response has changed the meaning of the cue-bid. The reason for this is so that the cue-bid can be used to show four cards in the other major and a long minor – it is not possible for two no-trumps to mean this without forcing the bidding right up to the three level on all these hands.

Responding to a take-out double when the next hand has bid a new suit

What happens if my right-hand opponent responds in a new suit at the one level: for example, 1♡ – Dble – 1♠?

This sequence, 1♡ – Dble – 1♠, is often what is referred to as a 'baby psych'. It is possible that responder does not have spades at all, but he thinks that we do and he is trying to stop us finding our fit. It is important that we do not let him. A double of one spade in this position should show at least four spades and the values to have willingly responded one spade to the double ourselves; for example, a working 6 or 7 HCP. Thereafter opinions diverge and there are two schools of thought:

1   Double shows precisely four spades and with five spades we should bid two spades instead. If we wish to make a take-out bid with both minors, we just bid two hearts.
2   Double shows at least four spades, after all we will probably be able to bid spades again on the next round to show five.

This allows us the luxury of two take-out bids, two hearts and two spades, which can be played as either:

- the lower cue-bid (two hearts) shows better clubs and the higher cue-bid (two spades) shows better diamonds – this can be helpful in deciding whether or not to sacrifice and with the choice of opening lead;
- the lower cue-bid (two hearts) merely shows a wish to compete with both minors, whereas the higher cue-bid (two spades) shows a full-weight game force – this can be useful because after a game force is established both hands can bid naturally without fear of stopping prematurely.

Whichever of the last two is adopted, it should be amended slightly when the opponents have been bidding suits of unequal rank. Suppose the bidding goes 1◇ – Dble – 1♡, two diamonds would show better clubs and two hearts better spades, but with many hands with better spades we would simply bid two spades, so to use either cue-bid would imply that the clubs were worth mentioning. If the last method is adopted, two diamonds would imply at least one club more than spade, otherwise we would simply bid two spades.

After a sequence such as 1♡ – Dble – 1♠ – Dble, it is important for partner to tell us if he also holds four spades. So, for example, a sequence such as:

West	North	East	South
1♡	Dble	1♠	Dble
2♡	2♠		

does not show any extra values, it merely confirms that there is a 4–4 spade fit. A pass of two hearts on this sequence would be tantamount to a denial that he held four spades.

Does it make any difference if the next hand has bid a new suit at the two level: for example, 1♡ – Dble – 2◇?

These days most people play that a new suit at the two level is natural and forcing, just as it would have been without the take-out double. In that case it is unlikely that we would want to bid anything very often, for we would have very little in the way of high cards.

There is certainly much to be said for treating a new suit at the two level in much the same way as we did at the one level – i.e. double would show four cards in the suit and the two cue-bids would show the same sort of hand as they did before. This would ease the memory strain, since modern-day opponents sometimes play that their responses over a take-out double are not natural at all. If two diamonds was not natural then a double would surely show at least four diamonds and a few values.

However, assuming that the response is natural, it is slightly illogical to play the same methods. There is much less reason for the opponents to be psyching against us – even after the bidding 1♠ – Dble – 2♡, if responder had sufficient spades to make a psych reasonably safe, he would probably do better to pre-empt in spades to as high a level as he could. If our opponents play the aforementioned methods whereby a two-level response is natural and forcing, then it seems foolish to tell them how their suits are breaking. If our opponents play the slightly old-fashioned style, whereby a new suit at the two level is merely a rescue, showing a long suit and few values, then we do not want to be able to double them only when we have four trumps.

Our scheme should be:

1 If their response is artificial, then a double shows four cards in the suit they have bid and a smattering of values.

2 If their response is natural, then a double is penalty, but based on the assumption that partner, the take-out doubler,

holds three cards headed by an honour in their suit (after all, he did make a take-out double of a different suit).

3   Cue-bids of either opponent's suit retain the same meaning as before.

4   Two no-trumps is probably best played as natural, but if you choose it as showing a weak hand with a long suit after a sequence such as 1♡ – Dble – 2♡, you may also choose to play it similarly here.

Responding to a take-out double when the next hand redoubles

What if responder redoubles: for example, 1♡ – Dble – Rdble?
When the opponents have made some show of strength, we are in a different situation. We may wish to do one of three things:

1   Find the best place to play at a low level – they are threatening to take a penalty from us and we would like to find our best spot.

2   If we have some distribution we would like to pre-empt as high as possible in order to make it difficult for them to find their best contract.

3   We may wish to show some general values, if we have them, in order perhaps to compete later or even double them, particularly if the opening bidder removes the redouble, thus announcing a weak hand in terms of high-card strength.

All immediate bids after the next hand redoubles are weak, even jumps. It could even be said that a jump to two spades after the sequence 1♡ – Dble – Rdble should be mandatory with any five-card suit, though perhaps a passing thought should be paid to the vulnerability.

If I pass the redouble, does this mean that I want to defend against one heart redoubled?

A pass of the redouble is played this way in some parts of the world, but generally in Great Britain it merely says that we have no preference for any suit and suggests that partner should bid his cheapest four-card suit. Let us say that the auction begins:

West	North	East	South
1 $\heartsuit$	Dble	Rdble	Pass
Pass	1 $\spadesuit$	Pass	?

Two clubs merely shows both minors and asks partner to choose, but two diamonds shows reasonable values, say a working 6 or 7 HCP with a diamond suit; otherwise we would have bid two diamonds directly over the redouble.

A pass of a redouble either shows a very weak hand with little preference between the other suits, or it shows a hand with a few values which it will try to express later.

If a pass of a redouble does not show length in the opponent's suit, what should I do when I would have liked to pass for penalty?

It is moderately likely in this position that we will find ourselves with a hand with little in the way of high cards (everybody else at the table has announced some strength) but with great length in our left-hand opponent's suit (partner has implied shortage and the redouble traditionally shows little fit for opener). It would seem logical that either an immediate bid in the opponent's suit or a pass followed by such a bid should be natural. It doesn't matter much which way round we play these two bids, but it seems more in keeping with the rest of our bidding that an immediate cue-bid should be natural, to play.

What can I bid to tell partner I have some values after the redouble?

We have arrived at a situation which is very similar to the forcing-pass situation we discussed after partner had doubled a one no-trump opening and our right-hand opponent removed to two of a minor. Immediate bids are all weak, and pass followed by a voluntary (not merely correction) bid shows some values. Thus an immediate one no-trump would be light in high cards but very solidly packed in the opposition's suit; an immediate two no-trumps would be weak but with at least 5–5 in the minors. To make a simple bid and follow it with a double on the next round would be for take-out.

Conversely, to pass and then bid one no-trump would imply more high cards and less no-trump suitability; to pass and bid two no-trumps would be natural; to pass and cue-bid would show a good raise in partner's suit. To pass and then double would be penalty – strict penalty if opener rebid his suit, but assuming partner held three cards to an honour if opener bid a new suit.

Why do we need bids to show a good hand? Surely we can't really hold one on this auction?

Normally there aren't enough high cards left for us to have many of them but there are two possible exceptions:

1 When our opponent has psyched (or opened extremely light in third seat).
2 Some players nowadays play short-suit redoubles whereby responder's redouble did not necessarily show a good hand but just showed at most a singleton in opener's suit. Clearly, if this is our opponents' agreement, there may be plenty of high cards left for us to hold.

If our opponents are playing short-suit redoubles, it may be wise to change the meaning of our pass of the redouble. Since they have announced a misfit and may have very few values, there is a strong case to be made for playing the pass of the redouble as showing a wish to defend.

Responding to a protective double when opener makes a rebid

What happens when the opponents bid again after a protective double: for example, 1♡ – Pass – Pass – Dble; 2♡?

Many pairs have had misunderstandings (hopefully only once!) about the meaning of a double in this sequence. There is a case for playing it as penalty, and a case for responsive. The most important thing is for both halves of a partnership to agree.

If we decide to play it as responsive, and we have seen already how very useful a responsive double can be, then it is important that the doubler should double again if the two-heart bid is passed round to him. Even if partner holds a minimum 8 or 9 HCP double, if he has a singleton or less in the opponent's suit he knows that we wanted to make a penalty double. Provided that he has sufficient high cards to have left in a penalty double had we made one, then he should double again.

If we agree to play the double as responsive, we can play a two no-trump bid as natural. There can be no point in using it to define the strength of the responding hand because if we had a long suit we are known not to be very strong for we did not overcall in the first place. However, if we agree to play the double as penalty, we should probably give up a natural two no-trump bid in order to have some way of competing when we have two possible trump suits to offer partner.

What if opener bids a new suit: for example, 1♡ – Pass – Pass – Dble; 2♢?

If opener bids a new suit after our take-out double, a double should be suggestive of penalties, but more because of length in the suit opened than in the second suit. We should assume that partner has three to an honour in opener's second suit. In this situation we have a cheap cue-bid of the suit opened at our disposal as a take-out manoeuvre.

What if opener rebids one no-trump: for example, 1♡ – Pass – Pass – Dble; 1NT?

If opener bids one no-trump after partner's take-out double, all our bidding is just as if the double had been in second seat, but we need more to double, say 13 HCP instead of the 9 we needed before. Again we need some values in opener's suit.

What if opener redoubles: for example, 1♡ – Pass – Pass – Dble; Rdble?

If opener redoubles, we are in a position slightly different from any we have seen previously. This is because we are quite likely to want to pass for penalties. In the previous redouble situation, our opponents had shown more than half the points in the pack (say 12 for the opening bidder and 9 for the redoubler) and even if we did have length in their suit, this was going to be under their trump suit, making defensive prospects weaker. Here, not only is our trump length, if we hold it, over opener's, but the opponents have also announced less in the way of high cards. Opener may have redoubled on as little as 17 HCP (perhaps unwisely) and responder may have none at all. Also, in the previous situation, the opponents' high-card strength was fairly evenly divided (say 9 facing 12), ours was not (say 14 facing 5), whereas here our strength is evenly divided (say 10 facing 10) and theirs is not (say 18 facing 2). All this makes it much more likely that we have a profitable penalty to collect.

After a sequence such as 1♡ – Pass – Pass – Dble; Rdble, we should only pass when we wish to defend one heart redoubled. If we do not wish to do so then we must bid something, just as we would have done without the redouble.

Doubles after our side has overcalled (by responder)

What does a double mean if partner has overcalled and my right-hand opponent raises, for example, 1◇ – 1♠ – 2◇ – Dble?
A double in this position has much in common with the responsive doubles we have looked at earlier. The opponents are at a low level and have found a fit, so there is likely to be little profit from doubling them for penalties. A more useful meaning for the double is to express values, a wish to compete, but no clear action to take.

The first meaning (i.e. the meaning partner should assume when making his first response) of a double in this position is to show the other two suits plus tolerance for partner. However, we do not live in a perfect world and are not always dealt the perfect hand. Often we have to compromise and a double may often be used to show the other two suits with no tolerance for partner, an unbid major with tolerance for partner or even just a good raise in partner's suit with only three-card support.

The following hands would all be suitable for a double after the sequence above, 1◇ – 1♠ – 2◇ – Dble:

(a) ♠ K 6 5
   ♡ A 7
   ◇ A 6 5 3
   ♣ Q 10 8 2

(b) ♠ 5
   ♡ K Q 7 5 4
   ◇ 7 6
   ♣ A K 10 8 2

(c) ♠ K 6
   ♡ K J 7 5
   ◇ 7 6
   ♣ Q J 10 8 2

(d) ♠ A 6 5
   ♡ K Q J 7 5
   ◇ 7 6
   ♣ 10 8 2

With hand (a) we would bid three spades over any minimum response partner makes. With hand (b) we would bid three clubs over partner's two-spade rebid and become more enthusiastic over any other response. Hand (c) is the classic distribution for this type of competitive double – we would pass any response. With hand (d), we would pass two spades or proceed with three hearts (depending on our overcall style), and if partner responded three clubs we would bid three hearts to show a good heart suit with spade support. Note that if we start with a double and then bid a new suit, partner always knows that we either have both other suits or support for his first suit, otherwise we would simply have bid our suit in the first place.

If our double can conceal any of the above distributions, how is partner supposed to respond to it?

The following two points must be borne in mind:

1   With a minimum hand he should not bid above the next level of his first suit except to bid a second four-card suit. If he is not going to rebid above the next level of his first suit, he should choose an intervening three-card suit (headed by an honour) before rebidding his own five-card suit.

2   With a good overcall he should jump in a new suit or cue-bid the opponents' suit.

Let us suppose he holds one of the following hands for his one-spade overcall, after the bidding has started 1◇ – 1♠ – 2◇ – Dble; Pass:

(e) ♠ K J 10 6 5   (f) ♠ K J 10 6 5   (g) ♠ K J 10 6 5
    ♡ A 4   ♡ Q J 4   ♡ A 4
    ◇ 8 6 4   ◇ 8 6 4   ◇ 8 6
    ♣ Q J 3   ♣ A 3   ♣ Q J 6 3

With hand (e) he should simply rebid two spades, not wishing to go beyond the two level with his minimum overcall. With hand (f) he can afford to introduce his three-card heart suit since it is below the level of two spades. This leaves us free to choose between the majors. With hand (g) he should bid three clubs on his four-card suit.

What if he holds a stronger hand?

Let us look at some stronger hands, after the same auction:

(h) ♠ K J 10 6 5   (i) ♠ K Q J 6 5 2   (j) ♠ A K 6 5 2
    ♡ A Q 4 2   ♡ A J 4   ♡ A 4 2
    ♢ 8 6   ♢ 8 6 4   ♢ 8 6
    ♣ K 6   ♣ 6   ♣ Q J 6

With hand (h) he should jump to three hearts. With hand (i) he should jump to three spades. With hand (j), he has extra values but no extra distribution. He should express this by bidding three diamonds to let us choose the suit.

What if the opponents compete further?

In the same way that a second responsive double could be made after the sequence 1♡ – Dble – 2♡ – Dble; 3♡, after the sequence 1♢ – 1♠ – 2♢ – Dble; 3♢, double would also be competitive, tending to show a hand such as (j). Note that while described as competitive, this double denies further distribution, so partner will occasionally be able to judge to pass it.

What if the next hand makes a jump raise: for example, 1♢ – 1♠ – 3♢ – Dble?

In the same way that our responsive doubles continued as far as the level of four diamonds, so do our competitive doubles in this situation. However, the higher the level the bidding has reached the more likely it is that we are simply interested in the majors. After the proposed sequence 1♢ – 1♠ – 3♢, if we were simply to bid three spades, partner would think that this was merely a competitive gesture, rather than a serious try for game. Consequently, with any hand that wishes to make a positive try for game, we would have to start with a double. Partner should not proceed beyond the three level in his suit without extra values – i.e. with:

♠ K J 10 6 5
♡ A 4
♢ 8 6
♣ Q J 6 3

he should simply respond three spades.

What if the next hand responds one no-trump: for example, 1♢ – 1♠ – 1NT?

The traditional meaning of a double in this position is penalties. If we are going to play this as a penalty double, we need to be clear in our minds just how strong a hand it shows. This needs us to determine how strong an overcall can be assumed to be. We all know that an overcall may be made on as little as K-Q-J-x-x, but if this was all we ever played partner for we would never get anywhere. It is reasonable to assume that an overcall shows 10 HCP, and therefore that a double of a one no-trump bid in this position shows about 11 or more HCP. This does not mean that partner can no longer overcall with K-Q-J-x-x; it just means that he has to recognize that when he has less than 10 HCP, one no-trump doubled is quite likely to make and he should consider removing our double.

If partner has passed, rather than overcalled, we agreed that a double was not penalty at all. Why should this situation be any different?

Over the years many expert pairs have found that there was little to be gained by doubling one no-trump for penalty in this position – it seems that either partner or opener removes himself. Consequently many pairs have found it more useful to use the double as competitive, similar to the competitive doubles we have already seen – i.e. as if the bidding had gone 1♢ – 1♠ – 2♢ – Dble. Its first message is a desire to compete in one of the other suits and it need not have the values needed for a penalty double. Let us suppose we hold the following hands after the sequence 1♢ – 1♠ – 1NT:

(k) ♠ K 5
   ♡ K Q 10 9 5
   ◇ J 7 6 2
   ♣ 6 5

(l) ♠ 7
   ♡ K J 7 6 3
   ◇ 6 2
   ♣ K J 6 5 2

(m) ♠ 7 6 5
   ♡ K 7 6 3
   ◇ 6
   ♣ K Q 6 5 2

(n) ♠ 7
   ♡ A J 7
   ◇ K Q 10 9 6
   ♣ K 6 5 2

On hand (k), double one no-trump and, if partner bids two clubs, bid two hearts, showing our good heart suit and spade tolerance. On hand (l), double one no-trump and pass partner's response – if he rebids two spades he will usually have six spades, since he should rebid a three-card suit in hearts or clubs before rebidding a five-card spade suit. With hand (m), double one no-trump. If partner bids two clubs, pass; if partner bids two hearts, bid two spades, as he is quite likely to have only a three-card heart suit. This is better than an immediate spade raise for two reasons: first, if the opener rebids diamonds, which is quite likely, partner may well lead a spade if we raise directly; second, and this is a matter of style, partner may only have a four-card spade suit. The auction may proceed:

West	North	East	South
1 ◇	1 ♠	1NT	Dble
Pass	2 ♣	Pass	Pass
2 ◇	Pass	Pass	

and now we can bid two spades to offer partner a choice between the black suits. With hand (n) we would like to double one no-trump for penalties, but we can't. If the opponents are vulnerable, it is probably best to defend one no-trump undoubled and collect undertricks at 100 a time; if we are vulnerable and the opponents are not, we could choose to double one no-trump and rebid two no-trumps when partner removes us.

What if the next hand responds in a new suit: for example, 1♡ – 1♠ – 2♣ – Dble?

Most players play a change of suit by responder (two clubs here) in this position as forcing, so there is little point in doubling for penalties. All this will achieve is to tell our opponents that their suits are breaking badly. Even if we play against opponents who do not play such a change of suit as forcing, it is probably more useful to play a double here as competitive.

If a double in this position is competitive, what exactly does it show?

In principle, it shows the unbid suit plus tolerance for partner's suit. As usual, we place greater emphasis on majors than minors. Let us suppose we hold the following hands after the sequence 1♡ – 1♠ – 2♣:

(o) ♠ K 7
♡ 6 5 4
♢ K Q 10 4 2
♣ 7 3 2

(p) ♠ K 7 6
♡ 6 5
♢ K 10 5 4 2
♣ Q 7 3

(q) ♠ 7 6 2
♡ 6 5
♢ A K 10 5 4
♣ Q 7 3

(r) ♠ 7
♡ A 6 5
♢ K Q 10 5 4 2
♣ 7 3 2

(s) ♠ 7
♡ A 6 5
♢ A 5 4 2
♣ K J 10 7 3

With hand (o) we would like to show our diamond suit, but if partner doesn't like diamonds we would be quite happy to play in two spades, so we double two clubs and let partner choose the suit. With hand (p), although we do have a fair diamond suit, we have better spade support and should raise him directly. On hand (q), although we also have three-card spade support, we would be better advised to start with a double because we would rather partner led a diamond than a spade. With hand (r), we just bid a simple two diamonds. Partner will know that we do not hold any spade support, so he will not go back to spades unless he has a good six-card suit. Hand (s) is a hand on which we would have liked to make a penalty double, but we can't, so we have to pass. This may work out better for us in the end because the opponents will not know that the suits are breaking badly and we may later be able to double a higher contract more productively.

Is there any difference when partner has overcalled in a minor and the unbid suit is a major?
Let us consider the sequence 1♠ – 2♣ – 2◇:

(t)	♠ 6 5 4	(u)	♠ 6 5	(v)	♠ 6 5
	♡ K Q 10 4 2		♡ K 10 5 4 2		♡ A K 10 5 4
	◇ 7 3 2		◇ Q 7 3		◇ Q 7 3
	♣ K 7		♣ K 7 6		♣ 7 6 2

With hand (t), we have such a good five-card major that we should actually bid two hearts instead of doubling. If we double, we can hardly expect partner to bid hearts with J-x or x-x-x, when he knows we have some club support for him. On hand (u), we should double, even with our good club support, as we would be delighted if partner could bid hearts. On hand (v), we should again bid two hearts with such a good suit.

When a major is the unbid suit we should strain to bid it if we can do so at the two level, even if we have support for partner's minor. In this situation, a double tends to suggest a good four-card or poor five-card holding in the other major.

When partner has overcalled in a minor and the unbid suit is a minor, or when he has overcalled in a major and the unbid suit is a major, we are in middle ground. It would be normal to put greater emphasis on supporting partner unless our holding in the unbid suit was very strong.

How should partner respond to this type of competitive double?
Partner's response to this type of competitive double is usually fairly straightforward – he simply chooses between the two

suits, jumping with extra values. If he has a good hand with no clear direction he can cue-bid one of the opponents' suits – normal practice is to cue-bid where he has values.

What if opener bids again?
If opener bids again, either rebidding his own suit or raising responder, the overcaller can again make a further competitive double to show extra values with no clear direction. The implication of this further double would be that the overcaller had a balanced hand type – after all, he will not have six of his own suit and will not have four-card support for the suit we have implied – so this may be passed out for penalties if the original doubler has a balanced hand.

The opponents double partner's overcall

What if my right-hand opponent makes a penalty double of partner's overcall: for example, 1♡ – 1♠ – Dble?
The normal action to take when an opponent makes a penalty double is to pass and hope that partner has a good overcall and that the opponents have done the wrong thing. This is particularly the case when partner has overcalled at the two level, thus showing a good suit. However, there are exceptions:

1 With a long suit of our own which is quite likely to be better than partner's, we simply bid it.

2 With extreme shortage in partner's suit and length in both the unbid suits we can make an SOS redouble. This simply asks partner to choose between the other two suits. This can be an extremely useful convention and can often help us get out of trouble, but remember that partner may sometimes have to choose between two doubletons, so the redouble should be used with caution. It is often better to pass quickly, in order that partner may be able to remove himself (if we

pass slowly he may feel ethically bound to pass) – after all he has heard the double as well, and by the time the bidding gets to him, the opener will also have passed, so if he has a second five-card suit, for example, he should remove himself anyway.

What if my right-hand opponent makes a negative double: for example, 1♡ – 1♠ – Dble?

A negative double means different things to different people and is a subject we will discuss in detail in the next chapter. All that concerns us at this stage is that it is not a penalty double, and that it shows values in at least one of the remaining suits. Given that it is not a penalty double, it is unlikely to be passed out, therefore there is no need to play an SOS redouble. In principle all bids mean the same as they would have done without the double, with the exceptions that:

1   Redouble is now available to show a good hand that is interested in taking a penalty, in much the same way as if partner had opened the bidding and the next hand had made a take-out double.

2   Again, in the same way that after partner had opened and the next hand had made a take-out double, we had two no-trumps available to show a good raise, so do we here (in fact many players play this even without the intervening negative double, as with a natural two no-trump bid they can start with a cue-bid of opener's suit).

3   We had a fit-showing jump shift available after the sequence 1♡ – Dble, and so do we here (again, many players play this even without the intervening negative double, while others play the jump to show four-card or longer support for the overcall and a singleton in the suit jumped to) since a hand worth a forcing bid in a new suit would start with a redouble.

Doubles after our side has overcalled (by the overcaller)

Can I start by making an overcall and double on the next round?
We noted in Chapter 1 that modern-day practice tends to be to make a simple overcall even on a very good hand. If we do this it is important that we are able to show our extra values later in the auction.

Another thing to remember is that our use of competitive doubles in some auctions left partner without a bid when he wished to make a penalty double. On some of these occasions he will hope that we can make a take-out double which he will pass.

Do I need extra values to double, having made an overcall on the first round?
All second-round doubles, having merely overcalled on the first round, are for take out, but it is important to distinguish between those that are showing serious extra values and those that are merely 'balancing' – i.e. are allowing partner to make a penalty pass in a situation when he could not make a penalty double, or perhaps suggesting he competes in an unbid suit (remember, he will not strain to bid over our overcall without a fit for that suit).

1   If the opponents are still in a 'live' auction, i.e. their combined values are unlimited, then an overcall followed by double shows substantial values.
2   If the opponents are in a limited auction, i.e. their combined values are limited, then an overcall followed by a double is merely 'balancing' and shows a sound overcall, but nothing substantial in the way of extra values.

Let us look at some examples of a balancing double when we overcalled on the first round:

West	*North*	*East*	*South*
1♡	1♠	2♡	Pass
Pass	Dble		

West	*North*	*East*	*South*
1♡	1♠	1NT	Pass
Pass	Dble		

These two sequences would be consistent with a hand such as:

♠ A J 10 6 5
♡ 5
◇ A 6 5 3
♣ K 10 5

i.e. a sound overcall with good general defensive cards. Of course, it may be stronger, but we will come to that later.

West	*North*	*East*	*South*
		Pass	Pass
1♡	1♠	2♣	Pass
Pass	Dble		

This sequence would be consistent with a hand such as:

♠ A J 10 6 5
♡ K 10 5
◇ A 6 5 3
♣ 5

On all three occasions we are doubling for one of two reasons:

1 Partner may have a penalty double which he could not make himself on the last round, because we have decided to play it as competitive.
2 Partner may have some length in an unbid suit, but insufficient values or an insufficiently good suit to have bid it earlier.

None of the hands so far has been particularly strong. It seems I do not need extra values?

Here are some examples of take-out doubles in 'live' auction – i.e. doubles which show substantial extra values:

West	North	East	South
1 ♡	1 ♠	Dble★	Pass
1NT	Dble		

West	North	East	South
1 ♡	1 ♠	2 ♣	Pass
2 ♡	Dble		

West	North	East	South
1 ♡	1 ♠	Dble★	Pass
2 ♣	Dble		

★negative

With these three sequences the opponents' combined values are unlimited and they have also not yet found a fit, so we are in a very exposed position. We cannot safely bid without a good hand because we may be doubled and go several down. Consequently, these sequences show substantial extra values.

If partner is not going to pass our take-out double in any of the above sequences, is there some way that he can distinguish between when he has absolutely nothing and when he has a fair smattering of values?

If the opponents have alighted in one no-trump or two of a minor there is usually not much of a problem because he can jump when he has some useful-looking cards, but when they have alighted in two of a major, he has the same old problem that we have seen before.

We can use a two no-trump bid in an artificial way, but again we have to choose whether we wish to use it to help define the strength of a hand or whether we use it as a 'scramble' to offer more than one suit. We are in a similar situation to, for example:

West	North	East	South
1 ♠	Pass	2 ♠	Dble
Pass	2NT		

Here we agreed that, although it was certainly possible that on some hands we would prefer to have a 'scramble' available, the chances that game was on for our side were sufficient that it was more important to use two no-trumps to help define the range of the responding hand. We will do the same here. When we overcall and make a subsequent take-out double, a two no-trump response from partner would show a very weak hand, whereas to bid a suit at the three level would show some positive interest.

West	North	East	South
1 ♡	1 ♠	2 ♡	Pass
Pass	Dble	Pass	2NT

West	North	East	South
1 ♡	1 ♠	2 ♣	Pass
2 ♡	Dble	Pass	2NT

In both these sequences, the two no-trump bid would be used to show a very poor hand. Over two no-trumps we would usually bid three clubs, and partner would either pass or convert to three diamonds. If, instead of two no-trumps, partner were actually to bid a suit, this would show positive values and some game interest.

Let us look at some hands:

	Overcaller		Responder
(a)	♠ A J 10 6 5	(b)	♠ 7
	♡ 5		♡ J 8 3 2
	◇ A 6 5 3		◇ 9 4 2
	♣ K 10 5		♣ A Q J 6 2

	Overcaller		Responder
(c)	♠ A K 10 6 5	(d)	♠ 7
	♡ 5		♡ J 8 3 2
	◇ A 6 5		◇ 9 4 2
	♣ K 10 5 4		♣ J 7 6 3 2

In each case the sequence has gone:

South	West	North	East
1 ♡	1 ♠	2 ♡	Pass
Pass	Dble		

Both hands (a) and (c) are possibilities consistent with our bidding. If partner has hand (b) he responds three clubs, showing reasonable values, and if he has hand (d) he will respond two no-trumps to show very few values. If he responds two no-trumps we will bid three clubs with either hand (a) or hand (c) and he will pass. If we hold hand (a) we would pass if partner bid three clubs, as we do not have much to spare and eleven tricks are a lot to make. However, if we held hand (c), which is not much stronger in high-card points but has a much better fit, we would certainly be worth a move towards the laydown five clubs. If we did not play this two no-trump convention, we would not know what to do over three clubs – we could pass and find that five clubs was a good contract when partner held hand (b); or we could bid on, only to go down in four clubs when partner held hand (d).

What can he do if the bidding has reached the three level so he doesn't have this two no-trump bid available?

The use of this two no-trump bid is obviously only possible when the double has been made at the two level. If the bidding has reached the three level before we, the overcaller, double, partner just has to do the best he can, following the usual rules of overbidding slightly as far as major suits are concerned and underbidding slightly with minor suits.

Let us look at an example:

	Overcaller		*Responder*
(e)	♠ A 5 4	(f)	♠ 7 6
	♡ A Q 6		♡ K J 10 4 3
	◇ 7		◇ J 4 2
	♣ A K 8 7 4 3		♣ J 7 6

Let us suppose that the bidding has gone:

South	*West*	*North*	*East*
1 ♠	2 ♣	2 ◇	Pass
3 ◇	Dble		

Hand (e) is consistent with our bidding, though is perhaps a little stronger than necessary. When we double, partner has an awkward decision to make. He has a good heart suit and his jack of clubs may come in useful; on the other hand he knows we probably don't have four-card heart support (or we could have chosen three hearts instead of double). If he had the queen of clubs instead of the jack it would be clear for him to bid four hearts; if he was missing the jack and ten of hearts it would be clear for him to bid only three hearts (our good trumps will be forced out by our opponents' diamonds). On the hand in question it is a very close decision, and, in fact, facing hand (e), which is stronger than it might be, on best defence (top diamond followed by a spade switch, threatening to cut off dummy), game (and slam) depends on bringing in the club suit.

Doubles at the second opportunity

What does it mean when we pass on the first round and later double in a 'live' auction: for example, 1♡ – Pass – 1♠ – Pass; 2♠ – Dble?
When we pass on the first round of the bidding and subsequently double an opponent, the meaning of this double again depends

whether we are doubling in a balancing position (which we will discuss later) or whether we are doubling in a 'live' auction.

As we have seen in many areas, when we choose to play any sort of take-out double, we have problems on hands on which we would like to make a penalty double. This is true in many competitive double situations, but is also true in the most straightforward double position of all, that of our right-hand opponent opening in a suit. Suppose we hold, for example:

♠ A K 6 5
♡ 7
♢ A Q 6 5
♣ K J 10 4

If our right-hand opponent opens one heart, we have a perfect take-out double. But what if he opens one diamond, for example? The classic solution to this problem is to pass for the moment and hope to double later. As long as our opponents do not continue bidding our suits, we should be able to express our hand reasonably well later. The auction may proceed in any one of the following ways:

	West	*North*	*East*	*South*
(a)	1♢	Pass	1♡	Pass
	2♡			

	West	*North*	*East*	*South*
(b)	1♢	Pass	1♡	Pass
	2♢			

	West	*North*	*East*	*South*
(c)	1♢	Pass	1♡	Pass
	1NT			

	West	*North*	*East*	*South*
(d)	1♢	Pass	1NT	Pass
	2♢			

On all these sequences we can now double. After sequences (a), (b) and (c), partner should take us for opening-bid values with shortage in the *second* bid suit – i.e. more or less our example hand. Sequence (d) is slightly less clear. It certainly shows a good hand with length in diamonds, but less is known about the rest of the hand. We would also have to pass our right-hand opponent's one-diamond opening if we held, for example:

♠ A 76
♡ K J 10 3
♢ K Q J 98
♣ 6

If we hold this hand and we hear sequence (a), we will just have to pass two hearts – after all, partner is known to be very short in hearts and has not bid so we have probably not missed anything. With sequences (b) and (c), we could risk a double, since it is basically a penalty double but this is a little dangerous as partner may well remove to clubs. After sequence (d) we would happily double.

Let us look at some other sequences:

	West	North	East	South
(e)	1♡	Pass	1♠	Pass
	2♣	Dble		
(f)	1♡	Pass	1NT	Pass
	2♢	Dble		

Again, the classic meaning for either of these doubles is a good hand with length in the suit opened. For sequence (e), shortage in spades would be expected; for sequence (f), shortage in diamonds. In both cases, we are hoping that all the suits are breaking badly for the opponents and that we can take a penalty if partner has length and strength in the suit we are short in.

That sounds straightforward enough, but do these sorts of hand come up very often?

All the above is the classical meaning of such doubles. However, the cut and thrust of the modern game has led many pairs to modify the meaning of some of these sequences in order to use them with more frequency. It is all very well to have these doubles meaning that we have a sound opening bid with length in the suit opened, but we are not dealt the hand very often and also the bidding does not always develop in such a way as to make it easy for us to express our values. Nowadays, people open very weak hands against us and we may find that we miss easy games if we have to pass good hands ourselves. Let us consider some of the problems associated with retaining the classic meaning of the sequences already looked at. To revert to (a):

West	North	East	South
1 ◇	Pass	1 ♡	Pass
2 ♡			

As we will see when we move on to the subject of 'balancing', if we pass two hearts and it is passed round to partner, he is only likely to take some action when he is short in hearts. This means that if we are short in hearts and we pass, we are likely to defend two hearts and perhaps lose a part-score swing. Suppose we hold:

♠ J 7 6 5
♡ 7
◇ A Q 3
♣ K J 10 3 2

We are pretty sure that passing out two hearts will not be a good score for our side. If we pass two hearts, we cannot seriously expect partner to take any action with, say:

♠ A 4
♡ J 10 4 3
♢ J 10 6
♣ Q 7 6 5

With our combined hands we would expect to make ten tricks in clubs and we would expect our opponents to be able to make eight or nine tricks in hearts. It is a losing policy at any form of scoring or vulnerability to be unable to compete on these hands. Consequently, the values needed for a double of two hearts in sequence (a) have been considerably reduced in modern-day tournament play, although the distribution needed for a double has remained more or less the same, particularly if the opponents' minor-suit opening can be made on a three-card suit.

What about second-round doubles of one no-trump?
Playing teams scoring, it is sensible that these sequences such as (c) should retain their classic meaning.

West	North	East	South
1 ♢	Pass	1 ♡	Pass
1NT	Dble		

There is quite a case, however, for reducing the values needed when playing match-pointed pairs. Suppose, after the above sequence, we hold:

♠ A J 7
♡ 6 5
♢ K Q 10 9
♣ Q J 10 5

We know that the cards will be lying badly for declarer. We have good diamonds over his suit, we have a good opening lead (clubs), and where an opponent has bid hearts, our shortage suggests that partner may have length and strength there. Also, we have a sufficiently balanced hand not to be frightened should partner be weak with a long suit and wish to remove our double. It would be foolish to suggest that such doubles are not without danger, when East may have been about to raise one no-trump, but at match-pointed pairs one often has to take risks. What is undoubtedly true is that we will be dealt a hand such as the above much more often than we will be dealt a stronger, more penalty-oriented hand.

What about when my right-hand opponent has bid a new suit after a one no-trump response?

West	North	East	South
1♡	Pass	1NT	Pass
2♢	Dble		

When our right-hand opponent has bid two suits and his partner has responded, as on (f), there are quite a few hands you might hold where you would like to compete in the auction which do not have substantial values with length in the first suit and shortage in the second. The sort of hand you might hold on the above auction might be:

♠ Q 10 9 5
♡ A 5 4
♢ 7 6
♣ A Q J 7

If you held this hand after sequence (f), you would like to make a take-out double of two diamonds because it is very likely that your partner has some spades with you – neither East nor West will usually have four spades for this auction, and West has shown nine cards in two suits, making it quite unlikely that he holds as many as three spades.

Let us consider a slightly different auction:

(g)	West	North	East	South
	1♠	Pass	1NT	Pass
	2♣	Dble		

Again, we might be dealt a strong hand with spade length and club shortage, but we may also be dealt a hand such as:

♠ 7
♡ K 10 7 6 5
♢ A 10 7 6 5
♣ 5 4

If we are dealt this hand we would surely like to suggest that partner may like to compete in one of the red suits over two clubs, or even over three clubs.

It is always a little dangerous to enter an auction when the opponents have defined their hands well and they may not have a fit, but if we are to use a double in this type of sequence with any frequency, there is a strong case for playing it as take-out.

So, have all these second-round doubles become devalued?
In the other auctions already mentioned, for a variety of reasons it would be too dangerous to deviate from the classic treatment.

Reverting to (b):

West	North	East	South
1♢	Pass	1♡	Pass
2♢	Dble		

One could argue that this sequence is similar to 1♡ – Pass – 1NT – Pass; 2♢ – Dble, and one could play the double as take-out. However, it would be much more dangerous to do so. Not only have the opponents not yet found a fit, but East is completely unlimited.

Reverting to (d):

West	North	East	South
1$\diamond$	Pass	1NT	Pass
2$\diamond$	Dble		

Here the opponents have only bid one suit and it is the one which they bid on the previous round. If we wished to make a take-out double of two diamonds, we would surely have made a take-out double of one diamond on the last round.

Reverting to (e):

West	North	East	South
1$\heartsuit$	Pass	1$\spadesuit$	Pass
2$\clubsuit$	Dble		

Here the opponents are in an auction where they have bid three suits, have not found a fit and both of them are virtually unlimited. It is hard to see how we could ever wish to make a take-out double of two clubs.

Balancing doubles

What is a balancing double?
A balancing double is a double which is made in the pass-out seat, when the opponents' bidding has died.

Why is a balancing double different to any other double?
The purpose of a balancing double is to compete for a part-score, or possibly to push the opponents a level higher where they will be more likely to go down. The classical balancing double position is a sequence such as:

West	North	East	South
1$\spadesuit$	Pass	2$\spadesuit$	Pass
Pass			

Here we know that our opponents have a fit and limited values. It follows that we are also likely to have a fit and our side is likely to have close to half the high-card points in the pack. It will usually be to our advantage to compete the part-score. Let us consider the following hands after this auction:

(a) ♠7
   ♡KJ52
   ♢K103
   ♣QJ842

(b) ♠763
   ♡KJ52
   ♢K3
   ♣AQ82

(c) ♠763
   ♡5
   ♢AJ953
   ♣KQ82

(d) ♠763
   ♡AJ5
   ♢QJ53
   ♣A108

(e) ♠76
   ♡52
   ♢A53
   ♣K108542

Hand (a) is a perfect balancing double – just the right shape but not quite enough values to have made a double on the first round. Hand (b) should also double – partner probably has at most a doubleton spade so we are likely to have a fit somewhere. On hand (c), we certainly want to bid something but double is unsuitable because it tends to suggest tolerance for hearts, so here we bid two no-trumps to ask partner to choose between the minors. Hand (d) is again suitable for a double – any five-card suit partner holds will suit us fine. Hand (e) was not strong enough for an overcall on the first round, but now we know that partner has some values we can afford to bid three clubs this time.

How should I respond to partner's balancing double?
One thing to bear in mind when responding to a balancing double is that the one thing that partner will not have is a hand that should have made a take-out double on the previous round. He will either be shape-suitable but with less high cards or, more likely, he will not be perfectly shape-suitable. Here it is clear that a bid of two no-trumps can be used as a scramble because our side is

unlikely to have game values. Thus it is much more important to differentiate in terms of distribution than strength. If we have no long suit of our own, or if we hold two suits, we should respond two no-trumps, to allow partner to bid one of his suits. Let us suppose, after the sequence 1♠ – Pass – 2♠ – Pass; Pass – Dble – Pass, that we hold:

(f)	♠ 5 4	(g)	♠ J 8 5 4	(h)	♠ 4
	♡ A 6		♡ A 6 4		♡ K 6 4 3
	◇ Q J 8 7 4 2		◇ Q J 8 7		◇ K 8 7 4
	♣ J 9 6		♣ K 9		♣ Q 9 6 3
(i)	♠ A 5 4	(j)	♠ A 5		
	♡ 6		♡ K 6 4 3		
	◇ Q 8 7 4 2		◇ K 8 7 4		
	♣ K 9 6 3		♣ 9 6 3		

Hand (f) is straightforward: we simply bid three diamonds. When we are relatively short in spades this should always show at least a five-card suit. Even if partner holds hand (b), he should pass three diamonds, knowing that we are in the best fit available. With hand (g) we should also bid three diamonds. Our spade length and high cards suggest that partner will have a hand with short spades and support for all the other suits but without the values for an initial take-out double. Even if three diamonds is a 4–3 fit, say facing hand (a), it should play better when we are taking the ruffs with the short trumps. On hand (h), our distribution suggests that partner has length in spades and that his hand may be similar to hand (b) or (d) above. We should bid two no-trumps and pass his response. With hand (i) we would like partner to choose his best minor, so again we try two no-trumps and pass whichever minor he bids. With hand (j), we would like to play in a red suit, so again we bid two no-trumps. If he bids three diamonds we will pass, but if he bids three clubs we will bid three diamonds, allowing him to choose between diamonds and hearts.

Can I never try for game after a balancing double?
We should be very wary about doing so. There is little more infuriating than to have made an aggressive balancing action, succeeded in the objective of forcing the opponents up a level and then finding that partner bids one more and goes down when the opponents were also going down.

Sometimes we may be in a position to make an encouraging move and this is when we hold positive preference for the highest suit in response to one of these take-out doubles – i.e. hearts when they are bidding spades, or diamonds when they are bidding hearts. We can either respond in that suit directly or bid two no-trumps first and then remove whatever partner bids to our own suit. Let us compare the following two bidding sequences:

West	North	East	South
1 ♠	Pass	2 ♠	Pass
Pass	Dble	Pass	3 ♡

West	North	East	South
1 ♠	Pass	2 ♠	Pass
Pass	Dble	Pass	2NT
Pass	3 ♣	Pass	3 ♡

Normally, the second sequence would have been going to offer a choice of suits but, when partner chooses the lowest (clubs) and we bid three hearts, that can no longer be the case. It makes a great deal of sense, therefore, to use one of the sequences to show positive responding values (i.e. game interest), whereas the other should be weak.

Which sequence should mean which?

There is a logical answer to this question. On the second sequence, partner might have responded three diamonds rather than three clubs. If he had done so, we would have bid three hearts with our single-suited hand and he would not know whether we were single-suited or had actually been offering a choice between hearts and clubs. Partner will usually pass this three-heart bid so, if we had no game interest, we would not mind.

Consequently, it is better to play the direct three-heart bid in the above sequence as constructive, and the delayed three-heart bid, as in the second sequence, to show no game interest. This is also consistent with other Lebensohl positions.

Consider the following hands:

(k) ♠ A 5 4   (l) ♠ Q 5 4
    ♡ Q 10 9 6 3   ♡ Q 10 9 6 3
    ◇ A 6 4 2   ◇ K 6 4
    ♣ 6   ♣ 6 3

With hand (k) we have serious game interest, even though we know that partner probably has less than the values for an initial take-out double. With hand (l), we are much weaker and it would be very unlikely that we could make a game if partner could not bid over one spade in the first place. For the reasons stated above, we should bid three hearts with hand (k) and two no-trumps with hand (l).

Although this is clearly the logical way round to play these two sequences for constructive purposes, there is one drawback: bidding two no-trumps allows the opener a 'free' double, after which it will be easier for them to penalize us. Consequently, if we were going to be very aggressive with our balancing actions, there would be some case for choosing the immediate bid to be weak after all.

Is it any different when the opponents are bidding hearts?

The answer to this depends to a certain extent on our overcalling style. We have to consider the meaning of the sequence:

West	North	East	South
1♡	Pass	2♡	Pass
Pass	2♠		

Obviously this does not show a hand which should have overcalled one spade on the previous round. If we play a sound overcalling style, then this would just show a hand with five spades that was not worth an overcall in the first place. If, however, we play an aggressive overcalling style, this two-spade bid would suggest either a poor five-card suit or a good four-card suit. Some pairs who play an aggressive overcalling style even go as far as to suggest that the above sequence should show spades and clubs, whereas a double would suggest spades and diamonds. This seems a little restrictive. It is probably best for us to bid two spades in this auction whenever we would be happy to play in a 4–3 spade fit. Consider the following hands after the sequence 1♡ – Pass – 2♡ – Pass; Pass:

(m) ♠ QJ109
♡ 543
♢ A76
♣ K53

(n) ♠ J7632
♡ 543
♢ K7
♣ AJ5

(o) ♠ Q763
♡ 5
♢ AJ76
♣ Q1053

(p) ♠ Q763
♡ 543
♢ K7
♣ AJ53

(q) ♠ A76
♡ 54
♢ KJ76
♣ QJ53

With hand (m), bid two spades. Partner should not pass if he only holds a doubleton. If we have to play in a 4–3 fit, it is best to remain as low as possible and take the ruffs in the short hand.

Hand (n) would not be everybody's choice for an immediate one-spade overcall, but we can bid two spades now and, if partner removes this because he has only a doubleton, we do not mind too much. With hand (o) we can double, knowing that whatever partner bids will suit us. With hand (p) we can also double, knowing that if partner doesn't have a five-card minor he will bid two no-trumps and we can choose to play in clubs. With hand (q) we can double happily, knowing that partner will never respond in a three-card spade suit. If he bids two spades we will be taking ruffs in our short trump hand; if he responds in a minor that will also suit us.

Are there any other types of balancing position?
So far, we have looked exclusively at situations where we are balancing after an opponent has opened the bidding, his partner has raised and the auction has been passed round to us. There are many other balancing positions and the safest time to balance is when the opponents have a fit, because then there is every likelihood that our side will also have a fit. Consider the following situation:

West	North	East	South
1 ♦	Pass	1 ♡	Pass
2 ♡	Pass	Pass	Dble

We are now in a similar situation to the one above. The opponents have found a fit and have limited values. We probably also have a fit, so there are many hands on which we would like to compete the part-score. We failed to make a take-out double over one heart so, when we double two hearts, he should not expect us to have a very good hand. Consider the following hands after the auction above:

(r) ♠ Q 5 4 3   (s) ♠ Q J 5 4   (t) ♠ Q J 10 9
    ♡ 6   ♡ 7 6 5   ♡ 7 6 5
    ♢ A 7 3 2   ♢ A 8   ♢ A 7 3
    ♣ K J 7 5   ♣ K 7 5 3   ♣ K 7 5

(u) ♠ K 5 4   (v) ♠ Q 4
    ♡ 7 6   ♡ 7 6 5 4
    ♢ A J 7 3   ♢ A 7
    ♣ K Q 7 5   ♣ K Q 10 7 5

Hand (r) would be a perfect balancing double on this sequence. We would even be happy if partner wanted to bid diamonds, particularly if our left-hand opponent's diamonds might only be a three-card suit. Hand (s) is also well suited for a balancing double on this sequence. Hand (t) is best described with a bid of two spades, for the same reasons as we discussed above. We have not bid one spade immediately over one heart so partner knows we do not have a good five-card suit. He will pass two spades with three-card support, otherwise he can bid a suit of his own. Hand (u) is also suitable for a balancing double in this situation, even though it contains only three spades. Partner should only bid two spades when he has at least four of them. Hand (v) should bid three clubs. Because we have four hearts we know that partner is short in the suit, and this makes it very likely that he has some club support and that we can successfully compete the part-score.

Does a balancing double still occur at the three level?
Yes, sometimes the bidding will have proceeded to the three level before we get to a balancing position. The basic principles are the same, but obviously we need a slightly better hand to wish to compete at a higher level. The following are all sequences where you should consider balancing if you have suitable distribution:

West	North	East	South
1♡	Pass	2♡	Pass
3♡	Pass	Pass	

West	North	East	South
1♡	Pass	2♣	Pass
3♣	Pass	Pass	

West	North	East	South
1♡	Pass	1NT	Pass
2♣	Pass	3♣	Pass
Pass			

What about sequences when they have not shown a fit?

There are other sequences where the opponents have not actually bid and raised a suit, but where it is fairly likely that they have an eight-card fit. On these sequences it is slightly more dangerous to balance because you are more at risk of being doubled and going for a penalty, therefore you need a better hand before you take action. Here are some such examples:

West	North	East	South
1♡	Pass	1NT	Pass
2♡	Pass	Pass	

West	North	East	South
1♡	Pass	1NT	Pass
2♣	Pass	Pass	

West	North	East	South
Pass	Pass	1♢	Pass
1♡	Pass	Pass	

Double is for take-out on all these sequences and all suit bids would be natural, although obviously denying the values for earlier action. The lower the level and the more favourable the vulnerability, the lighter can be our values for any action. One thing to bear in mind is that when the opponents are not in a 'fit' auction, if we are very short in their suit, then partner is very likely to pass our double for penalties. He will not expect us to have any trumps for our balancing double, but we should have sufficient defensive values not to be frightened if he passes.

There are other balancing situations where the opponents are even less likely to have a fit and therefore it is even more dangerous to enter the auction. Consider the following auction:

West	North	East	South
1♡	Pass	1♠	Pass
2♡	Pass	Pass	

The opponents have stopped in two hearts. Opener has shown a six-card suit and responder surely has less than three-card support. Now we are in a position where the opponents' best fit is probably only eight cards and will often be only seven. When we double two hearts here we should be short in hearts with close to the values for an opening bid. We will often hold four spades and partner should certainly feel free to respond two spades if he also holds four. The opponents very often only have a 4–1 spade fit on this auction.

West	North	East	South
1♡	Pass	1♠	Pass
2♣	Pass	Pass	

Here East hasn't been able to raise to three clubs, so is quite likely to hold only three clubs. West could still have a very strong hand. Again double would show about opening values, short in clubs, and would be very likely to hold four spades.

What if a one no-trump response or rebid is passed round to us?
All doubles of one no-trump rebids or responses are penalty oriented, showing fair values and suggesting that the opponents' cards are lying badly for them. Here are some examples:

West	North	East	South
1♡	Pass	1NT	Pass
Pass	Dble		

The classic meaning for this double is to suggest a strong hand with good hearts and that partner should pass and lead a heart, but there is a modern idea that this double can be used as two-way – either classical, as described above, or a light take-out double. Partner should be able to work out which hand-type it is and take action accordingly. This can be a particularly useful treatment at match-pointed pairs.

West	North	East	South
1♡	Pass	1♠	Pass
1NT	Pass	Pass	Dble

Here South is suggesting that he has a strong hand with good spades and short hearts (which he expects his partner to hold). North should usually pass and lead a spade.

Classically, these doubles were played as almost a command to pass and lead the suggested suit. This was all very well but the frequency of such a hand was low. Many tournament players (especially playing match-pointed pairs) have chosen to devalue these doubles so that all that would be expected would be opening-bid values with a strong four-card holding in the relevant suit. This leaves partner much more free to remove the double when he has a long suit and a weak hand.

Points to remember

1 When partner has made a take-out double and the next hand raises, if we wish to bid but have no good suit, it is more flexible to use a responsive double than guess which suit to bid.

2 A responsive double of a major should, in principle, deny holding four cards in the other major; if the double has been of a minor, then it should show both or neither major.

3 When one side of a partnership has made a take-out double of one suit, then doubles of other suits by either side should be penalty-oriented, always assuming that the original take-out doubler has three trumps to an honour.

4 If an opponent redoubles a take-out double, it is important that partnerships agree when a pass is for penalty and when it simply shows no suit to bid.

5 When we hold a strong hand with a long suit, it is usually better to start with an overcall and double on the next round, rather than to start with a take-out double.

6 When partner overcalls and the next hand bids a new suit or raises, if we would like to bid but have no clear-cut action, we can make a competitive double.

7 Doubles on the second round in live auctions always show a good hand with length and strength in the suit opened.

8 Doubles in a balancing position – i.e. when the opponents' bidding has died – are merely competitive gestures and the partnership should work on the assumption that there is no game on for their side.

5

Doubles After Our Side Has Opened the Bidding

In the last chapter we covered a range of competitive doubles, all of which were in sequences when the opposition had opened the bidding. There is at least as much scope for competitive doubles when it is our side that has opened and these will be covered in this chapter.

Negative (Sputnik) doubles

What exactly is a negative double?
A negative (or Sputnik) double is a double of an overcall for take-out rather than for penalty.

What are some of the advantages of playing a take-out double in this position?
Often we are dealt sufficient values to want to enter the auction but we do not have a good suit to bid, or else we would like to offer partner a choice between two suits but do not have the values to make two bids on our hand. For example, suppose partner opens one heart and our right-hand opponent overcalls two clubs. If we held one of the following hands, we would be stuck for a bid:

(a) ♠ K Q 10 6   (b) ♠ K Q 10 6   (c) ♠ A Q J 5
    ♡ 8 7   ♡ 8 7   ♡ K 4 3
    ♢ K J 10 7   ♢ K J 10 7 6   ♢ J 6 5
    ♣ 9 6 2   ♣ 9 6   ♣ 9 6 5

With hand (a) we have sufficient values to want to bid, but partner will surely expect us to have a five-card suit if we bid a suit at the two level. On hand (b) we could bid two diamonds, but partner has no reason to suppose that we hold four spades and if he has a minimum hand a good fit may be lost. On hand (c) we could raise hearts but, especially if we are playing a four-card major system, a good spade fit could be lost.

If we use a double as take-out, what do we do if we hold a hand with a strong holding in the opponents' suit on which we would have liked to make a penalty double?

As usual in take-out double positions we have to pass and hope for partner to reopen with a double. Most top partnerships play that partner *must* reopen the bidding in this position if he has two cards or less in the suit overcalled. If he would have passed a penalty double, then he reopens with a double; if he had extreme distribution and would have removed a penalty double, then he reopens with a bid in a suit.

What exactly do I need to make a negative double?

This is a very difficult question to answer because there are many styles of negative double in widespread use. Some people play that the double guarantees four cards in both unbid suits; some play it guarantees four cards in any unbid major; some play it limited; some play it unlimited; some allow single-suited hands; some do not. Others play complex mechanisms such as transfers in this situation, which means that some of the hands that the rest of us would find difficult have been made easier.

One of the problems is that, once our opponents have entered the auction, it is even more likely that, after our negative double, the next hand will bid further. If our negative double could show practically any hand, it makes it very difficult for partner to know when and what he is supposed to bid if there is further competition.

How should I decide what style of negative double is best for my partnership?

There is no 'right' way to play negative doubles. The major consideration to take into account is what our basic bidding system is. If partner's opening bid guarantees four cards in the suit, it will be easier for us to bid naturally over it than if he may have three cards in the suit (presumably a minor) or maybe even less.

If this is the case and we insist that our negative double (at a low level) promises four cards in an unbid major, there will not be many hands on which we would like to bid but have no convenient action. However, we will have no easy bid after 1♣ – 1♠, holding, say:

(d) ♠ 6 5 4
    ♡ A Q 5
    ♢ K J 6 5
    ♣ 6 5 4

If we held this hand we would have to choose between one no-trump with no spade guard, two diamonds on a four-card suit, two clubs or three clubs with inadequate support, a cue-bid for which we do not really have the values or pass, which could lead to our side missing something.

Why, then, do some people like to insist that the double should show four cards in the other major?

The problem that occurs if the double carries no guarantee of any particular holding in any particular suit is that, if the next opponent pre-empts the auction further, it is very difficult to know when to bid on and when to defend. Many top players believe that, particularly after a minor-suit opening and a one-spade overcall, the double should guarantee four hearts. They believe that the advantages they gain when the next hand pre-empts further more than outweigh the disadvantages of having a problem in finding an initial descriptive bid on a few hands.

Is there anything else we should take into account when deciding on our style of negative double?
One further consideration should be our opening no-trump range, or, to be more specific our no-trump rebid range. If we make a negative double of a two-level overcall and partner is allowed to rebid two no-trumps with a balanced 12-count, obviously we need more values to make the negative double than we would if partner was only going to rebid two no-trumps with 15 HCP.

What style of negative double are we going to choose?
For the purposes of this section we will consider the implications of using negative doubles within the following basic systems:

1 Acol, four-card majors, weak no-trump
   Here, with a minimum opening bid, we would rebid a five-card suit in preference to rebidding no-trumps. Therefore a two no-trump rebid shows extra values (15+). For the purposes of this discussion, it will also be assumed that a one no-trump rebid shows extra values, but if you are used to managing a wide-range rebid with a two-club inquiry, there is no reason why you should not do so in this position also.

2 Natural, five-card majors, prepared minors, strong no-trump
   Again, with a minimum opening bid, we would rebid a five-card major (or possibly a three-card minor) in preference to rebidding two no-trumps, so after a major-suit opening, a two no-trump rebid should show extra values. A one no-trump rebid would be weak (but again could be wide range if you use that in an uninterrupted sequence). However, after a minor-suit opening and overcall at the two level, a two no-trump rebid would be made on a minimum hand.

The following is but one sensible scheme of bidding in this position:

1   A negative double after a minor-suit opening and a major-suit overcall guarantees four cards in the other major.

2   In other situations responder can make a negative double without four cards in an unbid major, but will not be unduly perturbed by a response in that major.

3   A negative double is never made on an extreme single-suited (i.e. six-card or longer) hand – with that we either bid the suit or pass and hope to bid it on the next round.

4   A negative double is unlimited in terms of high-card values, but if the hand contains a five-card suit and the values to bid at the appropriate level, then that suit is bid in preference to a negative double.

Could we have a look at some example hands?
Let us consider the following hands after the sequence: 1♦ – 1♠:

(e) ♠ 6 5 4
     ♡ Q 7 5 3
     ♦ K 6
     ♣ Q 7 5 3

(f) ♠ A J 9 6
     ♡ J 10 7 5
     ♦ 6 4
     ♣ K 7 3

(g) ♠ 6 5 4
     ♡ Q 10 9 7 5 3
     ♦ A 6
     ♣ 7 5

(h) ♠ 6 5 4
     ♡ K 7 5
     ♦ Q 6
     ♣ K J 10 5 3

(i) ♠ 6 5 4
     ♡ Q J 7 5 3
     ♦ K 6
     ♣ A J 7

Hand (e) is the perfect distribution for a negative double – four cards in both the unbid suits and honour-doubleton in support of partner should he wish to rebid his suit. We will happily pass any non-forcing response he makes.

With hand (f) it is best to bid one no-trump, despite the four-card heart suit. Our spades are so good that it is unlikely that partner will be able to rebid one no-trump and, if he doesn't have four hearts, he will have to rebid two of a minor, which we have insufficient values to bid over, and we will have lost our chance to play in one no-trump when that is our best contract.

Hand (g) is not strong enough for a bid. Some pairs include this hand-type in a negative double; others play a change of suit (two hearts here) as non-forcing in this position. Our structure forces us to pass with this hand. We just have to hope that we will get a second chance.

Hand (h) is tricky and the right bid depends on our system. If we are playing Acol with a weak no-trump, we have just enough values to bid two clubs. After all, partner will not rebid two no-trumps unless he has a 15-count. However, if we are playing a strong no-trump, partner may have to rebid two no-trumps with as little as 12 HCP, so we are not really strong enough for two clubs – the choice is between an aggressive two clubs and pass.

Hand (i) is strong enough for a two-heart bid whatever no-trump range is played.

Let us consider some different hand-types, again after the auction 1♦ – 1♠:

(j) ♠ A Q 5　　(k) ♠ A 10 5　　(l) ♠ A 75
　　♡ J 6 4　　　　♡ Q J 6 4　　　♡ K J 6 4
　　♦ K 7 5　　　　♦ J 10 7　　　　♦ J 10 7
　　♣ Q 9 8 6　　　♣ K 8 6　　　　♣ A J 6

(m) ♠ A 7　　　(n) ♠ K J 10 9 5
　　♡ Q J 6 4 2　　　♡ A 6 4
　　♦ 7　　　　　　　♦ 7
　　♣ J 10 8 6 4　　　♣ J 10 6 4

On hand (j), with our double stopper in spades, there is no need to do anything clever – bid two no-trumps, just as we would have done without the intervention.

Although hand (k) has more or less the same values, there are two important differences: first, it contains four hearts, and second, it is less suitable for no-trumps with only a single guard in spades. We should start with a negative double and rebid two no-trumps on the next round if partner does not respond two hearts. He should understand that, while we are balanced and have a spade guard, we also have four hearts and are quite suitable for anything else he might like to consider.

Hand (l) is worth forcing to game. We could start with a cue-bid of two spades, which would do just that, but the modern treatment of an immediate cue-bid is that it should contain four-card support for partner. Without such support we double to start with and cue-bid on the next round. This will set up our game force, and perhaps let partner play the hand in no-trumps, protecting his supposed queen of spades.

Hand (m) is not strong enough for a two-heart bid, whatever no-trump range we decide to adopt. However, we can start with a double. If partner rebids two diamonds, we can bid two hearts to show that we don't like his suit and have a fair heart suit of our own. Since we have not bid two hearts immediately, this cannot be forcing, and, since we established earlier that we never start with a double on a single-suited hand, partner will know that we also have clubs.

If a double of one spade is for take-out, we obviously cannot bid it on hand (n). As in other take-out double positions, when we have a penalty double we have to pass and hope that partner can reopen the bidding with a double, which we will pass.

So far we have only considered negative doubles after the sequence 1◇ – 1♠. Are there any differences if other suits are involved?
One question we have to decide is how many spades we show when we bid one spade after partner has opened one of a minor and the next hand has overcalled one heart. One camp argues

that we might as well bid one spade when we have four cards in the suit, in the same way as we would have done had there been no intervention. This frees the double to place emphasis on the minors. The other camp believes that in a competitive auction it is important to differentiate between four and five spades. They argue that one spade should show a five-card suit and with only four they would make a negative double. Both are valid arguments and have many expert supporters, but for the purposes of our scheme, and to be consistent with what we do after a one-spade overcall, we will assume that to bid one spade would show a five-card suit and we will double to show only four.

If other suits are involved, the double does not guarantee holding four cards in any particular suit. Many distributions are possible, but, again, never a weak single-suited (six-card or longer) hand. This is also the case if the intervention is higher – a jump overcall perhaps, or a pre-emptive jump.

To what level should we play negative doubles?
To what level we play our negative doubles is a matter for partnership agreement. In response to 'How high do you play negative doubles?', many top-class pairs write 'seven spades' on their convention cards! However, what they really mean is that a double is never made with a trump stack. It is probably best to play them in a similar way to take-out doubles over pre-emptive openings, as we saw in Chapter 2 – i.e. they should be strict take-out up to the level of four diamonds, suggest playing in spades over a four-heart overcall, and ideally have balanced values over an overcall of four spades or higher.

When the opponents pre-empt at any level in any auction, it is important to strive for 'the best result possible' rather than the 'best possible result'. We should content ourselves with playing in a sensible contract, or defending whenever we think we will get a reasonable plus score by so doing. When deciding whether or not to make a negative double over an opposition jump overcall, at whatever level, we should consider partner's problems and only double if we think that we can control the auction – i.e. there is nothing that partner can respond which will leave us completely stuck.

Let us consider the following hands after the auction 1 ◇ – 2♣ (weak):

(o) ♠ K J 6 4
♡ A 7 5 3
◇ K Q 6
♣ 7 5

(p) ♠ 6 4
♡ K J 7 5
◇ J 6 4 2
♣ A 7 5

(q) ♠ 6 4 2
♡ K Q 10 5
◇ 4
♣ K 10 7 5 3

(r) ♠ K 10 9 6
♡ K 7 5 3
◇ A 6
♣ 7 5 3

(s) ♠ 6 4
♡ J 7 5
◇ A 6
♣ Q J 9 7 5 3

With hand (o) we should just jump to three no-trumps. If we double instead, the worry is that partner will not think our spades are as good as this even if we rebid three no-trumps. It is possible that bidding three no-trumps will miss our 4–4 heart fit, but it is also possible that even if such a fit exists, three no-trumps will be the better game.

Hand (p) is fine for a double. We will be happy if partner bids hearts or diamonds, and if he rebids clubs we can give him preference to diamonds. If he rebids two no-trumps we have to decide whether bidding three diamonds is forcing. If the two no-trump rebid showed extra values, as in our Acol weak no-trump style, then three diamonds should probably be forcing – with less values we should have raised diamonds immediately. If the two no-trump rebid is consistent with a minimum balanced hand, then there is a strong case for three diamonds to be non-forcing.

Hand (q) is very difficult. If we double two spades we would not be happy to hear partner rebid three diamonds. Again, this depends on basic system. If we play an Acol weak no-trump style, we know that partner cannot have a balanced 12–14 HCP. Therefore, when he rebids three diamonds, he is known to have a six-card suit and we can just about afford to risk a double. If, however, we play the five-card major, strong no-trump style, partner may rebid three diamonds when he has a 2–3–5–3 12-count with no spade guard. This possibility makes a negative double with our hand (q) a poor risk.

With hand (r) we could bid two no-trumps, but we surely fancy our chances on defence with our good four-card trump holding and good controls. Pass two spades and wait for partner's reopening double – if it never comes we won't be missing anything.

Hand (s) is just not worth a bid. We know in our heart of hearts that if we bid three clubs, partner is going to bid three no-trumps and, even with a weak no-trump base, there is no guarantee that this is going to be anything like a sensible contract. We just have to pass and hope that we get another chance.

Responding to a negative double

How should I respond to a negative double?
There are varying opinions as to the best style of responding to a negative double, but the one that fits in best with our general scheme is very similar to the way in which we responded to competitive doubles in the previous chapter:

1   After a minor-suit opening and major-suit overcall – i.e. when partner has promised four cards in the other major – we should bid as if he had responded in that major.

2   If we can rebid one no-trump, we should do so on nearly all

balanced hands in the right range even without a full stopper in the opponents' suit.

3   We may rebid another four-card suit, even if it is above the level of our first suit, with minimum values, but this might give partner a difficult decision, so if our first suit is of good quality we should choose to rebid it on a minimum hand.

4   We may jump in another four-card suit, or in no-trumps with extra values.

5   We may cue-bid, if we have enough values to force to game.

6   If it is our best alternative, we may rebid a three-card suit, provided it is below the level of our first suit.

Let us consider the following minimum hands after we have opened one diamond, the next hand has overcalled one spade and partner has made a negative double:

(a) ♠ K J 6   (b) ♠ J 6 4   (c) ♠ 6 4
    ♡ Q 7 5 3   ♡ Q 7 5   ♡ A K 7 5
    ◇ A 6 4 2   ◇ A K 6 4   ◇ A J 6 4 2
    ♣ Q 7   ♣ Q J 7   ♣ J 7

(d) ♠ 8 6 4   (e) ♠ 8 6 4
    ♡ 7   ♡ A Q
    ◇ A K 6 4 2   ◇ Q 8 6 4 2
    ♣ A J 10 7   ♣ A J 7

With hands (a) and (b), if we were playing a weak no-trump, we would have opened one no-trump and would not be facing this particular problem. However, having opened one diamond, we should rebid two hearts on hand (a) – partner has promised four hearts, remember – and one no-trump on hand (b), even without a full spade stop.

With hands (c) and (d), a simple rebid in our second suit is called for, showing a minimum opening. Hand (e) would again have already been opened a weak no-trump by some, but if system has forced us to open one diamond, it looks very unattractive to have to rebid such a poor suit and one no-trump, with nothing at all in spades, looks equally unattractive. The best alternative is two clubs, which is unlikely to excite partner too much.

These are all minimum openings. What do I do with a better hand?

(f) ♠ K J 6
    ♡ A 7 5
    ♢ Q J 10 6
    ♣ A K 7

(g) ♠ 6
    ♡ A K J 7
    ♢ A K 6 4 2
    ♣ 7 5 3

(h) ♠ A 6 4
    ♡ K J 7
    ♢ A Q J 10 6 4
    ♣ 7

(i) ♠ 6 4
    ♡ A K 7
    ♢ A Q J 10 6
    ♣ A 7 5

(j) ♠ 6
    ♡ A K J 7
    ♢ A K 6 4 2
    ♣ A 7 5

With hand (f), we have a balanced 18-count and can tell partner this in just the same way as we would have done if he had made a natural one-level response – by jumping to two no-trumps. Hand (g) has substantial values and is well worth a jump to three hearts. Hand (h) is a straightforward three-diamond rebid, showing much the same as it would in an uninterrupted auction. Hands (i) and (j) are both very strong and worth forcing to game. We should cue-bid two spades and then we can proceed to show our suits naturally. It is wrong to jump to game with hand (j) because this takes away a lot of bidding space which we may need to bid a slam. A jump to four hearts should be reserved for a hand that either has five hearts (and six diamonds) or that has sufficient spade length (say A-x-x) to suggest that partner is very likely to have a ruffing value and that the 4–3 fit will play well.

The next hand raises after our negative double

What should I do if the next hand makes a simple raise after partner's negative double – say 1♢ – 1♠ – Dble – 2♠?

We have arrived in another area where confusion abounds. All expert partnerships are agreed that a double in this position would be 'competitive', but what exactly does this mean? Does it show four hearts? Does it deny four hearts? Does it show substantial extra values or just a suitable minimum? Would a double be consistent with a strong no-trump in this auction?

All these questions need to be answered, but the answers can be found only by looking at the style of negative double used and the rest of our system. Here are some questions we need to answer before looking at the meaning of a double after this sequence.

1   Did our negative double promise four hearts?
    Since the answer to this is yes, then if we also held four hearts, we would surely bid the suit. Therefore a double of two spades would deny four hearts. If our negative double had not promised four hearts, we would need to make sure that we could investigate a heart fit at a safe level.

2   Should a two no-trump bid over two spades be natural?
    If we play a weak no-trump structure, there is no reason in the world why opener should not hold a balanced 16–18 count on this auction and want to bid a natural two no-trumps. However, suppose we are playing a strong club system where we are known to have less than 16 HCP, or a natural method with a strong no-trump. Now there is less reason to play two no-trumps as natural.

If two no-trumps is not natural, what does it mean?

Once the opponents have entered the auction and found a fit, they have begun to exchange information. On the above sequence, they have exchanged more information than we have and it is important for us to try to catch up. If we have a distributional hand it is important to tell partner. If we were dealt a minimum, shapely opening bid with a good six-card diamond suit we would want to rebid three diamonds on the above sequence. If we were dealt a 16-count with a good six-card diamond suit – i.e. a hand where we would have bid 1◇ – Pass – 1♠ – Pass – 3◇ – we would also want to rebid three diamonds. The two no-trump bid can be used here in a similar way as in response to a take-out double of a weak two bid. It can be used to tell partner that we have a weak distributional hand, either with six diamonds, or perhaps with five diamonds and four clubs. If partner has no extra values he just bids three clubs (if that is where he would like to play facing five diamonds and four clubs) and we either pass or convert to three diamonds.

That sounds like a good idea. Are there any problems with it?
Yes, there are several drawbacks with the idea. First, we have to work out what further bids mean after the two no-trump rebid – what is forcing and what is not, whether partner should bid suits in 'Multi' style (i.e. bid suits which we may have when he would like us to pass if we have them) or whether he bids his suits naturally, etc. Second, he may decide that he wants to play in three no-trumps and may be playing it the wrong way up. The other drawback is that, if the opponents bid further, they have prevented partner from knowing what suits we hold, so making it very difficult for him to know whether to bid on.

For the purposes of the rest of this chapter we will assume that two no-trumps is natural in sequences such as 1◇ – 1♠ – Dble – 2♠. If playing a basic method where two no-trumps cannot be a balanced 16/17 HCP, then it should show a hand with at least one spade guard and a good long diamond suit – such a hand with 14 or 15 HCP will be the equivalent in terms of playing strength of a balanced 16/17 of count.

What should a double of two spades show when playing our agreed negative double style?

Since our negative double promised four hearts, when we, as opener, have hearts we can simply bid the suit. Therefore a double of two spades denies four hearts and shows extra values which cannot be expressed by a natural bid.

Could we look at some examples, please?

Let us look at the following hands after the sequence 1◇ – 1♠ – Dble – 2♠:

(a) ♠ 7
  ♡ A K 6 4
  ◇ A J 7 5 3
  ♣ 8 6 4

(b) ♠ 7
  ♡ A K 6 4
  ◇ A J 7 5 3
  ♣ K 8 6

(c) ♠ 7
  ♡ A K 6 4
  ◇ A J 7 5 3
  ♣ A K 8

(d) ♠ 7
  ♡ A 6 4
  ◇ A K 9 7 5 3
  ♣ A J 8

(e) ♠ 7
  ♡ A 6 4
  ◇ A K 7 5 3
  ♣ A J 8 6

With (a) we have a minimum hand which is suitable for playing in hearts. We can express this by bidding a simple three hearts.

Hand (b) is stronger and had there not been any intervention we would have raised partner's one-heart response to three. Here they have taken away our bidding space, but partner is likely to have little wastage in spades, so it is best to overbid a little by bidding four hearts.

Hand (c) is stronger again, worth a game force. Had the opposition remained silent, and partner responded one heart to our one-diamond opening, we would have been too strong simply to raise to game and would have had to use some artificial device to tell partner of this – perhaps a three-spade splinter bid. Here we cue-bid three spades to tell him that we have a full-weight game force with four-card heart support.

Hand (d) is too strong for a simple three diamonds, so we should start with a double and bid diamonds later. Hand (e) is too strong for a simple three clubs, so we should double first and bid clubs later.

This seems fairly straightforward, but suppose partner doubles after a sequence such as 1◇ – 1♠ – Dble – 2♠. How do I show him whether I am minimum for my original double or if I have extra values?

Once again we must consider the meaning of a two no-trump bid in response to partner's double of two spades. It is unlikely to be needed as natural since we did not bid a natural two no-trumps over one spade and now the opponents have raised spades and partner has shown shortage in their suit, we are even less likely to want to play in no-trumps. If we do wish to bid a natural two no-trumps, perhaps with a hand that also wished to explore for a heart fit, or perhaps only had a single spade guard, then we have to bid three no-trumps. Partner should have at least a sound opening bid for his double, so it won't matter if we overbid a little. Once again we can use the two no-trump bid to show a hand that has no game interest, even if partner has extra values. By doing this we have released all natural three-level bids to show some game interest. If we have sufficient for a game force we must either jump or cue-bid three spades.

Could we look at some examples, please?

Let us consider the following hands after the sequence 1◇ – 1♠ – Dble – 2♠; Dble – Pass:

(f)	♠ 8 6 4	(g)	♠ 8 6	(h)	♠ A 8 6
	♡ Q J 7 5		♡ Q J 7 3		♡ K Q J 7
	◇ Q 8		◇ Q 8 6		◇ Q 8
	♣ Q 10 7 5		♣ K Q 7 5		♣ 9 7 5 3

(i) ♠ A 8 6   (j) ♠ 8 6
    ♡ K 7 5 3   ♡ A 7 6 3
    ◇ Q 8   ◇ K J 8
    ♣ K 7 5 3   ♣ K Q 7 5

With hand (f) we are as minimum as we could be, therefore we bid two no-trumps and pass partner's response.

We are not ashamed of hand (g) and are well worth a constructive three-level bid. Whether we should bid clubs or diamonds depends on our basic system. If we play Acol with a weak no-trump, we can afford to bid three clubs since partner will know we don't hold five clubs (with constructive values we would have bid two clubs over one spade). If we play a strong no-trump, where we would have needed more values to bid two clubs over one spade, we are safer to bid three diamonds here.

With hand (h) we have the values for game and a strong four-card heart suit. We can express this by jumping to four hearts. Once we have shown extra values, partner will know that we have only four hearts or we would have bid two hearts on the previous round. This jump bid shows a good four-card suit, and suggests playing in a 4–3 fit. If his hand is unsuitable, he will remove to five of a minor.

With hand (i) our heart suit is less robust and we would not relish playing in a 4–3 fit. Three no-trumps could well be our best game, therefore we start by bidding two no-trumps and, when partner bids three of a minor, we can rebid three no-trumps to show a single spade guard. If we had a double spade guard we would bid three no-trumps immediately.

On hand (j) we again have the values to force to game but our heart suit is poor and we have no spade stopper. Here we cue-bid straightaway. If partner cannot bid three no-trumps, he can bid his hand naturally at the four level – it is likely that we belong in game in a minor.

Would my bids mean the same thing if partner had passed the raise to two spades instead of doubling?
No, this situation is different for two reasons:

1   We now have a double of two spades available ourselves.
2   Partner has not shown any extra values, so we are not forced to bid at all and if we do bid we show something extra in the way of distribution and/or high cards.

Often opener will hold a normal minimum opening bid after the sequence 1♢ – 1♠ – Dble – 2♠, and will have felt no need to take any action. This is particularly likely if the basic system used incorporates a strong no-trump.

There is no need to be complicated in this situation. Given our basic structure of negative doubles, we cannot hold a very long suit, nor can we hold a hand with a five-card suit that had the values to bid at the two level in the first instance. Therefore to bid a suit shows a five-card suit and is not very strong. There is no reason why a two no-trump bid should not be natural, showing a hand that was not suitable for an immediate two no-trumps, perhaps because of only a single spade guard or because the hand also held four hearts.

The only game-forcing hands we can hold on this sequence are balanced hands which can either be expressed by a cue-bid or by a second double. A cue-bid asks partner to bid three no-trumps if he has a stop in the opponents' suit and is the sensible action to take if our hand has little potential for playing in game in a minor. If our hand is potentially suitable for playing in game in a number of different denominations, then we should choose the more flexible double.

Could we have some examples, please?
Let us consider the following hands after the sequence 1♢ – 1♠ – Dble – 2♠; Pass – Pass:

(k) ♠ 8 6 4   (l) ♠ 8 6   (m) ♠ A J 8
    ♡ Q 10 3 2   ♡ A 7 5 3   ♡ K 10 7 5
    ◇ Q   ◇ Q 6 4   ◇ Q 6
    ♣ K Q 10 9 7   ♣ K 10 7 5   ♣ J 10 7 5

(n) ♠ 8 6 4   (o) ♠ 8 6
    ♡ A 7 5 2   ♡ K J 10 7
    ◇ K Q 6   ◇ A 6 4
    ♣ K J 7   ♣ K Q 7 5

Hand (k) is very minimum, but non-vulnerable it would be very tempting to bid three clubs. Our three-card spade holding suggests that partner will only hold a doubleton, so we may well have an eight-card club fit; even if we do not, our suit is good enough to play in a 5–2 fit. If we go down in three clubs, they would probably have made two spades, and they may go wrong and bid on to three spades which we have a greater chance of defeating.

Hand (l) is slightly tricky. We would like to make another bid, but would like partner to choose where to play. We have four cards in both the unbid suits plus reasonable support for diamonds. We should double again, asking partner to choose something.

Hand (m) was unsuitable for an initial two no-trump bid because of the four-card heart suit and the sort of spade guard which is also good for suit play. However, now we can bid two no-trumps, confident that partner will move if unsuitable. He already knows of our heart suit, so he can always bid the suit now if he also has four hearts. If we double again with this hand we won't know what to do if partner rebids three diamonds.

Hand (n) is a 13-count which is so balanced that there is little chance of game in anything other than no-trumps. We should try three spades, hoping that partner can bid three no-trumps. If he can't and bids four of a minor instead, we should probably pass, expecting there to be three top losers. Remember, if he is short in spades, he would have bid on most hands earlier.

Hand (o) is a different matter, although again it is a balanced 13-count. Here we are much more suitable for playing in a suit contract – clubs, diamonds or hearts. Here we should double again and listen to what partner has to say.

How should partner respond to this second take-out double?
He should just bid naturally. Two no-trumps should be natural, since a minimum hand with values in the opponents' suit is the most likely hand for him to hold on this sequence.

Does all this still apply even if the suits involved are different?
So far we have considered in some depth the sequence 1♢ – 1♠ – Dble – 2♠. In this sequence there was one unbid suit below the level of our first suit and one above it: also, one unbid suit was a minor and one a major. This is not always the case. Let us take a brief glance at other possible combinations of suits and see if there are any differences:

1♣ – 1♠ – Dble – 2♠

This is the same as the above situation, except that three diamonds would show extra values, since there is no guarantee of diamonds opposite.

1♣ – 1♡ – Dble – 2♡

This is similar to over a spade overcall, since the double guarantees four spades. We should bid two spades with nearly any minimum hand with four spades. Three diamonds or three spades would show extra values. Otherwise double to show extra values which cannot be expressed by a natural bid.

1♢ – 1♡ – Dble – 2♡

Here we can bid either unbid suit below the level of three diamonds. We should again bid two spades on nearly any hand with four spades and jump to three spades with invitational values. If we have four clubs, we can bid three clubs with a sound minimum opening, but should double with four clubs and, say, 16 HCP or more. We really need a very distributional hand – say 5–5 in the minors – to jump to four clubs.

$$1\clubsuit - 1\diamondsuit - Dble - 2\diamondsuit$$

Here partner will not have a five-card major, but could have one or two four-card majors. If he does not have both four-card majors, then he should have some support for clubs. Our possible actions here are:

1 We should bid a four-card major if we hold one on any minimum hand without too much wastage in diamonds.
2 Rebid our own suit (clubs) with a good suit.
3 Jump to three of a major – an invitational.
4 Bid two no-trumps – natural.
5 Double, and then:

> • pass partner's simple response – this would be our action on a minimum hand with both four-card majors, or possibly with 3–4–1–5 distribution;
> • convert a two-heart response to two spades – the meaning of this action depends on our basic method: if we are playing strong no-trump and five-card majors, this action would simply show genuine clubs; if we are playing weak no-trump and four-card majors this would be mildly invitational;
> • bid three of a major – forcing;
> • rebid three of our suit to show a hand too good to rebid it straightaway;
> • rebid two no-trumps – natural but less no-trump-oriented than an immediate two no-trumps;
> • cue-bid – a game force with no four-card major.

6   Cue-bid three diamonds to ask partner to bid three no-
     trumps with a diamond stopper.

1♡ – 1♠ – Dble – 2♠

We should bid a four-card minor with anything from a sound
opening up to about 15 HCP, otherwise we should double.

*So far we have considered only one-level overcalls and their consequent
raise to the two level. What difference does it make if the overcall is at
the two level and the raise at the three level?*

There are two significant differences. First, since we may have
to rebid in no-trumps over the negative double, even if the next
hand doesn't raise, if this no-trump rebid may be made on a
minimum opening (i.e. if we play a strong no-trump structure
when the opening bid has been in a minor), then partner needs
more values to make that double in the first place. Second, a
responsive take-out double from opener becomes less attractive
because the original negative doubler can no longer use two
no-trumps to define the range of his hand.

The good news, which we have seen before, is that the
opponents generally have a better fit to go to the three level
(usually nine-card, as opposed to eight-card at the two level). If
they have a better fit, so do we, and consequently are less likely
to come to harm by bidding more aggressively.

1◇ – 2♣ – Dble – 3♣

Here, with a sound, slightly above-minimum opening bid –
say 14–15 HCP – we should bid a four-card major if we have
one: if we have a stronger hand with a good four-card major we
should jump to game, trusting partner to correct if he has less
than three cards in our suit. A double here would show extra
values, and may or may not contain a four-card major.

We do not need to look at all the possible sequences individually.
The higher the level to which the opponents have pushed us, the

more we will have to guess, just as we saw in the chapter on bidding over pre-emptive openings. If they start with a jump overcall, we need either better distribution or more values to make a negative double in the first place. This does at least mean that partner has a chance of guessing right when the next hand pre-empts further.

Suppose that, instead of raising, the next hand makes an unassuming cue-bid: for example, 1◇ – 1♠ – Dble – 2◇?
On any sequence, if we have support for partner and choose to do something other than raise to the limit – make a splinter bid, bid a good suit of our own first, cue-bid the opponents' suit, etc. – the price we pay is that we leave them more room to bid their own hands. In all sequences we should be clear in our minds that this price is worth paying.

The corollary to this is that when the opponents do other than raise their suit to the limit, we need to make the best use of the extra space available to us. In the sequence 1◇ – 1♠ – Dble – 2◇, their two-diamond cue-bid, for example, has left partner free to bid two hearts, when, if they had simply bid two spades, he would have had to bid at the three level if he wanted to bid his hearts. They have also given us a double of two diamonds, a cue-bid of two spades, and a pass followed by a double of two spades on the next round.

How can we make best use of all this extra space?
Traditionally, a double of two diamonds just shows good diamonds, but this is not necessarily the best treatment (when playing a natural system). We have heard partner open one diamond and already know he has length and probably some strength there. It may be more useful for him to tell us if he has suitable distribution for us to wish to compete further – say a minimum opener with a 1–3–5–4 distribution (if he had four hearts he would surely simply bid two hearts). If he doubles two

diamonds and then bids on, he is making a constructive bid but is not forcing. This is perhaps a more useful alternative treatment of an immediate double.

What then is the meaning of an immediate cue-bid of two spades?
This should be a game force with shortage in the opponents' suit (only if the above suggested meaning of a double is employed – if not, then it will be needed for some other strong hands). With hands not worth a game force, start by doubling two diamonds and later make an encouraging descriptive bid.

What about a pass followed by a double of two spades on the next round?
This should show a more balanced take-out – say a 2–3–5–3 distribution. This also allows us the option of passing two spades doubled out when we have good defensive values.

After the bidding sequence:

West	North	East	South
1 ◇	1 ♠	Dble	2 ◇
Pass	2 ♠		

We are in an identical position to when the sequence was:

West	North	East	South
1 ◇	1 ♠	Dble	2 ♠
Pass	Pass		

and the same structure applies to both situations.

A structure of negative doubles when the minor-suit opening could be short

Are there any differences if the minor-suit opening was prepared – that is playing strong no-trump with five-card majors, or perhaps a one-diamond opening playing Precision?

So far we have been assuming that all the opening bids have been in suits of at least four cards. In today's world this is not always the case. Traditional 'strong no-trump five-card major' bidders have opened their longer minor (one club unless holding four diamonds or precisely 4–4–3–2). These days there is a tendency in some expert quarters to open one club on all weak balanced hands which do not contain a five-card suit in diamonds, hearts or spades. Also, there are those who play a Precision club-style system allied to a strong no-trump, and they have to open one diamond on all their weak balanced hands.

The 'traditional' strong no-trumpers can probably get away with little modification to the above, since their opening bids are usually natural. However, the 'modernists' or the 'strong club-bers' have more problems since they do not know anything about the length in the minor opened (some of the strong clubbers could even have a void in diamonds). This means that a 'raise' of the suit opened is not available to them in the normal way. A sequence such as 1♣* – 1♠ – 2♣, or 1♦* – 1♠ – 2♦, has to show a five-card suit and the values to bid at the two level, just as if the opening bid had been in a different denomination altogether. It is because this 'raise' has been taken away that it becomes impractical for the negative double to deliver any guar-antees about four cards in any unbid major(s). (Many pairs play transfer responses to opening bids in order to avoid some of these problems, but that is a subject for some other book.)

Let us consider the sequence we covered in some depth earlier, 1♦ – 1♠ – Dble – 2♠, when the one-diamond opener is always

11–15 points, but could be either single-suited with clubs, or single-suited with diamonds, or any balanced 11–13.

West	North	East	South
1 ◇★	1 ♠	Dble	2 ♠
?			

Dble always four hearts, either a suitable balanced hand, a minimum hand with four hearts and a long minor, or a very strong hand with four hearts and a long minor

2NT both minors

3 ♣ single-suited with clubs

3 ◇ single-suited with diamonds

3 ♡ medium range hand with four hearts and a long minor.

West	North	East	South
1 ◇★	1 ♠	Dble	2 ♠
Dble	Pass	?	

2NT both minors

3 ♣/◇ natural, five-card suit, insufficient values to bid the suit naturally the first time

3 ♡ natural, no game interest unless partner has the very strong hand, in which case he will proceed himself

4 ♡ to play

West	North	East	South
1 ◇★	1 ♠	Dble	2 ♠
Pass	Pass	?	

Dble always four hearts, tolerance for both minors

2NT either both minors, or one minor plus hearts without tolerance for the other minor

3 ♣/◇ natural, five-card suit

West	North	East	South
1 ◇★	1 ♠	Dble	2 ♠
Pass	Pass	Dble	Pass
?			

2NT no preference between the minors

Note that there is a different emphasis in these sequences. Strong club players are in a better position to open light hands than natural bidders because the upper limit of their non-one-club opener is less. When the one-diamond opening is usually 11–13 balanced, their partners expect this and therefore do not go overboard. Consequently, when they have opened one diamond when they are not 11–13 balanced, they have to strain to bid in order to inform partner of this. By the time East made his second bid in the above sequences, his partner had defined his hand quite accurately and East's further bidding can be directed to competing the part-score. Also, because the opening-bid suit is meaningless, it is sensible to play a direct cue-bid – i.e. 1♦★ – 1♠ – 2♠ – as a game-forcing balanced hand, thus eliminating all really strong hands from the negative double in the first place.

The next hand bids a new suit after our negative double

What about when the next hand bids a new suit: for example, 1♦ – 1♠ – Dble – 2♥?
This particular sequence, along with 1♦ – 1♥ – Dble – 1♠, is one where opponents are liable to psych against us. Whether or not our double guarantees four hearts, we are quite likely to have a fit there and an opponent may well hope to have a laugh at our expense by trying to get us in a muddle (see Chapter 1 after 1♥ – Dble – 1♠). It seems sensible, therefore, that when an opponent bids a new major after a negative double, a double by partner should show four cards in that suit. At least this agreement will enable us to find our 4–4 fit there.

Would this still apply if their new suit was a minor?
That is more open to question. It is unlikely that our opponent has psyched a minor suit in this position. However, there is little need for partner's double to be take-out – he can bid the fourth

suit or cue-bid either of the opponents' suits. The double is probably best played as a penalty-suggestion, but based rather more on the suit overcalled (where we have suggested shortage) than the new suit (where we have suggested length). After the sequence 1◇ – 1♠ – Dble – 2♣, partner might double holding, say:

♠ K J 10 6
♡ A 7
◇ A 10 6 4 2
♣ K 5

Doubles by opener after left-hand opponent has overcalled

If we open the bidding, the left-hand opponent overcalls and this is passed round to us, what sort of hands should we double on?

Assuming that we play negative doubles, partner has passed either because he is too weak to bid or because he has length and strength in the opponent's suit and would like to have made a penalty double, in which case he is unlimited. If our right-hand opponent has not bid over the overcall, and we are short in the suit overcalled, it is almost certain that partner wished to make a penalty double. Consequently, we *must* reopen on *any* hand that has a doubleton or less in the opponents' suit. If we have more than two cards in our opponents' suit, then we need substantial extra values, either in high cards or distribution, in order to reopen. This is because, when we have length in the opponent's suit, we know that partner has passed because he is weak.

Do we always reopen with a double when we are short in the opponents' suit?

We should reopen with a double only if we would have passed a penalty double, had partner been in a position to make one. For

example, consider the following hands after the sequence 1♣ –
1♡ – Pass – Pass:

(a) ♠ K Q J 6   (b) ♠ A 5 4 3   (c) ♠ A J 10 9 7
    ♡ 7   ♡ 7   ♡ A
    ◇ Q 7   ◇ Q J 6   ◇ 7
    ♣ K J 10 8 7 6   ♣ K J 7 6 4   ♣ K Q J 9 8 7

(d) ♠ 8 7
    ♡ —
    ◇ K Q J 7 6
    ♣ A J 10 7 6 5

With hand (a) we could risk a double and it is certainly
possible that that would be the winning action. However, we
are very weak defensively and in doubling we risk partner
passing on many hands where one heart will make. It is safer to
reopen with one spade. On hand (b), despite our minimum in
high-card points, we have fair defensive values and should
reopen with a double. Hand (c) is much too strong in playing
strength to double and we should show partner our strength and
extra distribution by jumping to two spades. Hand (d) also has
too much potential to double and we can show this by bidding
two diamonds. Note that bids such as jumps and reverses still
show hands that are strong, but in playing strength rather than
in high cards. If we held a hand that was more balanced but
stronger in terms of high cards, we would double.

How should partner respond to this double?

Much of the time he will simply pass because he would have
liked to have made a penalty double in the first place. If his
trumps are insufficiently strong to pass, then he simply makes a
descriptive bid. It is very important for him to keep in mind that
our double shows no extra values, so he should be very wary
about doing anything other than making a simple bid.

Can he never jump in response to my double?

There is only one type of hand he could have where he could not bid the first time and now wants to a make a jump response to our double: where he has length in the opponents' suit but is unsuitable for defence. Suppose we open one club and our left-hand opponent overcalls one heart and partner holds, for example:

♠ 7 6
♡ A 6 5 3 2
♢ K Q 10 9 7
♣ 6

He has a difficult bid to find. The trouble with bidding two diamonds is that, even if we are playing a weak no-trump structure, it is unlikely that we will be able to rebid in no-trumps. If we do anything other than raise diamonds he will be badly placed. This is the sort of hand that can be described well by passing on the first round. If we pass one heart out, then we will have at least three hearts and should get a plus score; if we reopen with a double he can jump to three diamonds, knowing that at worst we will hold a doubleton in support.

Is there any difference if the intervention is at the two level?

It is still obligatory that we reopen when we have a doubleton or less in the opponents' suit. However, there are certain problems concerning partner's response to our take-out double. He needs more values to bid or make a negative double, the higher the level of the intervening action: therefore there are some hands on which he has reasonable values but does not wish to pass our reopening double.

Can we use two no-trumps again to help us with this problem: for example 1♠ – 2♡ – Pass – Pass; Dble – Pass – 2NT?

Certainly, there is not much use for a two no-trump response in its natural sense. Since we have shown no extra values with our reopening double, it does not make sense for partner to suggest playing in two no-trumps with a hand on which he could not bid it in the first place. We have to decide what the best use of this two no-trump response should be. Assuming that we are playing a natural system, it is best to treat this just as we did after a take-out double of a weak two bid. This is because it is still possible that we have a game on. However, if we were playing a strong club system, where the opening bidder is limited, there is much less likelihood of our side making a game and there is much to be said for using two no-trumps as a 'scramble', denying a long suit and asking us to choose a suit.

Suppose I open the bidding, my left-hand opponent overcalls, partner passes and my right-hand opponent raises or bids a new suit: for example, 1♠ – 2♡ – Pass – 3♡. What does double mean then?

If our opponent has raised, then a double is for take-out, showing extra values, usually with shortage in our opponents' suit and support for all other suits. Very occasionally, it may just be the first move on some very strong hand.

And if my opponent has bid a new suit: for example, 1♠ – 2♡ – Pass – 3♣?

The double will still show shortage in the suit overcalled, but opinions differ as to how good a holding it should show in our right-hand opponent's suit. Assuming this new suit by the opposition is not played as forcing, there is a strong case for playing the double as penalty, assuming that partner has a penalty double of the suit overcalled. If the change of suit by the opposition is played as forcing, this is not a sensible treatment, and our double should be for take-out, suggesting four cards in the unbid suit, whereas to bid the fourth suit would show five cards. Indeed, this is the treatment adopted by many pairs regardless of how strong a hand our right-hand opponent has shown.

What if my right-hand opponent bids over his partner's overcall and this is passed back to partner: for example, 1♠ – 2♡ – Pass – 3♣; Pass – Pass? What would his double mean?

Any double made by partner would suggest positive values and a penalty double of the suit first overcalled. With any other hand worth bidding on he would have bid earlier. If the opponents have raised, partner's double would still be for penalty. If our right-hand opponent had bid a new suit, partner's double would not show length there, but rather that he is hoping that we have length there and will pass.

Doubles by opener after right-hand opponent has overcalled

What if my left-hand opponent and partner both pass my opening bid and my right-hand opponent balances: for example, 1♡ – Pass – Pass – 2♣; Dble?

There is little to say about this sequence; it is universally played as take-out and could cover a multitude of hand-types. It will usually have shortage in clubs and support for all other suits. However, in these modern times when many pairs do not play strong two bids, the one-heart opening can conceal some very strong hands that still have game interest even though partner has passed. They are best started with a double. For example, suppose we hold:

♠ K 6
♡ A K Q 7 5 3
♢ A Q 6 4
♣ 7

If we do not have an Acol two bid or its equivalent in our armoury, we have to start off by opening with one heart. If partner passes and the next hand reopens with two clubs, we should start with a double. If partner responds two diamonds we can jump to three hearts, trusting partner's diamond length to make that a fairly safe contract. Now partner, with a high card in spades or diamonds (say the ace of spades or king of diamonds), plus a couple of hearts, should press on to game. If we only bid two hearts, partner will not know that we are so strong as we might have doubled with a weaker hand with six hearts and four spades, say:

♠ A Q 6 4
♡ A K 9 7 5 3
♢ Q 6
♣ 7

What if partner has responded, say in a new suit, before my right-hand opponent overcalls: for example, 1♡ – Pass – 1♠ – 2♣; Dble?
There are three distinct schools of thought about how to play a double in this situation – two referred to here as 'British' and one as 'American'.

The 'British' take-out double
As suggested by the heading, the British style is to play a double in this position as for take-out, its exact meaning depending on which suits are involved.

In the sequence mentioned, 1♡ – Pass – 1♠ – 2♣, the opponents have not removed our ability to rebid diamonds naturally. Therefore, the (a priori) meaning of a double would be to show a diamond suit with three-card spade support – i.e. ideally a 3–5–4–1 distribution. However, it could also be used with 3–6–3–1 or 3–5–3–2 or 3–4–4–2. It does not necessarily show any extra values.

If the opponents have consumed more space – say in the sequence 1♡ – Pass – 1♠ – 2♢ – then the double shows four clubs, along with some spade tolerance, which may be only a doubleton. A bid of three clubs would show a five-card suit and not much in the way of extra values, whereas to double and then bid three clubs would show a good hand.

If we are in a situation such as 1♣ – Pass – 1♠ – 2◇, a double would show four hearts (a priori) and either a hand not worth a reverse or a hand worth a game force. Thus to bid two hearts instead would show reversing values but be non-forcing, say 16–18 HCP.

In response to these take-out doubles, everything is natural, a jump being invitational but non-forcing. If the intervention has been at the level of two of a major, it would be sensible to play two no-trumps as showing a 'bad' hand in the same way that we have seen earlier. If the initial response to the opening bid has been at the two level, a two no-trump response to the double should be the start on all non-game-forcing sequences and a direct three-level response to the double should be game-forcing.

The 'British' strong no-trump double

Whatever no-trump range we choose to play gives us some problems when we have a balanced hand which is out of the range of our one no-trump opening. Acol, weak no-trumpers can have problems when they have a medium balanced hand – say in the 15–16 range. If the bidding proceeds 1♡ – Pass – 1♠ – 2♣, for example, a balanced 15–16 count is substantially above a minimum opening bid but not strong enough to justify rebidding two no-trumps. These players use a double to show a strong balanced hand which is unsuitable for rebidding no-trumps. This may be because it is not strong enough to rebid no-trumps at the necessary level, or because it has no guard or an 'anti-positional' guard such as A–x–x in opponents' suit.

Because the double shows a strong no-trump, it can obviously be passed more frequently by responder. However, because it delivers no guarantees about distribution, it can be quite difficult to bid over since the responder needs to establish a sensible trump suit as well as defining level – the range of the double is 15–18. It is not very satisfactory to have to jump to show game interest when the suit we have jumped to is not suitable as a final resting place. For this reason, there is a lot to be said for incorporating a Herbert negative response to the 'strong no-trump double'. Thus the next available bid denies any game interest, all simple bids are natural, constructive but non-forcing, and all jumps or cue-bids are game-forcing.

The 'American' support double

The American style is to use a double in our above position, 1♡ – Pass – 1♠ – 2♣, simply to show three-card spade support. Consequently all raises promise four-card support. The double does not show any extra values, nor promise suitability for raising (such as a ruffing value); it merely shows the number of cards held in partner's suit.

In response to this double, all bids below the next level in responder's suit are correctional – i.e. showing four-card suits and suggesting a better spot. If responder rebids his suit at the two level this is a sign-off but does not necessarily show five cards in the suit. All bids above the next level in responder's suit are game tries (long or short, by agreement). If opener has extra values, he should bid on descriptively after a sign off or force to game via a cue-bid. For example:

West	North	East	South
1♡	Pass	1♠	2♣
Dble	Pass	2♠	Pass
?			

2NT natural, non-forcing, five hearts, three spades, good club guards
3♣ game-forcing
3♢ natural – say, 3–5–4–1
3♡ natural, six hearts and three spades

There can be a lot of accuracy gained in these sequences when both sides know how good the trump fit is. The gain is not only when opener doubles, but also when he raises immediately to show four trumps. Responder is well placed to try for a thin game, perhaps knowing of that vital and underestimated ninth trump.

Support doubles fit well into a strong no-trump, five-card major framework. After a sequence such as 1♣ – Pass – 1♠ – 2♦ we would like to show some support for spades on many minimum balanced hands, whether or not we have three- or four-card support. On the other hand, if we are playing a four-card major, weak no-trump base, after such a sequence as 1♣ – Pass – 1♡/♠ – any, the raise of the major will usually show only three-card support. For opener to hold four-card support he will have five cards in the suit opened, and with this extra distribution will usually be able to go to the three level.

What if partner's response had been 1NT: for example, 1♡ – Pass – 1NT – 2♣ – Dble?

There are some expert pairs who believe that all take-out doubles should go out of the window when our side has bid no-trumps, arguing that the no-trump bidder is quite well defined and therefore penalty doubles work well. No doubt there is much to be said for this argument, but the no-trump bid is never precisely defined, whether it is an opening bid, or a response, or a rebid. In the above sequence the one no-trump bidder will usually hold at least three clubs, so one could argue that opener can afford to double two clubs with a defensively oriented hand when he also has three clubs. No doubt a number of good penalties are achieved in this way.

However, what is often overlooked by avid penalty doublers is that the take-out doublers often achieve just as many penalties by making a take-out double and hearing partner pass for penal-

ties. They may not always achieve their penalties on the same
hands – take-out doublers tend to get penalties when the trumps
are in one hand and the strength in the other, whereas penalty
doublers tend to get penalties when the trumps and the high
cards are in the same hand.

When our side has bid no-trumps there is a strong case for
continuing to play take-out doubles, but to play them as
showing extra values and denying extreme distribution, thus
enabling partner to pass most of the time when they hold four
trumps. Thus, in the above situation, 1♡ – Pass – 1NT – 2♣, a
double would show the values for a game invitation with, say,
3–5–3–2, 2–5–4–2, 4–5–2–2, 4–4–3–2 or 3–4–4–2 distribution.
Partner should usually pass holding four clubs, but if not should
choose between the red suits – in this particular situation,
assuming he has neither four spades nor three hearts, if he has
only three clubs he will have at least five diamonds.

*We have chosen to start by looking at a situation when the intervention
has been in a suit where partner is very likely to hold length. Does the
situation change when partner has 'denied' four cards in the suit overcalled – say 1♡ – Pass – 1NT – 2♠? or in the situation where his
length is less certain: for example, 1♠ – Pass – 1NT – 2♢?*
It is best to stick to the notion of the one no-trump bidder only
passing when he has four cards in the suit overcalled. Even if our
style is *never* to respond one no-trump with an intervening
four-card major and thus the double will *never* be passed out, it is
still a useful tool for finding out more about the hand.

If our double is take out after a sequence such as 1♡ – Pass –
1NT – 2 any, then a two no-trump bid instead would be natural.
However, in response to the take-out double, we can use a two
no-trump bid in the same way as we have seen earlier – to show
a weak hand for our previous bidding, whereas to actually bid
three of a suit would be constructive.

There are those who argue that the best use of a double after partner has responded one no-trump is to show a raise to two no-trumps. This seems to be the worst of all worlds. When is partner supposed to pass it if it may contain any number of trumps from two to four? However, this method does gain one advantage which is that if a double shows a raise to two no-trumps, then clearly a bid of two no-trumps does not. This allows a two no-trump bid to be used artificially in the 'good/bad' way we have seen earlier.

Suppose we hold either:

(a) ♠ A 6   (b) ♠ A 6
    ♥ K Q 7 5 3   ♥ A K 7 5 3
    ♦ 8   ♦ 8
    ♣ Q J 7 5 3   ♣ A Q 7 5 3

If the bidding proceeds 1♥ – Pass – 1NT – 2♠, we clearly cannot bid three clubs on both of these hands. Those who play a double here as a raise to two no-trumps can use two no-trumps instead to show a hand such as (a) – i.e. a hand that merely wishes to compete in a minor; with a hand such as (b) they bid three clubs to show that they would have jumped to three clubs if there had been no intervention.

However, playing take-out doubles we need our two no-trump bid as natural. We can bid three clubs on hand (a), but with hand (b) we have to start with a double. When partner responds with the inevitable three diamonds we have to decide whether to go past three no-trumps to show our club suit, or make a totally non-descriptive three-spade cue-bid which will let us play in three no-trumps some of the time but may get us in a muddle otherwise.

The alternative solution to such a problem is to do without a way of raising to two no-trumps at all. In other sequences we have just had to overbid by jumping to three no-trumps when we did not have a natural two no-trumps available, and we may choose to do so here, freeing the two no-trump bid to differentiate between the good/bad hands.

The game-try double

Suppose partner's response to my opening bid was a simple raise: for example, 1 ♡ – Pass – 2 ♡ – 3 ◇; Dble?

In an uninterrupted sequence when partner has raised our opening bid of one of a major to two, we are free to make a game try in whatever way we choose – long suit, short suit, or a combination of the two. When the next hand intervenes he has taken some of our options away. If we have bid 1 ♡ – Pass – 2 ♡, and he intervenes with two spades, he has only removed one bid; if he bids two no-trumps he has removed two bids, three clubs three bids, but if he intervenes with three diamonds he has taken away all our space to make a game try.

It is in this latter situation that a game-try double is widely used. After the sequence 1 ♡ – Pass – 2 ♡ – 3 ◇ or 1 ♠ – Pass – 2 ♠ – 3 ♡ a double is used to say to partner, 'I have a good hand and would ordinarily have made some sort of game try. Are you maximum or minimum?' This convention is played sufficiently widely that it is listed in the World Bridge Federation Convention booklet and is allowed to be abbreviated on the WBF Convention Card. In their terminology, it is called a Maximal Overcall Double and applies only when the opponents have taken up all our bidding space.

In sequences such as 1 ♡ – Pass – 2 ♡ – 3 ♣ and 1 ♠ – Pass – 2 ♠ – 3 ♣, where there is still some room, then it is normal to bid any intervening suit as a game try. In the situation where the opponents have taken away nearly all our room – 1 ♡ – Pass – 2 ♡ – 3 ♣, for example – a bid of three diamonds would be any game try and would be totally unrelated to our diamond holding.

When we have more space we make the best descriptive bid available, choosing either the best of the remaining two suits, or the one where we need help, according to agreement.

What, then, is the meaning of a double when they have not taken away all our room – after, say, 1♡ – Pass – 2♡ – 3♣?

The normal meaning of this double is penalty-oriented – typically a balanced, defensive hand with length in clubs, say A-x-x-/K-x-x as a minimum. Partner will normally pass unless he has either four-card trump support for us (unless playing a four-card major system, where this is normal for a raise of one of a major to two), or extreme shortage in the suit overcalled (a singleton, say), or no defensive tricks at all.

This game-try double when they have taken all our space away seems a good idea. Can it be used in any other situations?

The most common type of situation is when our left-hand opponent has overcalled, partner has raised, and our right-hand opponent has also raised. For example:

West	North	East	South
1♡	2♢	2♡	3♢
Dble			

However, the same principle can be extended to any situation where our side has agreed a suit and the opponents have intervened in the suit which takes all our space away. Some other examples might be:

	West	North	East	South
(a)	1♡	Dble	2♡	3♢
	Dble			

	West	North	East	South
(b)	1♢	1♡	2♢	2♡
	3♢	Dble		

	West	North	East	South
(c)	1 ◇	1 ♡	1 ♠	2 ♡
	3 ◇	Dble		

	West	North	East	South
(d)	1 ◇	1 ♡	Pass	2 ◇
	3 ◇	Dble		

	West	North	East	South
(e)	1 ♣	1 ♡	2 ◇	2 ♡
	3 ◇	Dble		

	West	North	East	South
(f)	1 ♡	Pass	1 ♠	2 ◇
	2 ♡	3 ◇	Dble	

It can be seen from sequence (d) that our suit agreement may be inferential, via an unassuming cue-bid. Also it is not necessary for the opponents to have bid and supported their suit, as in sequences (c) and (d).

In auction (f), partner has freely rebid his suit, showing at least six cards and the opponents have bid and supported diamonds. By far the most useful meaning for a double in this position is to show a constructive raise to three hearts. If we merely bid three hearts in this position, partner will think we are just competing.

Doubles by responder on the second round

Suppose I respond to partner's opening bid, the next hand overcalls and this is passed round to me: for example, 1♡ – Pass – 1♠ – 2♣; Pass – Pass – Dble. What does this mean?

There is little disagreement among experts that a double of two clubs in this position would be for take-out. The disagreement comes when considering the differences between bidding a suit immediately – here two diamonds – and doubling before bidding a new suit. The method which will be described here would not receive universal approval.

Most pairs have the agreement that holding a hand such as:

♠ A Q 6 4
♡ 7
♢ K 10 9 6 4 2
♣ 7 5

their initial response to partner's opening bid of one heart would be one spade as the hand is not strong enough to bid two diamonds and rebid two spades. Some pairs even play that a responder's reverse (i.e. to bid two diamonds and then two spades) is game-forcing and no doubt they could have the same distribution with even more high cards.

If this is a hand that we could hold for responding one spade to one heart, it seems that we should be able to describe it if the next hand overcalls two clubs and partner passes. If we double to show this hand (among others), is partner really supposed to bid two diamonds on, say, a doubleton? No, of course he isn't. If we hold this hand we have to be able to bid two diamonds, showing at least five cards in diamonds, probably only four spades and not a great deal of strength.

Our scheme is as follows:

1 To bid a new suit instead of a reopening double shows at least five cards in the new suit and is likely to hold only four cards in the first suit – this new suit is non-forcing at whatever level it occurs. This obviously applies only when such an interpretation is possible. For example, if the bidding went 1♢ – Pass – 1♠ – 2♣; Pass – Pass – 2♡, obviously we hold at least five spades and at least four hearts – otherwise we would not have responded one spade in the first instance.

2   Double is for take-out and suggests that opener should
    choose between the unbid suit, rebidding his own suit or
    giving delayed support for responder's first suit – the double
    shows little in the way of extra values, particularly if the
    intervention has been at a low level, but if the doubler bids
    again he is showing extra values and to double and then bid a
    new suit is forcing.

Could we look at some examples, please?
Let us look at some possible hands for responder after the
sequence 1♡ – Pass – 1♠ – 2♣; Pass – Pass:

(a) ♠ A Q 7 5 3   (b) ♠ A Q 7 5 3   (c) ♠ K Q 10 7 5 3
    ♡ 6 4   ♡ 6 4   ♡ 6 4
    ◇ K 10 7 5   ◇ A K 10 7   ◇ 7 5 3
    ♣ 6 4   ♣ 6 4   ♣ 6 4

(d) ♠ K Q 10 7 5 3
    ♡ 6 4
    ◇ A 7 5
    ♣ 6 4

Hand (a) is the perfect distribution for a reopening double. We
will be happy whatever partner responds. If he chooses to pass
two clubs doubled, he should have a good four-card club suit
and our general defensive strength is adequate.

Hand (b) should also start with a double, but should then bid
three diamonds if partner responds two of a major. If partner
responds two diamonds, then we will cue-bid three clubs to
force to game.

Hand (c) is a very minimum responding hand but it would be
timid to pass out two clubs with such a good six-card suit. We
simply bid two spades.

Hand (d) is significantly stronger so we start with a double
and then bid two spades over partner's response. In this way we

have shown a hand about a trick stronger than if we had bid an immediate two spades.

The only really awkward hand to deal with using this method is a hand that is strong enough to double but is so short in the opponent's suit (clubs here) that we are afraid to double in case partner passes.

(e) ♠ A Q 7 5 3   (f) ♠ A K J 10 5 3   (g) ♠ A K 9 7 5 4 3
    ♡ 6 4   ♡ Q 6   ♡ 6 4 2
    ◇ K J 10 7 5   ◇ A Q 7 5 3   ◇ A 7 5
    ♣ 6   ♣ —   ♣ —

With hand (e) we should jump to three diamonds, showing 5/5 in our two suits, invitational but non-forcing.

Hands (f) and (g) are much too strong for a non-forcing bid and the void club strongly suggests that partner will pass for penalty (our right-hand opponent has not raised clubs). The only thing we have left at our disposal is a cue-bid of three clubs, forcing to game. It is never ideal to have to use a cue-bid, especially at the three-level, as an all-purpose game force. However, here it does tell partner quite a lot about our hand. First, it says we are extremely short in clubs, at most a singleton. Second, there is a strong likelihood of our holding a diamond suit since we neither forced immediately and nor have we jumped to game now. Of course, it is possible that we hold a hand such as hand (g), which was not quite worth an immediate force but still has serious slam interest, but in that case we will rebid our spade suit whatever partner does.

Suppose partner rebid two hearts over two clubs and the next hand raised: for example, 1♡ – Pass – 1♠ – 2♣; 2♡ – 3♣. What is the meaning of my various actions?

Here we are in a position where, if we bid three hearts, partner will think we are merely competing, so we have to decide what to do if we would like to make a game try. We also need a bid to show diamonds if we hold length in that suit. We could use double as a game try and play three diamonds as natural, but partner would rarely be able to pass the double as he would know that there was a heart fit.

It is perhaps better in this type of sequence to use the three-diamond bid as showing a fit for hearts, a hand such as:

♠ A 7 5 3 2
♡ Q 5
♢ 10 9 5
♣ A 6 5

The double would show extra values but no heart fit – i.e. a hand worth a bid in this position but suggesting that diamonds, spades or no-trumps may play better than hearts. This treatment will at least enable partner to pass some of the time.

Of course, as we saw earlier, if the opponents had been bidding diamonds rather than clubs, double would have been a game try in hearts as the opponents would have taken away all the space.

What if partner doubled two clubs and the next hand raised: for example, 1♡ – Pass – 1♠ – 2♣; Dble – 3♣?
Again we are in a slightly different situation, this time because partner has positively invited us to bid. A three-level bid in any of the three suits would be merely competitive and descriptive. A double would be used responsively to gain more information, perhaps on a purely competitive hand with no clear-cut suit to bid – say a 5–2–3–3 distribution with poor spades, or perhaps with a hand worth game but unsure which game to bid.

*Does it make any difference if I have responded one no-trump in the first
instance, rather than in a new suit: for example, 1♠ – Pass – 1NT –
2◇; Pass – Pass – Dble?*

Again, there is no reason why this double should not be for
take-out. If we have employed the method whereby a double
from partner would also have been for take-out, there will be
many occasions when he will have to with his penalty double
and hope that we can reopen. If we wished to make a penalty
double of two diamonds we cannot do so, but at least we know
that partner is minimum or he would have doubled for take-out
himself.

*What if my first response was a raise of partner's suit: for example, 1♡
– Pass – 2♡ – 3♣; Pass – Pass – Dble?*

Apart from the specific instances, which we have already discussed, when the opponents have taken away all our space, all
doubles when we have bid and agreed a suit should be for
penalty. There is no need for a take-out double when we have
already located a fit. It is best played as a defensively oriented
hand with three clubs to an honour and only three-card heart
support. Partner can pass or remove as he sees fit.

This double would retain the same meaning if we made it on a
slightly different sequence – say 1♡ – Pass – 2♡ – Pass; Pass –
3♣ – Dble. However, if our right-hand opponent were to
choose a balancing double rather than a three-club bid – say 1♡
– Pass – 2♡ – Pass; Pass – Dble – we would redouble to show a
balanced defensive hand and suggest that partner double anything that the opponents bid for penalty. If partner fails to
double for penalty, we should let the auction go unless we have
very good trumps and can make a penalty double ourselves.

Doubles of artificial overcalls

How should I bid if my partner opens the bidding and the next hand makes a Michaels cue-bid?

A Michaels cue-bid is a direct cue-bid of a one-level opening – in a minor it shows both majors and in a major it shows the other major plus one minor. The situation is different, depending on whether they have cue-bid a minor or a major because in the former case they have shown both their suits and in the latter only one suit. However, in either case a double should be directed towards a penalty in at least one of their suits.

When the opponents make any two-suited overcall the hand-types we may want to describe are:

- balanced or semi-balanced, interested in taking a penalty;
- strong and weak raises of partner's suit;
- strong and weak bids in the fourth suit.

A Michaels cue-bid of a major suit makes this rather difficult. We know we want to bid only one of the minor suits naturally, but we don't know which one! Undoubtedly the best method of bidding over a Michaels cue-bid in a major is to use transfers, but that is outside the scope of this book. The simple thing to do is to play all bids as natural, using a cue-bid of the suit they have shown as a good raise in partner's suit.

We will then have to decide whether we want to play a simple bid in a minor as forcing or non-forcing. Whichever we choose will give us a problem when we have the other; on frequency grounds it is probably better to play a bid in a minor as constructive but non-forcing – this is the hand we will be dealt more often and if we are too strong for that we will just have to start with a double and hope for the best.

When the Michaels cue-bid has been made in a minor, the situation is rather easier because we have a cue-bid of both of their suits available.

Hence, after 1♣ – 2♣:

- Dble   Dble shows a wish to take a penalty in at least one of their suits;
- 2♦   natural, non-forcing;
- 2♡   either a forcing bid in diamonds or a hand with diamonds and club support – partner can bid two spades to find out:
- 2♠   a value raise to three clubs;
- 2NT   natural;
- 3♣   a weak raise;
- 3♦   constructive, non-forcing with a good diamond suit;
- 3♡/♠   singletons and club support.

After 1♦ – 2♦:

- Dble   shows a wish to take a penalty in at least one of their suits;
- 2♡   either a forcing bid in clubs or a hand with clubs and diamond support – partner can bid two spades to find out;
- 2♠   a values raise to three diamonds;
- 2NT   natural;
- 3♣   constructive, non-forcing;
- 3♦   a weak raise;
- 3♡/♠   singletons and diamond support.

The above structure assumes that the opening bid of one of a minor always shows at least four cards. If this is not the case, you may wish to adapt some of the cue-bid responses to show varying lengths of minor suits.

An alternative treatment would be simply to use bids of the opponents' major suits to show stoppers in a hand suitable for no-trumps.

If we double the Michaels cue-bid and the next hand gives simple preference, then a double by either side should be for penalty. If, however, they show real support by jumping, then it is better to play take-out doubles.

Would it be the same if they overcalled with an unusual two no-trump?
Yes, we can follow a very similar structure to that of a Michaels cue-bid of a minor-suit opening, since both suits are known.

For example, after 1♠ – 2NT:

- Dble   shows a wish to take a penalty in at least one of their suits;
- 3♣   shows either a forcing hand with hearts or a hand with hearts and three-card spade support – partner can bid three diamonds to find out;
- 3♢   shows a value raise to three spades;
- 3♡   is constructive but non-forcing;
- 3♠   shows a weak raise.

The principles used are that a bid in the fourth suit is constructive but non-forcing. When there are two cue-bids available the lower one shows either the fourth suit plus support for partner or just the fourth suit in a hand too strong to make a non-forcing bid; the higher cue-bid shows a sound raise in partner's suit (less space is needed when trumps are known.) All the bids which show the fourth suit should show a six-card suit, since with a more balanced hand it is better to start with a double.

When the opponents bid an unusual two no-trumps over a minor suit opening, we do not have the same amount of space.

After 1♣ – 2NT:

- Dble   penalty-oriented;
- 3♣   any raise;
- 3♢   spades plus club support or just spades, forcing;
- 3♡   a good raise in clubs, obviously forcing to four clubs (or three no-trumps) and a better hand is needed than when the cue-bid can be made below the level of three clubs;
- 3♠   is constructive but non-forcing.

After 1♢ – 2NT:

- Dble   penalty-oriented;
- 3♣   is a good raise in diamonds;
- 3♡   is either spades plus diamond support or just spades, forcing;
- 3♠   is constructive but non-forcing.

Here we see the exception to the rule. When only one of the cue-bids can be made below the level of the suit opened, then priority is given to showing a good raise to partner's suit.

How should I bid if my right-hand opponent makes a double jump cue-bid, asking for a stopper for no-trumps: for example, 1♡ – 3♡?

In recent times, most good pairs have adopted the use of an immediate jump cue-bid – for example, 1♡ – 3♡ – as a request for partner to bid three no-trumps if he has the opponents' suit guarded. Sometimes the bid is used on quite a good hand, but also can be made pre-emptively on a solid suit and little else. The very nature of the jump cue-bid has taken away much of our bidding space and we need to use what little we have left as efficiently as possible. Here is a possible scheme, after 1♡ – 3♡:

- Pass   initially shows nothing in particular, but if fol-
            lowed by a double shows good (semi-) balanced
            values without a heart honour or good heart sup-
            port. If the double is made of three no-trumps,
            partner should be directed away from a heart lead;

- Dble   shows a heart honour, suggesting the best lead
            against three no-trumps. This shows very little in
            the way of values unless followed by a second
            double, which would suggest a good all-around
            hand, or a bid of four hearts, which would suggest
            a good raise to four hearts, or a bid in a new suit
            which would be a cue-bid in support of hearts;

- 3 ♠   natural, forcing;

- 3NT   two-suited take-out (it cannot be natural when an
            opponent has announced a solid suit against us);

- 4 ♣/♦   natural, forcing;

- 4 ♡   weak raise to game.

This is all common sense and you should be able to work it
out for yourself, using logic and general principles, but it is
worth discussing with your partner – many top pairs have come
unstuck because they didn't know how to suggest values with
nothing in partner's suit, or alternatively, wanted partner to lead
his own suit but had very few values.

Doubles after we have opened one no-trump

*What does a double mean if partner opens one no-trump and my
right-hand opponent makes a natural overcall?*

In these modern times, most tournament pairs play either some
form of Lebensohl or transfers when an opponent overcalls their
one no-trump opening. Whichever of these options they go for,
one thing is inevitable – they lose the use of a natural raise to two
no-trumps.

Where all these pairs differ is on how to use a double. Some choose penalties, some choose take-out and some choose to define it simply as a raise to two no-trumps. The trouble with this latter idea is that if all it shows is a raise to two no-trumps, when is partner supposed to pass it? It would certainly be reasonable to play the double as penalties, but this leaves us with a problem if we have insufficient trumps for this action. No, as we have chosen to do in most other areas, we will also choose to play a double as take-out here. With a real penalty double, we can always pass and hope that partner will reopen with a double – there is no reason why he should not do so just as freely as he would if he had opened one of a suit – i.e. when he has good defensive values and a small doubleton in the opponents' suit.

If the double is take-out, what exactly does this mean?
It means that the no-trump opener should remove the double unless he has a good four-card holding in the suit overcalled. He should bear in mind that we might only have a singleton for our take-out double, and also that we have not promised the values for two no-trumps. After the sequence 1NT – 2 ♡, the following would be perfect for a take-out double:

(a) ♠ A 6 5 3   (b) ♠ A Q 6 5
    ♡ 7   ♡ 7 6
    ◇ Q 10 6 5   ◇ K Q 6 5
    ♣ K J 6 5   ♣ K J 5

With hand (a) we intend to pass partner's response, but with hand (b) we intend to raise a two-spade response to game, and to cue-bid over any other response.

The lower the suit overcalled, the lower might our values be. For example, after a natural two-club overcall over a weak no-trump there is no reason why we should not make a take-out double on a 4–4–4–1 8-count.

How should I respond to partner's take-out double?

If we are not going to pass, we should respond in our lowest suit at the two level. If we cannot bid a suit at the two level (either we don't have one or the overcall was two spades), we have to decide whether a response of two no-trumps should be natural or a 'scramble', as we have seen in many other situations.

There are arguments to be made for both treatments. If we are not allowed to pass the double unless we have a good four-card holding in the suit, then we will often have quite a strong holding in the opponents' suit and want to bid two no-trumps naturally. On the other hand, if our best four-card suit is, say, J-x-x-x, we would much prefer to bid a two no-trump 'scramble' than bid such a poor suit.

Since we have chosen to play a take-out double, which doesn't promise great values, we have also chosen to put greater emphasis on competing for the part-score than finding game. It seems logical, therefore, that we should concentrate on finding the best part-score. If our best part-score is two no-trumps, then we probably should have defended two spades doubled. We will choose to play two no-trumps as a 'scramble', thus a bid of a suit at the three level is either a five-card or a very good four-card suit.

Could we look at some examples, please?

Let us consider the following hands after the sequence: 1NT (12–14) – 2♠ – Dble – Pass:

(c) ♠ K Q 10 9
    ♡ A 6
    ♢ A 7 5
    ♣ 8 6 4 2

(d) ♠ K Q 7
    ♡ Q 6 4
    ♢ A 7 5
    ♣ J 8 6 4

(e) ♠ A 7 5
    ♡ Q 6 4
    ♢ A 7
    ♣ Q J 8 6 4

(f) ♠ A 7 5
    ♡ K Q 6 4
    ♢ Q 7
    ♣ Q 10 4 2

(g) ♠ A 7 5
    ♡ K Q J 6
    ♢ Q 7 5
    ♣ J 4 2

With hand (c) we have good enough spades to pass the double. We expect to make five tricks in our own hand, and can reasonably rely on partner to provide at least one more. On hand (d) we would like to be able to bid a natural two no-trumps, but would much prefer to bid a two no-trump 'scramble' than our poor four-card club suit. Partner will bid a four-card club suit if he has one, otherwise he will no doubt play in three diamonds, a suit in which he may well have five cards. On hand (e) we can happily bid three clubs on our five-card suit. On hand (f) we genuinely have two suits to offer partner, and so should bid two no-trumps. If he bids three clubs we will pass, but if he bids three diamonds we will correct to three hearts. On hand (g), we should bid three hearts immediately. Even though we have only a four-card suit, it is sufficiently strong to be unafraid of playing in a 4–3 fit, particularly with the ruffs being taken in the short trump hand.

One of the advantages of playing a take-out double of natural intervention over one no-trump is that it can be the first move on all balanced hands in the game-invitation or stronger zone. It thus obviates the need for starting balanced hands with a cue-bid or a Lebensohl two no-trumps.

What if the overcall was conventional: for example, 1NT – 2♣ (Astro, hearts and another)?

There are several sensible schemes in operation in the above situation, all of which have something to recommend them:

Double is Stayman

The simplest way to deal with any two-club overcall of one no-trump is simply to ignore it! A double is Stayman (or however you play a direct two-club response without the overcall) and all other bids are just as you would normally play them. This idea has much merit in simplicity, unfortunately it doesn't work so well if they overcall two diamonds, so, since you have to put in a bit more effort to decide how you are going to cope when they intervene with two diamonds, you may as well do so over two clubs as well.

If, instead of double, you pass, and later double on the next round, this should say that you have a take-out double of hearts.

Double is take-out of the suits they have shown

In this method a double of an Astro two clubs would be a take-out of hearts: a double of an Astro two diamonds would be a take-out of spades; a double of a two-club overcall which showed both majors would show both minors, etc.

The drawback with this method is that we already have a low-level take-out bid of the suit(s) they have shown – i.e. we can cue-bid it at the two level. In the instance of an Astro two-diamond overcall, it would be much more convenient to be able to double to show a take-out of spades than to have to bid two spades for take-out, because it allows us the option of playing in two hearts. However, at least we do have some weak take-out available, whereas we are unnecessarily stuck if we just have a balanced hand with the values for two no-trumps. We managed without this when they overcalled in a major, but did not do so very happily and it would be convenient to have this facility back at our disposal.

If we choose to play a double as take-out of the suit(s) they have shown, then we can use the cue-bid to show a raise to two no-trumps, but of course we will lose some penalties in the process. If they have shown more than one suit – say two clubs for the majors – then we have two cue-bids to decide a meaning for; one possibility would be to cue-bid in the suit that we are strongest.

Since with a take-out of the suits they have shown, we would have doubled on the first round, a pass followed by a double should show a penalty double of hearts with shortage in the suit where they have actually alighted.

Double shows the values for two no-trumps

With this scheme, we cue-bid the suit(s) that they have shown for take-out and double to show the values for two no-trumps. The double invites partner to double any suit they bid for penalty, which he should do whenever he has four trumps or a good three-card holding with general defensive strength.

The double can also be used as the first move on a number of different hands. We will we make the reasonable assumption that if we have a balanced hand with the values for two no-trumps, then we will pass if partner doubles; and if partner does not double, we will either double or bid two no-trumps. What then is the meaning of the following sequences?

West	North	East	South
1NT	2♣★	Dble	2♡
Pass	Pass	3♣	

West	North	East	South
1NT	2♣★	Dble	2♡
Dble	Pass	2♠	
*Astro			

In the first sequence we have shown invitational values with a six-card club suit. Thus, if we play transfers, a two no-trump overcall (instead of double) would either be weak or strong; if we were playing Lebensohl (whichever version we choose), our weak three-club bid would be really weak and our strong one would be game-forcing. In the second sequence, we have been able to show (mildly) invitational values with four spades and five clubs.

Again, pass followed by double should show a penalty double of hearts. if they land in somewhere other than hearts, a double still shows a penalty double of hearts and shortage in the suit they are in, inviting partner to pass with length there.

What about if they make a jump overcall over partner's one no-trump opening: for example, 1NT – 3♡?

Here our opponent has made a jump overcall in a very exposed position. He is probably not afraid of being doubled for penalty, certainly not unless we have a strong trump holding over him. Our opponent has stolen all our bidding space and unless we have a five-card spade suit or a long minor or a heart stop we have no option but to double on any hand where we have the values for game. It is better that this double should be played for take-out. In the unlikely event that we have a heart stack, we should just pass and hope to beat him – if his heart suit is not very robust, he is likely to have a second suit and may make more tricks than we thought anyway.

What if I pass partner's one no-trump opening and the next hand balances: for example, 1NT – Pass – Pass – 2♡?

Again we have to choose between playing this as take-out or penalties, a decision which may be affected by the strength of our opening no-trump. If we choose to play double as penalty we need to have at least five defensive tricks in our own hand and this is not very likely if we are playing a 12–14 one no-trump; but it is possible if we are playing a stronger no-trump.

There is no reason not to play a double as penalty in this position, but if we are to do so then it makes sense that a double by us, if partner were to pass two hearts round to us, should also be penalty. If we play our double as take-out-oriented, then there is less need to play a double by him as penalty, because some of the time we will reopen with a double and collect our penalty anyway.

It is more consistent with the rest of our style to play a double as take-out in both positions. If the one no-trump opener doubles, this should show a maximum one no-trump with a doubleton in the suit overcalled; if the hand who has passed one no-trump doubles, this is for take-out, but should not be too distributional. If he is afraid of his double being passed he should bid a suit instead – here, say, two spades – which cannot be a five-card suit for he passed one no-trump in the first place.

If the opponents protect with a conventional bid, such as Astro, then a double should be take-out of the suit they have actually shown.

Points to Remember

1 A negative double of one of a major after a minor-suit opening shows four cards in the other major. Other negative doubles make no promises about any particular distribution, but they will not be made on a weak hand with a long (six-card) suit.

2 In response to a negative double, with a minimum hand we can rebid our first suit, bid a lower ranking suit, bid the 'other major' if partner has guaranteed holding it or rebid one no-trump (assuming we play a strong no-trump opening). With extra values, we can jump in our first suit or a new suit or rebid two no-trumps (or one no-trump if we play a weak no-trump opening). To force to game we must cue-bid the opponents' suit.

3 If the next hand bids further after a negative double – for example, 1♢ – 1♠ – Dble – 2♠ – we can double to show extra values which cannot be expressed by a natural bid. In response to this second double, partner can bid two no-trumps to show a minimum negative double, bid a suit to show extra values or cue-bid to force to game.

4 If partner passes instead of making a negative double and the overcall is passed round to us for example, 1♢ – 1♠ – Pass – Pass – *we must reopen the bidding when we have two cards or less in the opponents' suit*. This is because partner may have a very

strong hand that wished to make a penalty double. This reopening double by opener does *not* show extra values.

5 If right-hand opponent intervenes after partner has responded – for example, 1◇ – Pass – 1♠ – 2♣ – a double should not be for penalty. Choose between double being for take-out, showing a strong no-trump with no stopper or insufficient high cards to rebid no-trumps (useful when playing a weak no-trump structure) or showing three-card support for partner (useful when the opening has been in a minor and we are playing a five-card major system).

6 If we have bid and supported a suit and the opponents intervene with the highest suit, thus depriving us of all our bidding space – for example, 1♡ – 2◇ – 2♡ – 3◇ – then double is best played as a general game try, whereas to simply bid our suit would be merely competitive. This is the only situation when a double after we have agreed a suit is not for penalty. Generally, *when we have agreed a suit all doubles are for penalty*.

6

Doubles of Artificial Bids

So far, most of the doubles we have discussed have been doubles of natural bids, with the exception of a few conventional overcalls. In this chapter we are going to look at doubles of conventional bids.

Doubles of Stayman and transfers

What does it mean if I double Stayman?
When defending against opponents playing a strong no-trump, most pairs play a double of Stayman to show clubs. However, if the opponents are using a weak no-trump, expert opinion is divided between it either showing clubs or a balanced hand which would have doubled one no-trump.

If it shows clubs, how good a hand do I need?
Even if it is agreed that the double shows clubs, it also needs to be agreed whether this is for lead-directing or competitive purposes. If double shows clubs, the last thing partner is going to lead when the opponents bid to three no-trumps and we haven't doubled Stayman, is a club, so it is best to place emphasis on lead-direction – K-Q-10-x-x and nothing else would be sufficient. If the next hand bids a suit, partner can compete with a club fit but should be wary of doing too much bidding just because he has, say 12 or 13 HCP.

So, does it always show a weakish hand?

Just because the double might be as weak as K-Q-10-x-x and little else does not mean that we cannot use it as our initial action with various other types of hand including clubs. We can double two clubs and later double whatever the opponents land in for take-out, just as if we had made an ordinary overcall. We can double two clubs and later bid three clubs to show a different range of hand to an initial three-club bid. We can double two clubs and later bid another suit to show a two-suiter including clubs.

What do I do if I don't hold clubs?

If we do not hold clubs and do not have a good suit to bid we have to pass the opponents' Stayman and hope to get a chance to bid later. We then have to decide the meaning of a double in a sequence such as:

West	North	East	South
1NT	Pass	2♣	Pass
2♡	Pass	Pass	Dble

The meaning of a double in this sequence should depend on the strength of the opposing no-trump.

1   If the opponents are playing a strong no-trump (say 15–17 or stronger), then a double in this position should merely be for take-out, just like any other balancing double – the opponents probably have a fit and limited values, therefore we have a fit (or can take a penalty) and also have some values.

2   If the opponents are playing a weak no-trump this double should show at least three hearts to an honour and a strong no-trump-type hand which would have doubled one no-trump. It is more likely that East will be removing one no-trump out of extreme weakness and certainly need not

have four hearts, if the opponents are playing a weak no-trump. Also it is more likely that our side may have a game on.

What is the alternative to a double of Stayman showing clubs?
The flaw in the above method, when defending against a weak no-trump, is that it was necessary to stipulate that if we passed two clubs and later doubled the opponents, to show a double of one no-trump, we had to have at least three hearts to an honour. If we do not make such a stipulation, then we will hardly ever collect a penalty because partner will never know when to pass; however, having made such a stipulation we are now stuck when we have a hand which would have doubled one no-trump but has a less good holding in the opponents' suit, and we may well miss a game.

This is one of the reasons that many pairs prefer to play a double of Stayman as a hand which would have doubled one no-trump, arguing that at least they have shown their good hand straightaway.

However, those who choose this method have not altogether solved their problems. Consider the following sequence:

West	North	East	South
1NT	Pass	2♣	Dble
2♡			

Let us suppose that North holds, for example:

♠ Q 6 4 2
♡ 7 5
♢ A 6 4
♣ Q 7 5 3

He has a fair smattering of values, sufficient to consider that his side might be able to make a game, but does not have any hearts to speak of. What is he to do? He cannot afford to pass and hope that his partner has good hearts and can make another double, partly because his partner may well hold only three hearts and simply pass two hearts out, and even if his partner does have a good four-card heart holding, he will not know that he is facing any values at all.

The solution to this problem, although it is not without danger, is to play a double of any suit to which the opponents might remove themselves as take-out by either side; the corollary of this is that a pass by North in the above auction would be forcing on South whenever he had two hearts or less.

So, with the above hand North could double two hearts for take-out, but when he has, say:

♠ Q 6 4
♡ A Q 7 5
♢ 6 4
♣ Q 7 5 3

he has to pass and wait for his partner to reopen with a double.

Our policy on taking penalties in this awkward situation, when only one partner, here North, has any idea of our side's defensive strength, is that we have to decide at what point we wish to try for a penalty. What we have effectively decided to do here is to be able to try for a penalty whenever the opponents are in a seven-card fit which breaks 4–2. If they are in a seven-card fit which breaks 3–3 or an eight-card fit which breaks 3–2, we will never be able to take a penalty. North, in the above sequence, can never afford to pass with values when he has three trumps because his partner may also have three trumps and not reopen.

If we choose to play a double of Stayman as showing a strong no-trump type hand and we do not double Stayman but double on the next round, it is clear to play this delayed double as being a normal balancing action. However, if a double of Stayman shows clubs, then we lose our balancing double because we need it to show a strong balanced hand.

What does it mean to double a transfer response to one no-trump?
There are similar arguments about the meaning of a double of a transfer after a weak no-trump, as there are about Stayman. However, here most players choose to use the double to show the suit bid. This is for two reasons:

1 The hand who has used the transfer probably has some real distribution, reducing the possibility of a substantial penalty.
2 An opponent who uses Stayman is usually either very weak (when a penalty, can be hoped for) or has a hand with real game interest. In both cases we are relatively unlikely to want to compete the auction. An opponent who uses a transfer may well have a few values, opener may well have a fit and we may well want to compete in the bidding, which will be made easier if we can at least start off by showing a suit.

A double of a transfer shows length and strength in the suit our right-hand opponent has actually bid. Again, it does not necessarily show a particularly strong hand but because the emphasis here may well be on competing a part-score, it should show the values for a sound one-level overcall. As before we can double and then double again for take-out, or we can double and then bid a suit to show a two-suiter.

What do I do if I want to make a take-out bid of their suit?
If we wish to make a take-out bid of the suit the opponents have shown, we can simply bid it – for example, 1NT – Pass – 2♦ (transfer) – 2♥. This may be as weak as a 4–1–4–4 11-count, but should have more high cards if the distribution is less suitable. Over this take-out bid, partner should bid in the same way as we

saw when we were defending against weak two bids – i.e. a two no-trump response would be a negative, whereas to bid three of a minor would show constructive values.

What does it mean to pass a transfer and then double on the next round?
There are two schools of thought here. The first plays this second double as showing at least three to an honour in the opponents' suit and a strong no-trump type hand – i.e. penalty-oriented. The second (and most players when defending against a strong no-trump) prefers to play a pass followed by a double as a straightforward balancing double, on a hand not good enough to have made an immediate cue-bid. This is particularly useful at match-points as it is a common sequence and it is important to be able to compete for the part-score.

Doubles of relays, cue-bids, fourth-suit forcing, etc.

What about doubles of relays, cue-bids (in slam auctions), fourth-suit forcing, etc.?
All these doubles are primarily lead-directing. With the possible exception of some low-level relays which do not promise much in the way of high cards, they do not invite partner to bid, just suggest what partner might lead.

One thing to note, in particular in slam auctions, is that there is a lot of difference in doubling a cue-bid (probably an ace) when you have a king, than there is in doubling, say, a Black-wood response when you have a king. In the latter case you have no reason to suppose that your king is well placed.

Does a double of a cue-bid issue a command to lead that suit or is it merely a suggestion?
This is a matter of partnership philosophy. Some partnerships like to play a style where they make such doubles very freely – i.e. it is only a suggestion. The advantage of this style is that if

we are on opening lead against a slam and partner has not taken the opportunity of doubling a cue-bid or Blackwood response, then we can forget about leading that suit unless we have a good holding. However, the disadvantage of this style is that it may direct us towards a non-winning lead. If, playing this style, we hear partner double a cue-bid and then the opponents confidently bid a slam anyway, we should give serious consideration to an alternative lead – and have partner's prior assurance that he won't kill us when we are wrong!

Other partnerships prefer to double only when, as far as they can tell, they are 100 per cent certain it is the lead they want – i.e. they have a very solid holding in the suit concerned and very little outside. There are advantages in this method in that if partner has doubled a cue-bid we know what to do, but the disadvantages are that partner will not double often and when he doesn't we are much less well placed.

One other point to consider is that the frequent use of doubles of opposing cue-bids might make our life easier in terms of helping us decide on our choice of opening lead, but it also makes life easier for our opposition. By doubling a cue-bid we may persuade them to bid a making slam they would not otherwise have bid, or stay out of a losing one they would otherwise have bid. If they do still bid a slam our double may well help declarer in the play.

What about doubles of splinter bids?
When an opponent's cue-bid in a slam auction is known to be a singleton or void, there is much less point in doubling it for the lead. Even if we have the ace in that suit, if partner leads the suit, when we win our ace we may set up discards for declarer. If we have lesser honours, one of them will be picked up by partner's lead, and even if we have a very solid holding, such as K-Q-J, a lead of the suit is unlikely to achieve very much.

A modern idea is to play the double of a splinter bid as a request for a lead in the lower of the other two suits which are not trumps. If the bidding has gone, say, 1♡ – Pass – 4♣ (splinter) – Pass; 6♡, most of the time partner is going to choose between leading a spade and a diamond. It can be very useful if our pass of four clubs suggests a spade, whereas a double would have suggested a diamond.

What about doubles of four no-trumps?

Any double of Blackwood has to be treated with a little caution, since one has to be pretty confident that four no-trumps doubled will not make – although few pairs will be well equipped to exercise this option. Most people play that if Blackwood is doubled, all bids are related to how many aces they hold rather than a desire to play in four no-trumps doubled.

There are four main uses of a double of four no-trumps:

1 That the double of four no-trumps should itself be Blackwood – this only applies when our side is bidding constructively.
2 That the double of four no-trumps suggests a sacrifice in at least one suit bid by our side.
3 If our side have bid no suits, a double of four no-trumps suggests a sacrifice either in the other two suits, or if three suits are unbid, in two of the other suits.
4 That if it is clear that we cannot have a profitable sacrifice, the double should be lead-directing – say for the lowest-ranking unbid suit – obviously only relevant if it is partner who will be on lead.

Any of the above uses are likely to be on highly distributional deals. Here are some examples:

West	North	East	South
1 ♠	Pass	4 ♠	4NT
Dble			

Here, because East/West have bid to game themselves, double would itself be Blackwood.

West	North	East	South
1♡	2♠	4NT	Dble

South does not wish to bid 5♠ himself but wishes to suggest a sacrificed.

West	North	East	South
1♡	Pass	4NT	Dble

South's double cannot be lead–directing since he will be on lead against hearts, therefore it shows a two–suiter and suggests a sacrifice.

West	North	East	South
1♡	Pass	1♠	Pass
3♡	Pass	4NT	Dble

Here it is expected that North will be on lead so the double asks for a club lead.

What about doubles of cue-bids of suits our side has bid (in non-slam auctions)?

Here we are covering a wide range of situations, such as:

	West	North	East	South
(a)	1♡	1♠	2♠	Dble

	West	North	East	South
(b)	1♡	1♠	Dble	Pass
	2♠	Dble		

	West	North	East	South
(c)	1♡	1♠	Dble	2♡
	2♠	Dble		

(d) *West*	*North*	*East*	*South*
1♡	1♠	2♣	Pass
2♡	Pass	2♠	Dble

The important thing to decide is whether the double is simply lead-directing or whether it shows a hand that wanted to bid but the opponents have taken that bid away.

The thing that distinguishes the fourth auction from the other three, is that South has chosen to double two spades when he had a perfectly good opportunity to bid two spades on the previous round. The first three auctions show a desire to bid.

On auction (a), South has just shown a hand that was well worth a constructive raise to two spades, but East has taken his bid away. South probably holds a spade honour, but the main purpose of his bid was to show a few values and some spade support, in case West wants to bid on.

On auction (b), even though West has forced to game, North can still have a pretty good hand with a six-card spade suit, and this is what his double suggests.

On auction (c), South has made an unassuming cue-bid and the meaning of West's cue-bid is unclear. However, North's double suggests a desire to bid on if South has extra values.

On auction (d), however, South has not bid two spades when he had an opportunity to do so. Here, his double merely suggests a top honour in spades which should be the ace or king because his partner is quite likely to be on lead to a contract of four hearts and needs to be able to know that he can underlead his A-x-x-x-x – if he starts with the ace he may have given up the opportunity to give his partner a ruff if he started with K–x. South may not have another high card in his hand and he is certainly not inviting North to bid.

It seems clear to double this sort of cue-bid to ask partner to lead the suit, but doesn't it help the opposition in much the same way as it does when we double in a slam auction?

One of the problems that occurs when doubling a cue-bid of a suit our side has bid is that it often allows the opponents further definition. For example, let us consider the sequence:

West	North	East	South
1 ♣	2 ♡	3 ♣	Pass
3 ♡	Dble		

If we double three hearts on this sequence to make certain that we get a heart lead, we are offering the opponents the opportunity to establish the precise nature of their heart stop and perhaps play three no-trumps from a different side than they otherwise would have done. Suppose, here, that West has Q–x of hearts – he knew when he bid three hearts that this could well result in his partner's playing three no-trumps when it would be better if he did so, but he took that risk in the hope that his partner could bid three spades, whereupon he would bid three no-trumps to show his positional half-guard; if his partner couldn't bid three spades, then he would have to take his chances elsewhere. If we now double three hearts to insist on a heart lead, this gives East the chance to redouble to show A-x, A-x-x or K-x-x and West can happily bid three no-trumps.

'Un-lead-directing' doubles

Is there any way round this problem?

The 'un-lead-directing' double has been developed to avoid this problem. Playing this convention, a pass of three hearts would be the best that North could do to suggest a heart lead, thus affording East/West no such opportunity of sorting out the precise nature of their heart stop(s). A double of three hearts by

North in this position would strongly suggest that his partner did not lead a heart. If North doesn't want a heart lead, he hardly cares who plays three no-trumps and, indeed, he may do well from this if his opponents are not sufficiently clued up. Suppose he has overcalled two hearts on a suit such as J-10-9-x-x-x-x and South has K-x – the opponents may use the double in order to play three no-trumps from the West seat when West has Q-x and East A-x, and may be sadly disappointed.

Also, in normal circumstances, if we overcall partner tends to lead our suit anyway, whether or not we have taken up an opportunity to double a cue-bid. He will usually not have a very good alternative. How nice to be able positively to suggest he does something different – in the above auction, North might have overcalled two hearts with J-10-9-x-x-x in hearts and K-Q-x-x-x in diamonds.

The main drawback with this use of a double of a cue-bid is that it is very important to agree exactly when it applies.

Does its use mean that we can never double a cue-bid to suggest that we would be interested in hearing partner make a bid?
When the choice was between a double meaning 'lead this suit' and 'bid this suit if you feel like it', if we had a misunderstanding with partner it was quite likely not to matter; but if the alternative meanings were 'don't lead this suit' and 'bid this suit if you feel like it' we could be on very dangerous ground. One expert pair had the following costly misunderstanding, playing this method:

West	North	East	South
1 ♣	1 ♡	1 ♠	2 ♠
Dble	4 ♡	4 ♠	

East thought that West was doubling two spades to show a modicum of support in a minimum hand. West thought he was doubling because he didn't want a spade lead – he had a singleton spade, a certain heart trick, Q-J-10, and very good clubs. The result was an 1100 penalty against a non-making game.

Partners should decide on their own rules, as it matters more that they agree than that they arrive at any 'correct' answer. However, here are some suggestions.

1   When the player who has bid the suit doubles, this always suggests an alternative lead.
2   When the player who has not bid the suit doubles, this only suggests an alternative lead if he has had a chance to support the suit earlier and has not done so.
3   If both partners have bid the suit a double always suggests an alternative lead.

A simpler agreement to have is that all doubles of two-level cue-bids are for competitive purposes, but all doubles of higher cue-bids are 'un-lead-directing'.

Doubles of strong one/two-club openings

What does it mean to double a strong one-club or two-club opening?
There are nearly as many methods of defending against strong club openings as there are days in the year and it is beyond the scope of this book to go into them in enormous detail.

Once an opponent has opened with a strong one-club or two-club opening, the whole strategy of our defensive bidding changes. No longer do we have much interest in bidding our hands constructively; our prime consideration is to do as much as we dare to disrupt their constructive bidding. To this end a double of a strong one-club or two-club opening achieves little. Whatever the double means, our opponents will just ignore us and carry on just as if we had not bothered to open our mouths. Indeed, we have probably helped them. No longer do they have to respond, say, one or two diamonds with any negative hand; they now also have the opportunity either to pass or to redouble to show different hand-types. Whatever the conventional, disruptive bids we may have in our armoury, they will cause them more inconvenience than the simple double.

Indeed, some pairs play a double of a strong club opening to show a good hand of at least opening-bid values, reserving it for the time when it may indeed come in handy to have a way of bidding constructively. This is far from being a silly idea.

Whatever we use the double to mean, if it is to make sense to bid at all, then it needs to have a meaning which may at least enable partner to join in when the bidding gets to him. We may have given them more space, but perhaps partner can take some of it away. Whatever the double means it should show reasonable values (say normal overcall values) so that partner is not too frightened to bid aggressively opposite.

One of the best meanings for a double in this position is the old-fashioned one of it showing both majors. At least if partner does have a fit for one of the majors, he may be able to bounce to the two or three level pre-emptively.

What does a double of the response to a strong one-club or two-club opening mean?
If the opponents respond with a one-diamond or two-diamond negative, there is no reason why a double should not retain its meaning of showing both majors. Again it is taking up no space, but at least it may enable partner to bid up on the next round.

If the opponents respond with a natural positive response, a double is best played as take-out, but in the same way that we decided that it was best for a take-out double of a strong two opening to show a two-suited rather than a three-suited hand, so is that true here. When we are seriously outgunned in high-card strength, there is only any point in entering the bidding if either we can direct a lead, which double does not, or we can deprive our opponents of some useful space to describe their hands, which double does not, or we can pave the way for a useful sacrifice, which double may do, but only if we reserve it for two-suited hands, as three-suited hands are much less suitable for sacrificial purposes.

If the opponents respond with an artificial positive response, a double is best played as simply lead-directing.

Doubles of a Multi

What is the best way to play a double of a Multi-coloured two diamonds?
A Multi-coloured two diamonds is an opening bid which shows either a weak two in a major or some variety of strong hand. These days the Multi is losing much of its effect since more and more pairs are developing methods of coping with it successfully. Indeed, there are few top pairs in Britain who still use it in anything like its original form. Again, there are many different varieties of defence to it. The scheme below is the one most widely played by British experts:

1   A double of a Multi two diamonds shows either:

- 13–15 HCP balanced;
- 19+ HCP balanced;
- any hand too strong for a natural overcall, say 17+ HCP.

Partner always assumes it is 13–15 balanced until told otherwise. In response to the double, partner assumes we have opened a 13–15 1NT and the opponents have intervened with whatever the last bid suit is – i.e. if the bidding goes 2◇ – Dble – Pass, partner bids as if it had gone 1NT – 2◇; if the bidding goes 2◇ – Dble – 2♡, partner bids as if it

202

had gone 1NT – 2♡, etc. If the bidding has actually gone 2◇ – Dble – 2♡/♠, this is straightforward but if it starts 2◇ – Dble – Pass, partner must pass on the first round with a balanced hand. 2◇ – Dble – Pass – 2♡ and 2♠ are both natural; 2NT and higher bids are as if we had opened 1NT and the opponents had bid two diamonds.

2   A 2NT overcall (in either second or fourth seat) shows 16–18 and subsequent bidding is just as if we had opened 2NT.

3   A simple overcall is natural and non-forcing, up to about 16 HCP. After a major suit overcall, the other major can be used as an unassuming cue-bid. After a minor-suit overcall, bids of major suits should be treated, in the first instance, as showing guards rather than suits.

4   A double of a major suit bid when it is the first bid by our side is always for take-out. Thus in the following sequences double is for take-out: 2◇ – Pass – 2♡ – Dble, 2◇ – Pass – 2♠ – Dble, 2◇ – Pass – 2♡/♠ – Pass; Pass – Dble and 2◇ – Pass – 2♡ – Pass; 2♠ – Dble. If we wish to make a penalty double in any of these sequences, we just have to pass and hope that partner can reopen.

5   A pass followed by a bid of two no-trumps shows both minors – i.e. 2◇ – Pass – 2♡/♠ – Pass; Pass – 2NT or 2◇ – Pass – 2♡ – Pass; 2♠ – Pass – Pass – 2NT, although in the latter case it cannot be a very good hand as it risked two hearts being passed out.

6   An immediate overcall of four of a minor by either hand (provided it is a jump) is forcing with five cards in the minor bid and an unspecified five-card major.

7   A pass by the hand immediately over the Multi followed by a cue-bid – for example, 2◇ – Pass – 2♡ – Pass; Pass – 3♡ shows a good two-suiter, but not one worth an immediate bid of four of a minor.

8   A pass by the hand immediately over the Multi followed
    by a bid of three of a minor shows at least a good five-card
    holding in that minor (usually six) and four cards in the
    other major, and a hand of the same sort of strength to
    warrant action on the first round.

Doubles of prepared minors

*If my opponents play a system whereby an opening bid in one of the
minors is prepared – for example, strong no-trump, five-card majors
or maybe a Precision-style one diamond opener – should my double be
normal take-out or should it be different in some way?*

When the opponents open one club or one diamond against us
and it promises three or more cards, it is probably best to treat
it as natural and play take-out doubles in the normal way.
However, when the opening bid promises only two cards (or
less) in the suit, it seems wrong to play normal take-out
doubles when the opponents may not hold that suit at all.

Many pairs use this prepared minor-suit opening when they
have a weak no-trump hand-type (among others) and are
nearly as likely to have any other suit as clubs. One new idea is
to treat this minor-suit opening in a similar way to a Multi.
This has the advantage of allowing us to double with a (semi-)
balanced hand, even with some length in the minor opened.

Over a prepared one club opening:

- ● Dble 12–15 balanced, 19+ balanced or any hand too strong for an overcall. Over this double the next hand is likely to bid a suit at the one level. Now partner can either double for take-out, bid naturally at the one level, or bid at the two level or higher just as he would have done over a one no-trump opening bid – i.e. two clubs is Stayman, two diamonds a transfer, etc.;

- ● 1 ◇ shows a genuine takeout double of a one-club opening;

- ● 1 ♡/♠ normal overcalls;

- ● 1NT 16–18;

- ● 2 ♣/◇ natural overcalls – a two-diamond overcall should be intermediate even if we usually play weak jump overcalls;

- ● 2 ♡ & up just as usual.

Over a prepared one-diamond opening, the scheme is exactly the same, except we have no 'take-out double' of diamonds available and just have to struggle along the best we can. If we are really unhappy with that idea, we can always choose to use a direct cue-bid as a strong take-out of diamonds.

If we are in the fourth seat, after a sequence such as 1♣/◇ – Pass – 1♡, we are best to ignore the opening bid completely when choosing our action – i.e. double would just be take-out of hearts, a cue-bid of left-hand opponent's suit would be natural, a cue-bid of right-hand opponent's suit would be Michaels or Ghestem or whatever.

Doubles of other artificial two bids

What about if my opponents play 'funny' two bids (other than the Multi)?

Artificial, weak two openings, usually showing some sort of two-suiters, can be subdivided into three categories:

1 Those that show the suit that has been bid: for example two hearts shows hearts and a minor.
2 Those that deny the suit that has been bid (or at least deny it in any of the weak options): for example, two diamonds is either a weak two in hearts or some strong options.
3 Those that may or may not have the suit that has been bid: for example two clubs shows a major/minor two-suiter, or two hearts shows the reds or the blacks.

Those that show the suit that has been bid

In order for there to be any artificiality about this variety, they must also show another unspecified suit. The best defence to this type of two bid is to treat them like weak two bids, with the exception that a take-out double is only likely to contain support for one minor. In response to this double, the only difference is that two no-trumps should be a request for the doubler's minor. A response at the three level still shows constructive values, but also shows a good suit; with a hand worth a response at the three level but no good suit, first bid two no-trumps to find the doubler's minor and then bid on.

Those that deny the suit that has been bid

The most common artificial two openers that deny the suit opened (in any of their weak options at least) are ones where the weak two bid is opened in the suit below the one held: for example, a two-diamond opening shows either a weak two in hearts or various strong options. The straightforward defence to this type of two bid is to play a double in the same way as over a

Multi, with a bid of the suit they probably hold (here two hearts) as take-out. If the bidding goes, say, 2◇ – Pass – 2♡, then double would also be for take-out. The only thing to be decided on is the meaning of a pass followed by a double. Since we could have made a take-out bid on the previous round, there is much to be said for a delayed double to be penalty. It is not a safe position for a balancing double, since the opponents have not shown a fit.

Those that may or not hold the suit that has been bid

If the suit that has been opened is a minor – for example, two clubs shows a major and a minor – then the best treatment is to use a double as we did over a Multi. All delayed doubles must be take-out: for example, 2♣ – Pass – 2♡ – Dble, or 2♣ – Pass – 2♡ – Pass; Pass – Dble, as we had no other take-out bid available.

If the suit that has been opened is a major we have to be a little more careful, because it is a much bigger disaster if they make two of a major doubled. Also, if we double to show 12–15 balanced there is less room for us to escape when we are outgunned. We have to decide whether a double of an artificial two of a major (say two hearts shows either the red suits or the black suits) should show that suit – i.e. penalty, or be for take-out.

One of the dangers in defending against this type of two bid is that, because they usually promise a weak hand, responder is in a good position to pass when he knows his side does not have the values for game, even if by passing he may be in a silly contract (particularly non-vulnerable). He will not mind if his partner goes, say, five down in two hearts for −250 when we were cold for four hearts and he would have lost 620. However, in this instance – i.e. when we have had to pass when we had hearts – at least we have scored +250, if we have to pass when we don't have hearts, we may find that they make two hearts when we are cold for four spades, and that we have lost 110 when we could have scored 620.

The conclusion, therefore, is that it is better to play double for take-out. We will play double for take-out in both positions. However, if we double on the second round, this shows length in the suit opened. Thus 2 ♡★ – Dble is take-out; 2 ♡★ – Pass – 2♠ – Dble is take-out. For example:

West	North	East	South
2 ♡★	Pass	2 ♠	Pass
Pass	Dble		

Here, North's double is take-out, his previous silence explained by his heart length.

West	North	East	South
2 ♡★	Pass	2 ♠	Pass
2NT	Dble		

Here West has shown the red suits or the black suits and East has shown a preference for playing in two spades if West has both black suits. West has bid two no-trumps to show both red suits and now North can double to show sound values with hearts, thus enabling South to double when he has diamonds.

What about if the artificial two opening is two no-trumps?

There are two types of artificial two no-trumps openings in reasonably common usage:

1 To show a minor suit pre-empt.
2 To show both minors.

Two no-trumps shows a minor suit pre-empt

Here double should show a strong balanced hand. We have had our natural two no-trump overcall taken away, so now cannot afford the luxury of being able to take action with a weak no-trump hand-type. So, double shows 16+ HCP – in principle balanced, but maybe unbalanced if too strong for other action. If we wish to make a take-out action, we should use our better minor. Thus a three-club overcall is a take-out of diamonds, and a three-diamond overcall is a take-out of clubs.

Two no-trumps shows both minors

Here again, double should show a strong balanced hand. We have both three clubs and three diamonds available for take-out. There are various alternatives for these two bids, but one of the best is to play both three clubs and three diamonds as take-out, with the difference between the two depending on strength. Over three clubs we can then use three diamonds as a shape inquiry: three hearts/spades show five cards in that suit, three no-trumps denies a five-card major, four clubs/diamonds show five-five in the majors with a singleton in the bid minor.

Opinions differ as to which should be the stronger bid. Some people argue that three clubs should be the stronger, because it may also be more balanced, thus the extra space is needed to find out the distribution. Others argue that three clubs should be weaker, because then the best fit can be found for part-score purposes, whereas the stronger hand will more often lead to a game contract when the distribution can be discovered at a higher level.

Higher artificial openings

What about higher artificial openings: for example, transfer pre-empts?
Artificial three-level openings seem to have gone out of fashion recently. However, they still crop up from time to time.

Transfer pre-empts are easier to deal with than ordinary pre-empts (which is perhaps why they have gone out of fashion). If our opponents make an ordinary pre-empt against us, our only take-out mechanism is to double immediately. When they open a transfer pre-empt, we have the options of an immediate double, an immediate cue-bid of their suit and a delayed double. It merely remains to decide how best to use these bids.

The simplest thing to do is the same as we did over what was effectively a transfer weak two bid. Double shows 12–15 balanced (though we may prefer to up that range a little since we are at the three level); a cue-bid of their suit is for take-out; a delayed double is penalty.

I have come across three level openings which show either the suit opened or a different suit. How should I deal with these?
A convention in vogue at one time and now largely vanished was to play an opening three-club bid as either clubs or diamonds, or perhaps a three-heart opening bid as either hearts or spades. This is a little like Russian roulette. Over such a three-club opening, the best defence is probably to give up a natural three-diamond overcall, thus double is take-out of diamonds and three diamonds is take-out of clubs. Over a three-heart opening, a natural three-spade bid is too valuable to give up, and we should defend in the same way we do to an opening two bid which may or may not hold the suit – i.e. double is take-out.

What about a three no-trump opening which shows a minor suit pre-empt (perhaps solid suit, perhaps not)?
We can defend this opening in just the same way as we did a two no-trump opening which showed either minor: double is strong balanced, and four of a minor is a take-out of the other minor.

South African Texas is a widely played convention. How should I defend against this?
South African Texas is a convention whereby a four-club opening shows a hand with hearts, stronger than a four-heart

opening. Four diamonds is similar, but with spades. Again our opponents have made life easier for us than if they had opened a straightforward four hearts or four spades. Here it is best to play that a double is a takeout of the suit they have shown and can be quite light – say a 1–4–4–4 11-count. Pass and double shows a strong balanced hand, and an immediate cue-bid of the suit they have shown is a two-suiter including the other major. With both minors we can bid four no-trumps.

Strong pass systems

I have heard that at international level some pairs are starting to use 'strong pass' systems, whereby they pass on good hands and actually open the bidding with bad hands (HUMs.) How on earth am I supposed to defend against those methods?

HUM is a recent acronym, devised to describe Highly Unusual Methods – nearly always used to described strong pass systems. Many pairs will never come into contact with strong pass systems, and it is not yet clear whether they have come into the game to stay or whether they will eventually fade into obscurity. Some strong international teams use at least one strong pass pair – Sweden and Poland in particular. However, there is much interest in these methods in many other areas – notably Britain, Scandinavia and the Antipodes. Some bridge clubs have special nights when pairs are allowed to play whatever systems they like, provided notice is given. As with most unusual methods, when we first play against them, there is a tendency to panic. However, again as with most unusual methods, after a while sensible defences are developed and they are no longer so fearsome, and in fact it can be quite fun to play against a pair doing something different.

How should I bid when they 'open' the bidding with a pass?

Although the strong pass itself is not difficult to defend against – we could after all choose to ignore it completely – our motives for entering the auction have changed. For example, we want to be able to 'overcall', rather than need opening bid values to enter the auction. Also, it would be foolish to continue to play weak no-trump when our right-hand opponent has announced opening values. If we wish to bid whenever we have the strength to overcall, we need one bid for when we have a good hand. Even if we normally play a natural method, there is much merit in adopting a simple strong club structure when the hand in front of us has opened a strong pass. The following is such a structure:

After a strong pass:

- 1 ♣ shows 16+ HCP unbalanced or 17+ HCP balanced – in response, one diamond is a negative showing 0–7 HCP, other responses up to two diamonds are natural, 8+ HCP and forcing to game, higher responses show 5–7 HCP and long suits;

- 1 ◇/♡/♠ are natural, overcall strength, say 8–15 HCP, and we will play whatever methods we usually adopt over an overcall – however, we do need a 'cue-bid', and we will use two clubs for this purpose;

- 1NT is natural, 14–16, with whatever system we usually play over it;

- 2 ♣ is natural, overcall strength – a two–diamond response should be like an unassuming cue-bid;

- 2 ◇/♡/♠ are weak.

If the next hand intervenes over our 'overcall', as far as system goes we should just assume the pass hadn't happened. So, after

Pass – 1 $\diamondsuit$ – Dble, say, we bid as after 1 $\diamondsuit$ – Dble, always remembering, of course, that partner may be substantially short of opening bid values and will not have more than 15 HCP.

That seems straightforward enough, but how should I deal with their weak openings?
Of course, it is not the strong (though often limited and non-forcing) pass that is difficult to defend against; it is what the opponents open when they are too weak to pass!

These HUM players pass whenever they have opening-bid values (though they also sometimes play a strong club, so that the pass is limited to 11–15 points), but what they do when they do not have opening bid values varies enormously. They usually have one bid which shows, say, 0–6 HCP, and the rest all show hands in the 7–11 range. These weak bids are known as 'fertilizers' or 'ferts'. When they bid hands in the 7–11 range, they may bid them naturally or they may not. If they bid them naturally, then we just treat them as we would normally treat a natural bid. However, when they are not natural, we will treat them just the same way as we are going to deal with the hands in the 0–6 range.

When the 'fert' is one club, life is very easy. We double when we would have opened one club and otherwise we make our normal opening bid. In this way our bidding has been totally unaffected by our opponents.

When the 'fert' is something else, they have taken some space away from us and we have to do something different. Most pairs now play some sort of transfer defence to these 'ferts', a method of defence originally developed in Sweden. After a fertilizer opening of 1$\diamondsuit$/1$\heartsuit$/1$\spadesuit$:

● Dble   13–19 or 23+ balanced. In response partner always assumes 13–15 until told otherwise.

        If the 'fert' is one diamond:

    – 1 ♡   is a negative, showing 0–5 HCP and thereafter all bids are natural and non-forcing, except 2NT, which is forcing, showing 23+ balanced;

    – 1 ♠   is an unbalanced semi-positive, 6–9 HCP, over this all bidding is natural, but a 1NT rebid is forcing (since partner is known to be unbalanced in some way) so may be bid with a strong hand;

    – 1NT   6–9 balanced, then two clubs is Stayman.

Other bids are normal responses to a 13–15 1NT (but since they all show in excess of 10 HCP, transfers may be broken freely, even with no fit).

        If the 'fert' is one heart:

    – 1 ♠   is a negative, 0–5 HCP;

    – 1NT   6–9, sufficiently balanced to have passed a 13–15 1NT.

Other bids are normal responses to a 13–15 1NT (but could be as weak as 6 HCP).

        If the 'fert' is one spade:

    – all responses are as to a 13–15 1NT.

● 1 suit   natural opening bid, but always a five-card suit.

● 1NT   transfer to clubs. In response:

    – 2 ♣   negative, say 0–7 HCP;

    – 2 ♢   forcing to game, any distribution.

Other bids are natural, constructive but non-forcing.

- 2 ♣ transfer to diamonds. In response:
  - 2 ♦ negative;
  - 2 ♡ forcing to game, any distribution.

  Other bids are natural, constructive but non-forcing.

- 2 ♦ transfer to hearts. If the 'fert' was one diamond (when a natural one-heart overcall was available), this shows the values for a strong club (16+) opening. If this is the case, the ranges for the responses are 0–4, 5–7 and 8+. In response:
  - 2 ♡ negative;
  - 2 ♠ forcing to game, any distribution.

  Other bids are natural, constructive but non-forcing.

- 2 ♡ transfer to spades. If the 'fert' was one diamond or one heart, this show the values for a strong club opening (see above). In response:
  - 2 ♠ negative;
  - 2NT forcing to game, any distribution.

  Other bids are natural, constructive but non-forcing.

- 2 ♠ shows a 16–19 HCP three-suiter, 4–4–4–1 distribution with shortage in the suit opened.

- 2NT 20–22 balanced.

- Others as normal openings.

The above structure is intended only as an outline. If you are going to play against a strong pass system with any regularity, you will need to put in some more work.

7

Lead–directing Doubles of Final Contracts

Sometimes a double of a game or slam contract is made in order to try and direct partner to make a specific opening lead. In a sense it is a penalty double, because the doubler certainly expects the contract to go down, but only if his partner leads a particular suit. As one may imagine, this is an important area for partnerships to sort out and there is plenty of scope for expensive misunderstandings.

Whenever my partner doubles three no-trumps I seem to lead the wrong thing. Can you give me some guidelines?
Any double of three no-trumps by the hand that is not going to be on lead should be taken as lead-directing. If we just have a good hand, we should either pass unless we think the contract will go down whatever the lead, when we can double anyway.

Doubles of three no-trumps can be subdivided into four sections:

1   We, the doubler, have bid a suit.
2   Partner has bid a suit.
3   We have each bid a suit.
4   Neither of us has bid a suit.

What about if we, the doubler, have bid a suit?
There are two distinct schools of thought in this area, one saying that the double of three no-trumps should ask for the doubler's suit to be led, the other saying that the double should ask for a different suit.

There is no real 'right' way to play such a double. We should look at what we are trying to achieve. We would like to double any contract that we think is going to go down, but we would also like to use the double to suggest a particular lead – i.e. we do not think the contract will go down *unless* we double. The biggest swings come in this second category, so it is to this that we must direct our attention.

The best way to play a double when the doubler has bid a suit depends on general partnership style. If we always have a good suit when we overcall, or if we are very rude to partner when he doesn't lead our suit, then over the years he will have developed a very strong tendency to lead our suit when the opponents end up in three no-trumps. If this is the case, we would be best to play the double as asking partner to try some other suit.

On the other hand, if we overcall freely, not caring much about suit quality, and if we are very philosophical when partner doesn't lead our suit, then he will usually listen to the auction carefully and perhaps often lead some other suit. If this is the case, then we are better to play the double as a request to have our suit led.

What if I double when partner has bid a suit?
A double of three no-trumps when partner has bid a suit is generally played as a request for partner to lead his suit. It is highly unlikely that we have a suit of sufficiently good quality to hope to beat three no-trumps should partner lead it, if we have not bid it. It is much more likely that we have a holding such as K-x or A-x in partner's suit along with other good defensive values and suspect that as long as partner leads his own suit, we will beat three no-trumps.

What if we have each bid a suit?
The normal practice when both players have bid a suit is for a double to suggest that partner leads his own suit. Left to his own

devices partner would be more likely to lead our suit than lead his own. If our suit is poor and we have undisclosed honours in partner's suit it may well be preferable for him to lead his own suit.

What if neither of us has bid at all?
Assuming dummy has bid a suit, then the normal meaning of a double in this situation is to ask for a lead of dummy's first-bid suit. This is logical for two reasons: first, it is the most difficult suit for us to bid naturally, and second, it is not a very likely lead for partner to find left to his own devices.

If neither side has bid any suits – for example, after the sequence 1NT – Pass – 3NT – then opinions vary. Most people play that a double asks partner to lead his shortest major – it is not guaranteed that partner will pick the lead we were hoping for, but it is unlikely that the opponents have more than a seven-card fit in each major, so when we have, say, five or six of one major and two or three in the other, partner is likely to be significantly shorter in the suit in which we have length.

The other opinion is that we can improve on these odds. First, we have to make an assumption: when partner is looking at a virtually worthless hand (which he must have if we have enough to consider a double) after the auction 1NT – Pass – 3NT, he is likely to try to find our major suit with his opening lead anyway. If this assumption is accurate, then we could say that double called for a specific lead – say, a spade – and then if we don't double, partner will usually lead a heart.

Either one of these ideas has a great deal of merit and which we choose is a matter for partnership agreement.

What does it mean if we have made a lead-directing double (or non-double) in the auction and then double three no-trumps?
This is an interesting question and one for each partnership to decide. There are two possible meanings for this double:

1   It merely reinforces the initial request – i.e. the early lead-directing double merely suggested a lead; the double of three no-trumps declares that that contract will go down if partner leads the suit requested.

2   It cancels the first message. There is only any point in playing this if you are of a particularly devious persuasion. Suppose you had overcalled one heart with J-10-9-x-x in hearts and A-K-Q-10-x in a minor. If your opponents look as though they are heading for three no-trumps, you may like to help them on their way by doubling a three-heart cue-bid for the lead (or not making an un-lead-directing double, according to agreement). However, once they have reached their doomed contract, you want to double to tell partner that you were not serious.

The situation is slightly different depending on whether our first lead-directing action was a double, whatever that double means, than if it was a pass. When our opponents cue-bid our suit, we need a neutral action – i.e. one which neither particularly suggests partner should lead that suit nor particularly suggests otherwise. This obviously has to be pass. When playing normal doubles of cue-bids, a double is quite a strong command, whereas a pass is neutral. When playing un-lead-directing doubles, double is quite a strong command to lead a different suit, whereas pass is only a suggestion that we lead that suit. If we make an un-lead-directing double, there is a case for the double of the final contract to be directing partner's attention to a particular suit, perhaps asking for a lead of the lowest unbid suit, say.

What about doubles of slams?
A double of a freely bid slam alerts partner to one of two possibilities:

1 We have a void somewhere and would like to be given an immediate ruff.
2 We do not have a void, but our values are not where partner is likely to expect them and thus suggests an unusual lead.

It is sometimes possible to arrive in a position where this applies against a lower-level contract.

If we have a void somewhere and would like partner to lead that suit, there are several other things to bear in mind before we decide to double. This is difficult because we cannot afford to pass too slowly if that is what we choose to do instead of double, because partner may then be ethically barred from leading what we want him to. If we have a void in a side-suit and the opponents start bidding strongly towards a slam when partner is going to be on lead, we should do our thinking early, and decide under what circumstances we will double. The other things to bear in mind are:

1 Is it likely that if we double a slam in a suit contract that the opponents can (or will) convert to a different making slam – six no-trumps, say? If this is the case we may well be wiser just to hope that partner leads the right suit anyway.
2 Are we really sure that we want the suit led? Partner will assume that we are telling him that the slam will go down if he gives us a ruff. Sometimes he will possibly give up a trick in the suit he leads and if we have some trump length which may embarrass declarer later, we may find that to give us our ruff straightaway was the only way to let declarer make his slam.
3 Often when we are void in a suit all the suits are breaking badly for declarer and he will simply go down if left to his own devices. If we double and partner does not find the right lead, it may be helpful to declarer to know that we are void in a different suit.

Occasionally, partner should be able to work out that even though we are void in a suit, it is not right for him to lead it. Consider what you would lead from the following hand which cropped up in the 1989 Common Market Championships:

♠ 7 5
♡ 6 4
◇ A 10 8 7 5 3 2
♣ 8 6

You are West, vulnerable against non-vulnerable opponents, and the bidding goes:

West	North	East	South
—	—	—	1 ♡
Pass	4 ♣*	4 ♠	Pass
Pass	5 ◇	Pass	5 ♡
Pass	Pass	Dble	All pass

*splinter bid

Partner has overcalled four spades, passed five diamonds (to double might have suggested diamond values and invited you to bid five spades) and then doubled five hearts. This must be a penalty double and, in the light of the earlier four-spade bid, must surely indicate a void somewhere. This void cannot be in clubs as dummy has a singleton there, so must be in diamonds. At the table the West hand led the ace of diamonds, which was not a success as this was the full deal:

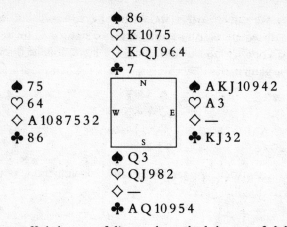

```
                    ♠ 86
                    ♡ K 10 7 5
                    ◇ K Q J 9 6 4
                    ♣ 7
  ♠ 7 5                              ♠ A K J 10 9 4 2
  ♡ 6 4                              ♡ A 3
  ◇ A 10 8 7 5 3 2                   ◇ —
  ♣ 8 6                              ♣ K J 3 2
                    ♠ Q 3
                    ♡ Q J 9 8 2
                    ◇ —
                    ♣ A Q 10 9 5 4
```

Declarer ruffed the ace of diamonds, cashed the ace of clubs, ruffed a club and led the king of diamonds. East ruffed but South overruffed, ruffed another club and led the queen of diamonds. The best East could do was to ruff high and cash one spade but there was no further defence.

West should have argued that his partner expected to beat five hearts doubled if he received a diamond ruff without knowing of West's ace of diamonds. There could be no rush to take the ace of diamonds and West should just have led a spade, hoping to take East's outside defensive tricks and wait for his ace of diamonds later. If he felt that it was important to lead a diamond, perhaps he should have led a low one!

These sorts of disaster can seriously test the strength of a partnership. West argued that he would have led a spade routinely without the double and thus beaten five hearts. East then argued that he didn't know that and how was he to know that declarer was also void in diamonds, etc.

When we double when we do not have a void but we have strength where partner is not likely to expect it, there is even more scope for misunderstanding. Look at this hand from a local league game:

```
                    ♠ 863
                    ♡ K65
                    ◇ QJ42
                    ♣ KJ6
    ♠ 1097              N          ♠ AQ542
    ♡ AQJ732                       ♡ 10984
    ◇ K          W        E        ◇ 8753
    ♣ 754                          ♣ —
                    S
                    ♠ KJ
                    ♡ —
                    ◇ A1096
                    ♣ AQ109832
```

West	North	East	South
—	—	Pass	1♣
1♡	2NT	3♣	6♣
Pass	Pass	Dble	All Pass

West led his singleton king of diamonds and that was −1090. What went wrong here?

East thought a spade lead might well be needed to beat the contract and was worried that he had no values in hearts for his unassuming cue-bid. He thought that if he had diamond values he would have bid three diamonds over two no-trumps which, since he was a passed hand, must also show a heart fit. Consequently, he thought the double was clearly asking for a spade lead.

West thought that a spade was the obvious lead on the sequence, for exactly the same reasons. He also thought his partner would have bid three diamonds over two no-trumps with diamond values. He also knew his partner didn't have any values in hearts anyway. However, when East doubled, West thought he was asking for an unusual lead – hence the king of diamonds.

The real disagreement here was the precise nature of the double. West thought that the choice lay between the two unbid suits (with or without the final double) and understood the double to mean 'lead the most unusual'. East thought that a passive lead – a 'safe' heart or a trump – was quite likely and thus was using the double in order to wake his partner up to the possible need to be active, but did not want him to 'be active' in a particularly unusual way.

This is an area fraught with scope for possible misunder-standings. Experience suggests that often the contract would have gone off on normal defence and the double often gives partner scope to make an imaginative lead to let it through. Unless we are prepared to spend hours discussing this position with partner, we are probably better using such a lead-directing double with extreme caution. On the above deal, whatever the merits of West's lead, East had no real reason to suppose that declarer had an undisclosed source of tricks and there was no real reason to suppose that any spade losers were going anywhere. His partner knew that declarer probably had a void heart and that dummy would have strength in the suit. Consequently West was very likely to lead a spade anyway. East would have had a much better result had he refrained from doubling.

What does it mean if we have made a lead-directing double of a cue-bid or Blackwood response in the auction and then double the slam?
Again we are in a situation where there is more than one school of thought, one thinking that it merely reinforces the first mes-sage, while the other thinks it should cancel the first message. As

in this situation when we discussed such doubles of three no-
trumps it is simply a matter of partnership agreement. There is
one situation when it is clearly right that the second double
should cancel the first and that is when the final denomination is
different from the one that looked likely when the double of the
cue-bid occurred. Suppose the bidding proceeds:

West	North	East	South
1 ♦	Pass	1 ♠	Pass
2 ♡	Pass	3 ♡	Pass
3 ♠	Pass	4 ♣	Dble
6 ♦	Pass	Pass	Dble

This double would clearly suggest that South has a void in one
of the majors. When South doubled four clubs he thought that
his opponents were headed for a slam in one of the majors and
clearly thought a club lead would be a good idea. When it
appears that West was intending to play in diamonds all along,
he changed his mind.

Points to remember

1 Partnership agreement in this area is much more important
   than the actual agreement itself. Discussion with your partner about these situations will pay dividends.
2 If we make an unexpected double of a game or slam, then
   either the contract is going down, in which case it doesn't
   matter what you lead, or an unusual lead is called for.
3 The double should be an attempt to defeat a contract that
   would have made on a normal lead, not to increase the
   penalty.

8

Redoubles

Having covered a great number of different doubles, we will now look at these situations from another perspective. Whenever our opponents double us, they present us with the opportunity to redouble and in this Section we are going to look at some situations where we can usefully employ this extra bid.

When our side has opened the bidding

If the opponents double partner's opening one bid, what do I need to redouble?
In the early days of the game, when an opponent had the temerity to double partner's opening bid, we used to bid suits for rescue, and either jump or redouble with all good hands. Modern theory has changed that style somewhat, but it is still normal to play a redouble as showing a fair hand of at least 10 HCP and either:

- interest in taking a penalty from the opponents (certainly at the two level or above) – after a redouble, both partners should feel free to double anything the opponents bid with a four-card holding in their suit;
- a three-card fit for partner in a hand too strong to raise to two;
- any hand in the 10–12 range which would be difficult to bid naturally; or
- any strong balanced hand.

If we redouble and the opponents bid a suit, what is the meaning of a subsequent double by our side?

Any subsequent double by either side is for penalty, usually showing at least four trumps. The exception to this may be when the opponents voluntarily raise the level – for example, the response to the double is a jump – or the initial doubler raises his partner's simple response. In these instances, a double should be penalty-oriented, but more because of general defensive values than great trump length.

How should the bidding proceed if neither of us wishes to make a penalty double?

If we redouble and the next hand bids something, partner should double with a four-card holding and otherwise pass in case we wish to double. Only if he has a hand which is very weak in terms of high cards and very strong in terms of distribution should he bid in front of us (perhaps jumping to show extreme distribution). If he passes and then removes our penalty double, he shows a hand which is unsuitable for taking a penalty, but which has at least the normal high cards required for an opening bid, if the redoubler bids a new suit when it is his next turn, this is best (but far from universally) played as constructive but non-forcing – say a hand in the 10–12 range.

What should I bid over my opponent's double if my hand is not suitable for a redouble?

Let us look at possible alternative courses of action:

1   Pass – nothing in particular to say, but a pass followed by a subsequent double would be for take-out.
2   One no-trump – natural, say 7–9 HCP, more or less as without the double, but we would be more inclined to bid one no-trump on a balanced hand in the right range rather than a four-card major.

3   A new suit – natural, forcing, just as without the double. The suit is more likely to be five cards in length than previously (see last paragraph) and should be readily raised with only three-card support. Otherwise bidding should continue exactly as it would have done had there been no double.

4   Raises – a raise to the two level shows more or less the same as it would have done without the double, but it is very much more likely to contain only three-card support and will not be top weight for, with a nine or ten-count, we would prefer to start with redouble.

5   A jump raise – pre-emptive, always four-card or longer support, say in the region of 5–8 HCP.

6   Two no-trumps – a normal limit raise to the three level with four-card support.

7   Jumps in a new suit – here there are a number of alternatives:

   ● a normal force (not very frequent);
   ● weak (can be useful, but remember that this will be a suit that has at least been implied by an opponent so it is a little dangerous, especially if you do not have a fit for partner);
   ● natural, showing the suit bid plus a three-card fit for partner, forcing for one round, but only promising the values for a raise to three of partner's suit (this can be very useful if the opponents jump around, as it puts partner in a good position to judge what further action to take).

I have played against pairs playing 'negative redoubles'. What does this mean?

Instead of our ascribed meaning of 10+ high-card points and a number of possible hand-types, a negative redouble shows shortage in partner's suit and could be made on any strength of hand.

Are there any advantages of this style?

It can help with the decision as to whether to compete for the part-score and can certainly help with the defence (although it will sometimes help declarer). When playing this style it is normal to play that a pass followed by a subsequent double by either partner is for take-out, whereas a redouble followed by a double from either partner is for penalty.

Do we not do this anyway, with our normal style of redouble?

Yes, but we will not always have had the values for the redouble in the first place. If we are not strong enough to redouble we will have had to pass or bid a suit, after which our doubles will usually be for take-out.

Is this style widely played?

No, it is mainly used by players who use a prepared minor, perhaps a Precision-style one-diamond opener. Since opener has not actually shown diamonds with his opening bid, it is often useful for responder to indicate his tolerance for the suit.

Remember that, if you do come across people playing this method, you need to agree with your partner on the meaning of a pass of the redouble.

What does it mean if my left-hand opponent and my partner pass my opening bid, the next hand doubles and I redouble: for example, 1♡ – Pass – Pass – Dble: Rdble?

This is usually played as showing a good hand and inviting partner to take some action, perhaps doubling the opponents for penalty or volunteering a long suit or some support for our suit.

What if partner has responded and the next opponent doubles: for example, 1♡ – Pass – 1♠ – Dble; Rdble – 2♣?

If your partner has bid a new suit, the redouble should show either a wish to penalize the opponents or any good hand. As usual, after auctions where a redouble has occurred, the first priority is one of doubling the opponents for penalty. The redouble invites partner to double the opponents when he has a generally defensive hand with three or more trumps, or else, unless he has an exceptionally weak distributional hand, to pass in case we wish to double. If we do not wish to penalize the opponents we can just bid our hand naturally, often at a lower level than we would otherwise have had to because we have already told partner that we have extra values.

If I start with a redouble in this position with any good hand, what does it mean if I bid, say, two no-trumps, which cannot now be a strong, balanced hand?

This is a matter for partnership agreement, but if we accept the premise that a redouble is the first move on any good hand, then the following is a sensible scheme after a sequence such as 1◇ – Pass – 1♠ – Dble:

1   Pass – any minimum opening bid without significant extra distribution.

2   One no-trump – whatever normal one no-trump rebid range is played but it should be a hand based more on playing strength than defensive values: if a wide-range rebid is usually played, then this should show a hand in the upper range with reasonable playing strength. With a balanced hand which does not fit into this category, then pass or redouble according to strength.

3   A simple rebid in a suit – for example, two clubs or two diamonds here – this is natural, as without the double, but caution should be exercised. Remember, our right-hand opponent has announced club length and if partner does not have a diamond fit for us, the opposing length will be poised dangerously over us.

4   Two hearts – i.e. a reverse – this should be natural with extra distributional values, at least 6–4 distribution, more likely

6–5, and non-forcing. Remember, if we had normal reversing values we would surely start with a redouble, since our right-hand opponent has advertised a heart suit.

5   Two spades – a normal raise, usually with only three-card support.

6   Two no-trumps – as this is no longer needed to show a strong balanced hand, it can be used in much the same way as after a redouble of a second-hand take-out double – i.e. a limit raise to three spades.

7   Three clubs – again this is not needed to show a strong hand with clubs for such a hand would start with a redouble. It can either be played as some sort of descriptive spade raise, or perhaps a very distributional two-suiter with both minors.

8   Higher bids – either a jump rebid in our own suit or a jump raise for partner should show extra distribution but little extra in high cards. A jump to three spades can be made on any sound opening bid with four-card spade support.

There are some alternative modern ideas. First, in the United States redouble is often used in much the same way as we saw the support double (after, for example, 1♡ – Pass – 1♠ – 2♣) – i.e. to show three-card support for partner. All other hands make their normal rebid (or pass). A rather better idea, in my opinion, is to use a one no-trump rebid in the same way – i.e. a one no-trump rebid shows three-card support for partner. Other hands either make their natural rebid or, if balanced, pass or redouble according to strength.[1] Again, as with 'support doubles', these ideas both work best in conjunction with strong no-trump, five-card major style.

[1]See *Partnership Bidding*, Andrew Robson and Oliver Segal, 1993.

Does it make any difference if partner's response was one no-trump?
No. A redouble would suggest taking a penalty, or a strong hand that was going to bid something later. A jump in a new suit would show plenty of distribution but less high cards than would have been the case without the double and redouble.

What if partner's response was a raise?
A redouble would show a strong balanced hand, again suggesting taking a penalty.

Are there any other common situations where a redouble might be used when our side has opened the bidding?
One fairly common situation is when partner opens in a suit, we make a simple raise, which is passed round to our right-hand opponent who balances with a double. Here we can use a redouble to show a maximum raise, usually with only three trumps. If partner also has a balanced hand we may be able to extract a penalty when the opponents have picked the wrong moment.

What does it mean if my partner opens with a pre-emptive bid, such as a weak two or weak three bid, the next hand doubles and I redouble?
This is an interesting position and it is very different from when your partner opens at the one level. If he opens at the one level, it is quite likely that, whatever response you have made, he will feel that he wants to make another bid in certain auctions. Consequently, we sometimes use the redouble to warn off, to tell him that we do have some values but that our hand is more suitable for defence.

When he has opened with a weak two bid or a weak three bid, we are not expecting that he will bid again unless he is invited to do so. We do not need to redouble to warn partner about bidding again because he should not do so anyway. He has described his hand quite accurately with his opening bid and most of the time we will know what to do when the opponents enter the auction. However, the only way that we can invite him to take a further part in the auction without forcing him to do so is by redoubling. Let us consider the following hands after partner has opened a weak two in spades:

(a) ♠ 5
   ♡ A Q 10 9
   ♢ K Q 10 4
   ♣ K Q J 7

(b) ♠ K
   ♡ A J 5 4 3
   ♢ A J 6 4
   ♣ K 10 4

(c) ♠ Q 3
   ♡ A 10 9 4
   ♢ K Q 5
   ♣ A 10 7 5

When we hold (a) we wish to double the opponents for penalty wherever they alight. The way to achieve this is to pass. There is no chance of partner's bidding again in front of us, so we simply pass and double on the next round. This is a penalty double and partner should always pass.

Hands (b) and (c) are a different matter. We have good defence, but not sufficient to be certain that we will be able to beat our opponents if they land in their best spot; we have some tolerance for partner's suit so sometimes it may be best for us to bid on. We simply do not know and what we would like to do is enlist partner's co-operation. It is with this type of hand that we should redouble. If partner has a normal weak two he will still not feel it incumbent on him to enter the auction, but if he has either more playing strength or more defence than we might expect, then he is invited either to bid three spades or to double the opponents as he sees fit.

When the opponents have opened the bidding

What does it mean if partner overcalls, the next hand doubles and I redouble?
That depends on the meaning of the double.

Suppose it was a penalty double.

A good general rule to have is that when the opponents double you for penalty at the one or two level in a suit that you are known to hold, then a redouble is for rescue, provided that there are at least two unbid suits. In this straightforward situation, the redouble tells partner that we do not like his suit and asks him to choose something else. It should be noted, however, that caution should be exercised in this area. Remember that partner has chosen to overcall and, particularly at the two level, should have a good suit. It is quite possible that if you ask him to choose another suit he will be choosing a doubleton and you may be simply increasing the size of the penalty. He can always rescue himself if he thinks he is in trouble.

What if it was a negative double?

If it was a negative double then we do not need to redouble for rescue since it is very unlikely that our opponents will be passing the double anyway. Here we are in a similar position to that of a redouble of an opening bid. The redouble suggests values – say 12 HCP (since an overcall may be weaker than an opening bid) – and, in the first instance, suggests taking a penalty.

So it is exactly the same as a redouble of an opening bid?

There is one difference between a redouble in this situation and a redouble of an opening bid. After a redouble of an opening bid, it is quite likely that our side has a game on, therefore it is important that the redouble should set up an 'auction force' – i.e. after a sequence such as 1♠ – Dble – Rdble – 2♣, opener should feel free to pass two clubs with a very good hand, confident that partner will bid again.

That is not the case here. One opponent has opened the bidding and the other has also shown some values – let us say their combined values are in the region of at least 18 HCP. This makes it very unlikely that we have a game on unless we have a fit. Also, our redouble has shown 12 HCP, but the overcall could be very weak. It no longer makes sense for us to be in a forcing auction. After a sequence such as:

West	North	East	South
1 ♡	1 ♠	Dble	Rdble
2 ♡			

North can double if he has good defensive values and can make a positive bid with extra distribution, but if he has a very weak overcall he should just pass. Again, if two hearts is passed round to South, he can double for penalty with a defensive hand or make a positive bid if his distribution warrants it, but he is under no obligation to do so. It is possible, in this auction, simply to defend South's two-heart contract undoubled.

What does it mean if I overcall myself, which is passed round to the opener who reopens with a double and I redouble?
The classical meaning of such a redouble is to show a very good overcall, but caution should be exercised. In these days of negative doubles it is quite likely that our left-hand opponent was going to pass us out doubled and may still do so if we redouble. In order to make such a redouble it is important to hold a very good suit, since it is likely that our left-hand opponent will have most of the missing cards in the suit. Partner has not raised and our right-hand opponent has announced shortage.

If we regularly overcall at the one level with four-card suits, there is an alternative sensible way to play the redouble. It has now become even more likely that our left-hand opponent is going to pass us out for penalty. If we only have a four-card suit we know this is not going to be good for our side since partner has not raised. We can use the redouble as a request to partner to rescue us if he has a long suit of his own; if not we will hope to scramble our way into a better spot.

Redoubles of artificial bids

What does it mean if an opponent doubles partner's Stayman and I redouble?
We are now in a different situation. Here our opponent did not
know that we had clubs and doubled more because he wanted a
club lead than for any other reason. Sometimes we will have a
nasty surprise for him – we have good clubs over him, our
combined values are substantial and we can expect to make two
clubs redoubled. If we make the contract exactly, we will just beat
the other pairs in game (important at Pairs), and if we can make an
overtrick then we can expect a substantial gain at IMPs.

If an opponent doubles Stayman, we should bid a four-card
major, as requested, if we have one. If we do not then our action
should depend on our club holding. If we hold a very good club
holding, say a five-card suit or a chunky four-card holding, then
we redouble; if we hold an average four-card suit or very good
three-card holding we can pass to see if that knowledge is
sufficient for partner to wish to redouble; if our club holding is
weaker then we simply bid two diamonds.

Is it the same if they double a transfer bid?
It would certainly be possible to play the same style, but in this
situation our opponents are likely to be going to compete for the
part-score and it is important to let partner know how suitable we
are for bidding on. At this point, partner knows our combined
values and we know our combined trump fit; if we tell him about
our degree of trump fit he will be better placed to decide whether
or not to compete. The following is a widely-played scheme after
the opponents double a transfer – for example, 1NT – Pass – 2◇ –
Dble:

1   Pass shows no wish to compete further, usually because we
    have only a doubleton heart, but sometimes we may have
    three hearts if we also hold good diamonds.

2   Two hearts shows at least three-card hearts but in a hand
    unsuitable for further competition.

3   Redouble shows at least three hearts in a hand suitable for
    bidding to the three level. If we were sufficiently suitable to
    have 'broken the transfer' without the double, then we
    should still do so.

*Can't we ever punish them for entering the auction at the wrong
moment?*

Although the above scheme is widely played, there is a strong
case for playing the immediate redouble by the 1NT opener as
showing a wish to play there. The most likely time to want to
play in the opponents' suit redoubled is when the opener has a
good five-card holding in that suit. If we choose to play this
style, then all we have left is pass to show no wish to compete,
and two hearts to show suitability.

What if we pass to show no suitability for hearts and partner redoubles?

It is unrealistic to suppose that this should really be an attempt to
play in this suit. Partner has already shown a five-card suit
elsewhere, so is unlikely to hold four or more cards in our
opponent's suit. Even if he does, the opposing trump strength
will be over him. It is best to play this redouble as a request for
opener to bid hearts. One of the reasons we choose to play
transfers is so that the one no-trump opener can play the hand.
Why should we let a little thing like an opposing double prevent
us from doing just that?

What should we do if the opponents double fourth-suit forcing?

When partner uses fourth-suit forcing he does so for several
reasons. He either wishes us to describe our hand further, wishes
to know if we have a stopper in the fourth suit, or perhaps
merely wishes to set up a situation where he is able to make a
forcing bid in a suit. If an opponent doubles fourth-suit forcing,

we have two extra bids, pass and redouble, available to describe our hand. Let us consider the sequence: 1♠ – 2♣; 2◇ – 2♡; (Dble):

1 Two spades would show a six-card or strong five-card spade suit.

2 Two no-trumps would show a full heart guard, with no worries about the lead coming through partner's tenuous holding – say K-10-x, Q-J-x or K-x.

3 Three clubs would show three-card support.

4 Three diamonds would show five diamonds.

5 Redouble would show a full heart guard, but one which is probably better to go down in dummy – if partner has Q-x, say, and we have A-x-x or K-x-x, no-trumps will be much better played from partner's hand.

6 Pass shows any other hand. If we pass and partner redoubles, this asks us to bid three no-trumps if we have half a stopper – say Q-x or J-x-x.

What about if the opponents double a cue-bid?
It depends on what sort of cue-bid. If it is a cue-bid of the opponents' suit, asking for a stopper for three no-trumps, then it is the same as a double of fourth-suit forcing.

What about a cue-bid above three no-trumps in a slam auction?
The best way to play a redouble of a cue-bid in a slam auction depends to a large extent on our cue-bidding style.

If the control that has been cue-bid is *known* to be a first-round control, then a redouble should show second-round control. A pass would then deny second-round control. The choice between a pass, a return cue-bid and a return to the agreed trump suit would depend on the exact auction. A pass would usually suggest more enthusiasm than a sign off and an inability to cue-bid the next suit up (provided that suit was below the level of the agreed trump suit).

If the control that has been cue-bid could be first- or second-round, then a redouble should show first-round control, a return cue-bid or a sign-off would deny any control and a pass would be neutral, perhaps second-round control, perhaps not. After a pass, the cue-bidder can redouble if he has first-round control.

If the control that has been cue-bid is *known* to be second-round control, then a redouble by the cue-bidder shows a solid holding – i.e. a singleton or the queen as well as the king. The redouble is an assurance that the slam will not be defeated immediately by a lead of the suit.

Points to remember

1 Most redoubles of opponents' *take-out* doubles do not so much announce confidence in the specific contract the opposition doubled, but, rather express the wish to double the opponents by announcing the balance of high-card points and extra defensive values.

2 We must be careful about redoubling in situations where the opponents might be able to pass for penalty. The most common situation is when our overcall is passed round to opener who reopens with a double – it is quite likely that responder was intending to pass for penalty, and will still do so if we redouble.

3 After partner has redoubled a take-out double of an opening bid, he has promised another bid and may wish to make a penalty double, so there is no need to bid in front of him unless we have a weak, distributional hand.

4 Redoubles of low-level *penalty* doubles ask partner to try a different suit.

5 It is important to agree with partner the meaning of re-doubles of Stayman, transfers, cue-bids, etc.

9

Penalty Doubles

We have discussed in great detail many sequences where a double is for take-out rather than for penalty and in doing so have also covered some situations where a low-level double is for penalty. We are now going to look at situations when the opponents have had a more or less free run, when there is no question whatsoever what the double means, and it is just necessary to develop the *judgement* in order to pick the right moment.

In what sort of situations and under what conditions should I consider a penalty double?
There are two main situations when you might consider a penalty double of a freely bid game. For example:

1 When you have an unexpectedly long, strong trump holding.
2 When they have had an informative auction and your length and high cards are placed over their suits and your shortages in the other suits suggest that partner will have length and strength there.

Are there any particular dangers I should look out for which should dissuade me from doubling?
One of the fundamental things to bear in mind about this sort of double is that there is little point in doubling a freely bid game, particularly at teams, if the best you expect is for the opponents to go one down. We double because you suspect they might go

more down; we double to help direct partner's defence; or we double to try to put declarer off a possible winning line of play. Accordingly, you should bear the following points in mind:

1   If we double because we have long, strong trumps, we are going to alert declarer to this likelihood. If our trumps are *under* the hand where his main trump strength lies, he is more likely to be able to use this information to his advantage. Perhaps declarer would have gone two down if we hadn't doubled and will go one down because he has been warned. If partner has opened with, say, a weak two-bid, so declarer is already likely to place us with trump length, this becomes less of a consideration.

2   It is much safer to double the opponents when they have had a limited sequence than when they have had a forcing sequence. If they have bid, say, 1♡ – 1♠; 2♡ – 3♡; 4♡, they are in a limited sequence and may well have stretched to a thin game. Provided we have the right hand-type, with strength over our opponents' strength, we may well be able to score a substantial penalty – don't forget that, at teams, the scoring favours being in any game which is about 50 per cent, so that when bad breaks occur, even reasonable bidding can lead to a contract which goes two or three down. If the opponent have an unlimited sequence, however – say 1♡ – 1♠; 2♢ – 3♣; 3♢ – 3♡; 4♡ – where responder has used fourth suit to create a force, they could be nearly in the slam range and the bad distribution may only cause them to lose the odd overtrick. When you are wrong to double, they may make their contract redoubled, possibly with overtricks. This possibility, which is only likely in an unlimited sequence, changes the odds dramatically.

3   It is important to be sure in our minds that, having been warned by our double, our opponents will not remove

Double Trouble

themselves to a different contract which they will be able to make. They are unlikely to remove themselves to a suit which they have not yet bid, but before we double we should feel reasonably confident of being able to beat game in any other suits they have bid, or indeed, in no-trumps.

Could you give me some examples of this type of penalty double?
The easiest way to do this is to present some examples in the form of a quiz. First study the questions, all of which occurred in recent top-level events, and decide whether or not to double the final contract. then we will look at what actually happened.

1   East/West Game. Dealer West.

West	North	East	South
1 ♡	Pass	2 ♡	2 ♠
3 ♣	Pass	3 ♢	Pass
4 ♡	?		

North holds:

♠ Q J 2   ♡ K Q 10 3   ♢ 10 9 7 4   ♣ 8 2

2   Game All. Dealer North.

West	North	East	South
	2 ♢*	Pass	3 ♡†
Pass	3 ♠	Dble‡	Pass
5 ♣	Pass	Pass	?

*weak two in either major
†pre-emptive raise in partner's major
‡take-out

South holds:

♠ Q 10 8   ♡ 10 6 5   ♢ A 10 8   ♣ A 6 3 2

3 Love All. Dealer North.

West	North	East	South
	Pass	1♡	Pass
1♠	Pass	2♣	Pass
4♠	?		

North holds:

♠ A Q 8 6 ♡ Q 9 ◇ A 10 7 2 ♣ 10 9 5

4 North/South Game. Dealer South.

West	North	East	South
			1♡
Dble	1NT★	2♠	Pass
Pass	3◇	Pass	3♡
Pass	4◇	Pass	5◇
Pass	Pass	?	

★transfer, showing clubs

East holds:

♠ A 9 8 5 4 ♡ 8 6 5 3 ◇ 10 4 3 ♣ J

5 East/West Game. Dealer West.

West	North	East	South
Pass	1♡	2◇	3♣
Pass	3♡	Pass	4♡
?			

West holds:

♠ Q 6 4 3 ♡ 9 7 6 4 3 2 ◇ K 6 ♣ 4

6 East/West Game. Dealer North.

West	North	East	South
	Pass	1♣	1◇
1♠	2♡	Dble★	Pass
4♠	Pass	Pass	?

★three-card spade support

South holds:

♠ K Q 9 3 ♡ 9 4 ◇ A 8 7 6 2 ♣ 10 9

7   Game All. Dealer West.

West	North	East	South
1NT	Pass	2♣	2♦
2♡	Pass	2NT	Pass
3♠	Pass	4♠	?

South holds:

    ♠ K964 ♡ 5 ♢ A87643 ♣ A9

8   Love All. Dealer East.

West	North	East	South
		Pass	1♠
Pass	1NT*	2♠†	Pass
4♡	?		

*forcing

†hearts and a minor

North holds:

    ♠ J6 ♡ K954 ♢ 1063 ♣ A876

9   North/South Game. Dealer South.

West	North	East	South
			1♢
Pass	1♡	Pass	1NT
Pass	2♣	Pass	2♡
Pass	3♡	Pass	4♡
Pass	Pass	?	

East holds:

    ♠ 9653 ♡ KQ963 ♢ 982 ♣ A

10   Game All. Dealer West.

West	North	East	South
1 ◇	Pass	1 ♡	2 ♣
3 ◇	Pass	4 ◇	Pass
5 ◇	Pass	Pass	?

South holds:

♠ A 10 5   ♡ K Q 7   ◇ 8   ♣ A K Q J 8 3

11   North/South Game. Dealer West.

West	North	East	South
Pass	1 ♡	1 ♠	Pass
2 ♡	Pass	2 ♠	Pass
3 ♠	Pass	4 ♠	?

South holds:

♠ 8 4 3 2   ♡ 8 6   ◇ A J 4 3 2   ♣ J 4

12   East/West Game. Dealer North.

West	North	East	South
	2 ♠	2NT	3 ♠
4 ♠	Pass	5 ♡	Pass
7 ♣	Pass	7 ◇	Pass
Pass	?		

North holds:

♠ K 8 7 6 5 2   ♡ J   ◇ Q J 10 6   ♣ 10 7

When you have decided whether or not to double on the above auctions, read on and find out what actually happened.

1   East/West Game. Dealer West.

```
              ♠ Q J 2
              ♡ K Q 10 3
              ◇ 10 9 7 4
              ♣ 8 2
♠ 6                         ♠ 5 4 3
♡ A J 7 5 2     N           ♡ 9 8 4
◇ K 6 5    W        E       ◇ A J 3 2
♣ A Q 10 4      S           ♣ K 9 5
              ♠ A K 10 9 8 7
              ♡ 6
              ◇ Q 8
              ♣ J 7 6 3
```

West	North	East	South
1♡	Pass	2♡	2♠
3♣	Pass	3◇	Pass
4♡	Dble	All Pass	

This hand was played in the semi-final of the 1991 Bermuda Bowl. Our sequence featured the great Gabriel Chagas as North. He had no hesitation in doubling and the American declarer had to go two down, −500. Note that if we just look at the East/West cards, four hearts is not an unreasonable contrct, but the 4–1 trump break meant that declarer lost control. In the other room, it was the American North/South pair who bid aggressively – all the way to four spades before the Brazilians had had the chance to do more than bid to the two level. They were lucky not to be doubled in four spades but the swing was 12 IMPs – and it was the last board of a match which the Brazilians won by 8 IMPs.

2   Game All. Dealer North.

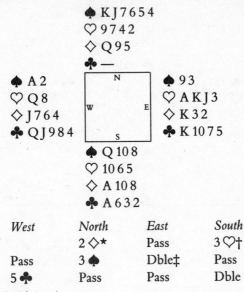

♠ K J 7 6 5 4
♡ 9 7 4 2
◇ Q 9 5
♣ —

♠ A 2
♡ Q 8
◇ J 7 6 4
♣ Q J 9 8 4

♠ 9 3
♡ A K J 3
◇ K 3 2
♣ K 10 7 5

♠ Q 10 8
♡ 10 6 5
◇ A 10 8
♣ A 6 3 2

West	North	East	South
	2◇*	Pass	3♡†
Pass	3♠	Dble‡	Pass
5♣	Pass	Pass	Dble

*weak two in either major
†pre-emptive raise in partner's major
‡take-out

Here East/West were given a push towards their final contract, which although poor, was difficult to avoid. East's take-
out double of three spades looks reasonable and West had a fair
hand with no invitational bid available so she took her chance at
her vulnerable game. South was Germany's Daniela von Arnim
and she knew that her opponents had been put in a difficult
position by her side's pre-emptive actions, hence she doubled
and five clubs went two down, −500. South had to double to
flatten the board, because her team-mates had also had problems
and had reached three no-trumps, a contract which had no
chance and eventually went five down when declarer mis-
guessed in diamonds.

3   Love All. Dealer North.

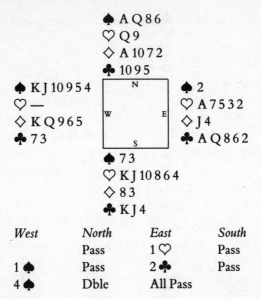

♠ A Q 8 6
♡ Q 9
♦ A 10 7 2
♣ 10 9 5

♠ K J 10 9 5 4
♡ —
♦ K Q 9 6 5
♣ 7 3

♠ 2
♡ A 7 5 3 2
♦ J 4
♣ A Q 8 6 2

♠ 7 3
♡ K J 10 8 6 4
♦ 8 3
♣ K J 4

West	North	East	South
	Pass	1 ♡	Pass
1 ♠	Pass	2 ♣	Pass
4 ♠	Dble	All Pass	

This deal occured in the final of the 1991 Bermuda Bowl.
After the same start to the auction at both tables, West had to
decide what to bid over two clubs. The Icelandic West went
quietly, bidding only two spades, but unfortunately he went
astray in the play and finished up one down. In the other room
the Polish West was more aggressive, opting for a jump to a
game, which again was not an unreasonable contract looking at
just the East/West cards. Jon Baldursson, North for Iceland,
liked his three certain defensive tricks and his relative weakness
in hearts and clubs, so risked a double and was rewarded with
+300.

4   North/South Game. Dealer South.

```
                    ♠ 7
                    ♡ J
                    ♢ K J 9 8 5
                    ♣ A K 8 6 5 4
    ♠ K J 6 3        ┌─────N─────┐        ♠ A 9 8 5 4
    ♡ Q 7 4          │           │        ♡ 8 6 5 3
    ♢ A 6          W │           │ E      ♢ 10 4 3
    ♣ Q 10 9 3       │           │        ♣ J
                     └─────S─────┘
                    ♠ Q 10 2
                    ♡ A K 10 9 2
                    ♢ Q 7 2
                    ♣ 7 2
```

West	North	East	South
			1 ♡
Dble	1NT★	2 ♠	Pass
Pass	3 ♢	Pass	3 ♡
Pass	4 ♢	Pass	5 ♢
Pass	Pass	Dble	All Pass

★transfer showing clubs

On this deal, from the same match, it was the turn of the Poles to extract a penalty. North was allowed to describe his hand, but his four-diamond bid was undoubtedly forcing and left South with little option but to raise to game. Yet again, five diamonds is not an unreasonable contract, but the bad club break spelled its doom. East doubled because he had an ace which was likely to be useful and also he *knew* that clubs were breaking badly because of his partner's original take-out double. Sure enough, five diamonds went two down, −500. In the other room diamonds were never bid and the Polish North/South ended up in the inferior contract of five clubs, but because they arrived there quickly, it was difficult for East/West to double.

5   East/West Game. Dealer West.

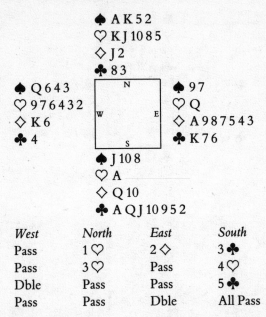

♠ A K 5 2
♡ K J 10 8 5
♢ J 2
♣ 8 3

♠ Q 6 4 3
♡ 9 7 6 4 3 2
♢ K 6
♣ 4

♠ 9 7
♡ Q
♢ A 9 8 7 5 4 3
♣ K 7 6

♠ J 10 8
♡ A
♢ Q 10
♣ A Q J 10 9 5 2

West	North	East	South
Pass	1 ♡	2 ♢	3 ♣
Pass	3 ♡	Pass	4 ♡
Dble	Pass	Pass	5 ♣
Pass	Pass	Dble	All Pass

This deal occurred in a Camrose match between Scotland and Wales. The Scottish West could not resist doubling North/South's four hearts, but he regretted it a moment or two later when his partner doubled five clubs which was unbeatable – and in fact made two overtricks on a heart lead. He was a little unlucky, for no doubt he imagined that his partner would be void in hearts so that even if his opponents did remove themselves to five clubs, a heart lead, ruffed, and a diamond back to his king for another heart ruff would mean defeat.

6   East/West Game. Dealer North.

```
                    ♠ 10
                    ♡ K 10 6 3 2
                    ◇ K 4 3
                    ♣ K 8 5 4
    ♠ A J 8 6 2        N          ♠ 7 5 4
    ♡ J 8 7                       ♡ A Q 5
    ◇ 10 9 5     W         E      ◇ Q J
    ♣ A 3                         ♣ Q J 7 6 2
                    S
                    ♠ K Q 9 3
                    ♡ 9 4
                    ◇ A 8 7 6 2
                    ♣ 10 9
```

West	North	East	South
	Pass	1 ♣	1 ◇
1 ♠	2 ♡	Dble★	Pass
4 ♠	Pass	Pass	Dble
All Pass			

★three–card spade support

This hand comes from the final of the 1991 World Junior Championships and West was duly punished for the exuberance of youth, for four spades is an extremely poor contract indeed. Despite having a minimum overcall, South had a good defensive hand: aces are always useful and the nine of spades was likely to be a severe hindrance to declarer's ability to pick up the trumps; his partner had announced some values in a suit in which South was short; and it was also likely that the opponents were in a 5–3 fit only. His judgement was rewarded with an 800 penalty and 12 IMPs.

7   Game All. Dealer West.

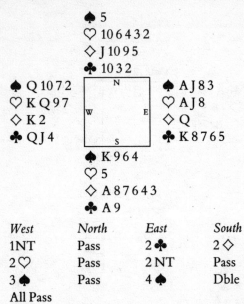

	♠ 5		
	♡ 10 6 4 3 2		
	◇ J 10 9 5		
	♣ 10 3 2		

West	North	East	South
West	*North*	*East*	*South*
1NT	Pass	2♣	2◇
2♡	Pass	2NT	Pass
3♠	Pass	4♠	Dble
All Pass			

This hand occurred in a Camrose match between Northern Ireland and Wales. In practice, South was damaged because West failed to alert East's two no-trump bid, which this pair played as forcing. South made an excellent double of what he thought was a limited sequence and, indeed, this type of sequence is one where a final double can often be lucrative. When the opponents have opened one no-trump, located a 4–4 fit via Stayman, and then made a game invitation which has been accepted, it is clear that they probably both have balanced hands and they will not have very many high cards to spare – if suits are breaking badly, they may well go several down. Detailed analysis will reveal that this is an interesting deal where the tiniest slip by declarer will lead to defeat, despite the wealth of high cards, however the defence went astray and four spades was allowed to make.

8   Love All. Dealer East.

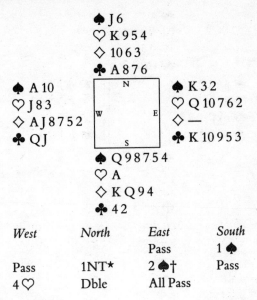

♠ J 6
♥ K 9 5 4
♦ 10 6 3
♣ A 8 7 6

♠ A 10   ♠ K 3 2
♥ J 8 3   ♥ Q 10 7 6 2
♦ A J 8 7 5 2 ♦ —
♣ Q J   ♣ K 10 9 5 3

♠ Q 9 8 7 5 4
♥ A
♦ K Q 9 4
♣ 4 2

West	North	East	South
		Pass	1 ♠
Pass	1NT☆	2 ♠†	Pass
4 ♥	Dble	All Pass	

☆forcing
†hearts and a minor

   North did not pick a good moment to double on this deal
from the final of one of the top American events as there was no
defence to beat the game. Perhaps he was unlucky, but perhaps
he should have been more wary – after all, his opponents had
been allowed plenty of room merely to invite game and had
chosen to bid it voluntarily instead, suggesting that at best the
contract was likely to go only one down.

9   North/South Game. Dealer South.

```
                    ♠ A 7
                    ♡ A J 10 5 4
                    ◇ 5
                    ♣ 10 9 5 4 2
    ♠ J 8 4 2          N           ♠ 9 6 5 3
    ♡ 8                             ♡ K Q 9 6 3
    ◇ Q J 10 4    W        E        ◇ 9 8 2
    ♣ K Q J 7                       ♣ A
                      S
                    ♠ K Q 10
                    ♡ 7 2
                    ◇ A K 7 6 3
                    ♣ 8 6 3
```

West	North	East	South
			1◇
Pass	1♡	Pass	1NT
Pass	2♣	Pass	2♡
Pass	3♡	Pass	4♡
Pass	Pass	Dble	All Pass

It may seem unnecessary for this pair of hands to reach game, which is certainly a poor contract, however both North/Souths arrived in four hearts after similar bidding sequences in the quarter-final match between USA and India in the 1988 World Teams Olympiad. It is surprising that only the Indian East doubled, for it seems to fit well with all our previously stated criteria – it does not sound likely that the opponents will be able to make a game elsewhere; also they have had a limited sequence so partner will have some values and four hearts may well go at least two down. The Indian East gained 7 IMPs for his side when four hearts went two down at both tables.

10   Game All. Dealer West.

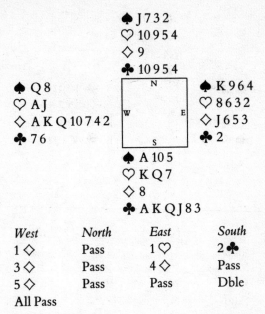

♠ J 7 3 2
♡ 10 9 5 4
◇ 9
♣ 10 9 5 4

♠ Q 8
♡ A J
◇ A K Q 10 7 4 2
♣ 7 6

♠ K 9 6 4
♡ 8 6 3 2
◇ J 6 5 3
♣ 2

♠ A 10 5
♡ K Q 7
◇ 8
♣ A K Q J 8 3

West	North	East	South
1 ◇	Pass	1 ♡	2 ♣
3 ◇	Pass	4 ◇	Pass
5 ◇	Pass	Pass	Dble
All Pass			

This hand, from the 1989 World Junior Championship semi-final between great Britain and France, illustrates another possible drawback in doubling a freely bid game. Here South's double succeeded in persuading North to make the only lead to let the contract make! Five diamonds will go down on a heart or a club lead, but North interpreted the double as suggesting that most of South's values were outside clubs and thought he was being asked to lead a major so he led the one in which he was strongest, −750.

Double Trouble

11 North/South Game. Dealer West.

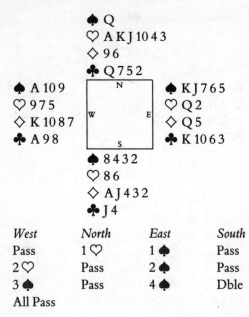

♠ Q
♡ A K J 10 4 3
◇ 9 6
♣ Q 7 5 2

♠ A 10 9
♡ 9 7 5
◇ K 10 8 7
♣ A 9 8

♠ K J 7 6 5
♡ Q 2
◇ Q 5
♣ K 10 6 3

♠ 8 4 3 2
♡ 8 6
◇ A J 4 3 2
♣ J 4

West	North	East	South
Pass	1 ♡	1 ♠	Pass
2 ♡	Pass	2 ♠	Pass
3 ♣	Pass	4 ♠	Dble
All Pass			

This example, on the other hand, illustrates another good reason *for* doubling. On this deal from the 1989 European Championships we see Daniela von Arnim again, this time as South. She doubled the final contract and the defence started with three rounds of hearts. Declarer ruffed the third round high and promptly led a spade to the ten and North's queen, eventually going two down in the doubled game. In the other room, declarer was in three spades only, and guessed spades right to make nine tricks. Thus, the judicious use of double can persuade declarer to lose a trick which he would otherwise have won.

12   East/West Game. Dealer North.

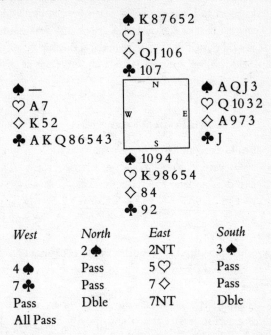

```
                      ♠ K 8 7 6 5 2
                      ♡ J
                      ◇ Q J 10 6
                      ♣ 10 7
   ♠ —                                   ♠ A Q J 3
   ♡ A 7                                 ♡ Q 10 3 2
   ◇ K 5 2                               ◇ A 9 7 3
   ♣ A K Q 8 6 5 4 3                     ♣ J
                      ♠ 10 9 4
                      ♡ K 9 8 6 5 4
                      ◇ 8 4
                      ♣ 9 2
```

West	North	East	South
	2♠	2NT	3♠
4♠	Pass	5♡	Pass
7♣	Pass	7◇	Pass
Pass	Dble	7NT	Dble
All Pass			

North's double on this deal from the 1989 Venice Cup Final, was one of the costliest on record. Her opponents had a mis-understanding and had arrived in a no-play grand slam. How-ever, they changed their minds quickly enough when North doubled, removing to seven no-trumps, which made on a spade/diamond squeeze against North. A swing of 17 IMPs to the USA was converted to a swing of 15 IMPs to the Netherlands.

This selection of hands will repay careful study. The difference between a good and bad double is often very subtle and, indeed, it may be that most of the unsuccessful doubles were unlucky to be so. It is said that if we never concede a doubled contract, then we are not doubling enough, so we should take heart if not all our doubles are successful.

Points to remember

1 We should consider making a penalty double when we have a nasty surprise for declarer – i.e. a trump stack. It would be better to double after the sequence 1♠ – 2♠ – 4♠, when we held ♠ Q J 10 9 ♡ 5 4 3 ◇ 6 5 4 ♣ 6 3 2 than when we held ♠ 5 4 ♡ A 6 5 ◇ A 7 6 3 ♣ A 8 7 6. With the first hand, we *know* we have two tricks and very few of the outstanding high cards; with the second hand we probably have three tricks but there is no reason to suppose we can contribute another.

2 We should also consider doubling when our side's pre-emptive action has caused the opposition to guess at a high level – we double when we think they've guessed wrong.

3 It can often be profitable to double when the opposition have had a hesitant, limited auction and we know that the cards are lying badly for them. If they had an unlimited auction it is much more dangerous as they may redouble.

4 We should not double if we think it is likely that they will remove to a better contract.

5 A penalty double may induce declarer to take a losing line of play.

10

The Shape of Things to Come

We seem to have covered doubles in every possible situation. Has this aspect of the game advanced as far as it possibly can, or is there scope for even more types of double?

We have covered very little in the way of high-level doubles. In Chapter 2 we discussed the basic requirements needed for a double of a four-level opening bid. In Chapter 1 we touched briefly on a double in a sequence such as 1♠ – Dble – 4♠ – Dble and in Chapter 9 we looked at when to make a penalty double of a freely bid contract. When the deal is very distributional and both sides are bidding to a high level, it is often not clear whether to defend or bid on and there is a great deal of scope for using double to help us decide.

Provided that the opponents are not clearly sacrificing, a double is only likely to net our side a fairly insignificant extra 50 or 100 points. Also, if we double a making game or slam, this only costs a small amount (provided they do not redouble). If the double can be used to help our accuracy in deciding whether to sacrifice ourselves or whether to bid on when both sides can make a high-level contract, it would be a small price to pay.

There are two ways in which double can be used to help us to make some of these decisions.

Non-penalty slam doubles

A non-penalty slam double is exactly what it sounds like – a double which says 'I have no defensive tricks and I think this slam will make.'

Why would I want to double a contract which I think is going to make?
To tell partner that, unless he has two defensive tricks himself, he should sacrifice.

What do I do if I have a defensive trick, or even two?
If we have one or more defensive tricks, we pass. If partner has no defensive tricks he will double and then we will pass with two tricks and sacrifice with one. If partner also has a defensive trick, he will pass and we will defend, albeit undoubled.

Does this idea apply to all slams the opponents bid?
It only works if our side is known to have a good sacrifice available – i.e. one that will go for a smaller penalty than their making slam.

In what circumstances does it apply?
In order for the non-penalty double to apply, three criteria have to be satisfied:

1　Our side has to have bid and supported a suit to at least game level.
2　It has to be clear from the auction that it is our side that is sacrificing.
3　It has to be clear that our sacrifice will be sufficiently cheap – i.e. attention must be paid to the vulnerability. It is unwise to play 'non-penalty' slam doubles when we are vulnerable and the opponents are not.

Could we look at some sequences when non-penalty doubles would apply?

West	North	East	South
1 ♠	2 ♡	4 ♠	5 ♡
Pass	6 ♡		

Here the opponents have bid a slam freely after our side pre-empted to game. If four spades were a good sacrifice over four hearts, then six spades must be a good sacrifice over six hearts. Double by West and East would be 'non-penalty'.

West	North	East	South
	1 ♠	4 ♡	4 ♠
Pass	4NT	Pass	5 ♢
Pass	6 ♠		

Here normal doubles would apply because East/West have not agreed a suit.

West	North	East	South
1 ♠	2 ♡	4 ♠	5 ♡
5 ♠	6 ♡		

Here normal doubles would apply because it is not clear whether East/West or North/South are sacrificing.

This sounds like a good idea. Are there any problems with it?
The biggest difficulty is deciding on how many defensive tricks we have. It is easy if we have aces or trump tricks; kings are slightly more difficult depending on how revealing the auction has been; but it is very difficult to know whether a holding such as Q-x is a defensive trick.

Playing normal methods, one seldom sacrifices against a slam unless one knows that the sacrifice will be very cheap, or if one has reason to believe that the slam will be laydown. Playing these methods we should also err in this direction.

Let us look at our first auction:

West	North	East	South
1 ♣	2 ♡	4 ♠	5 ♡
Pass	6 ♡		

This is a dangerous auction to sacrifice against anyway, because our opponents are guessing, but if they are vulnerable and we are not, it could easily be right. Suppose we, East, hold:

♠ Q J 6 5 4 3
♡ 5
♢ 7
♣ J 10 6 5 4

We should double because, first, we have no defensive trick, and second, we know that a sacrifice could be exceedingly cheap, maybe cheaper than the opposition's *game*. However, now suppose we hold:

♠ Q J 6 5 4
♡ 5
♢ 7 6 5
♣ J 10 6 5

Even though we also have the same lack of defence, it is much less clear that a sacrifice will be very cheap, particularly at equal vulnerability. Also, because we have less distribution, it is more likely that any defensive tricks partner may have will stand up. Taking all this into account, plus the fact that the opposition have clearly had to guess in the bidding, it is better to pass, expecting to defend unless partner doubles. Pass also allows partner to pass when he thinks the sacrifice will not be cheap, even if he doesn't have a sure defensive trick.

Let us look at a different bidding sequence:

West	North	East	South
1 ♣	2 ♡	3 ♢	4 ♡
4 ♠	Pass	5 ♣	Pass
5 ♢	Pass	5 ♡	Pass
6 ♠			

Here our opponents have had much more room to explore and there is good reason to believe that they will make their slam. In this type of auction, sacrificing is more attractive.

Does this type of double apply only to small slams?
No it works just as well when the opponents have bid a grand slam, provided, of course, that their suit is not above the level of ours. Indeed, sometimes we will make a non-penalty double of a small slam, partner will sacrifice and then the opponents will bid a grand slam. Now, when we have shown no defensive tricks, we can double again to show a hand that has no prospect at all of a defensive trick and is very suitable for sacrificing, or pass to show a hand on which we are less certain.

'Action' doubles

This type of double is only just beginning to be played by some expert partnerships. Its basic definition is that it says, 'Partner, I am sure that we should be taking some action here. My hand has more playing strength than you might expect, but I also have some defence. You look at your hand and decide whether it looks best to you to defend or bid on.'

What sort of auction are we talking about?
The sort of auction we are talking about is when it is clear that both sides have a fit in at least one suit and when it is not clear whose hand it is, perhaps an auction such as 1♡ – 2♠ – 4♡ –

4♠. On this auction the opener may have a hand where he is not sure whether or not to bid five hearts – after all, his partner may have a balanced hand with a fair number of high cards, or a distributional hand with less high-card values. If he is too good to pass, playing normal methods he has to guess whether or not to double or to bid on. Playing 'Action' doubles, he can double to ask his partner to make the final decision.

That sounds like a good idea, but what do I do if I want to make a penalty double?
As usual, when a double has a conventional meaning, if we wish to make a penalty double we cannot do so. The best we can do is to pass and hope that partner will feel able to make an 'Action' double himself. Note that on our example sequence it is unlikely that anyone will have sufficiently good trumps to want to double unilaterally, and any double which shows all-round high cards but not trumps by definition has some suitability for partner to remove it, if he is highly distributional.

Are there any rules to help decide when a double should be 'Action' and when it is just a normal opinion that our side has done enough bidding?
This is the most difficult part of this idea. many top-class pairs are experimenting with these 'Action' doubles and they have all developed different rules for its use. One wonders how some of them ever manage to take a penalty at all! One fairly straight-forward set of rules covers the most common situations and is that a double is 'Action' when:

- it is not clear that the opponents are sacrificing; and
- our side has bid to game level in a suit.
- We are not in a forcing auction.

Could we have some examples, please?

West	North	East	South
1 ♡	1 ♠	3 ♡	4 ♠
Dble			

West holds:

♠ 5   ♡ A Q J 10 6 5   ◇ Q 6 5 3   ♣ A 7

West would certainly feel like taking some action over South's four-spade bid, whatever the vulnerability. Playing normal methods, he would probably guess to bid five hearts, but that could be very wrong. If instead he makes an 'Action' double, he can cater to the possibility of his partner's holding either of these two hands:

(a) ♠ K J 6   (b) ♠ 7 6 4
    ♡ K 7 3 2   ♡ K 7 3 2
    ◇ 7 4   ◇ A 7
    ♣ K 6 3 2   ♣ K 6 3 2

With hand (a), East would surely look at his spade holding and pass quickly and East/West would probably beat four spades by two tricks rather than go light themselves. On hand (b), his three small spades look much more suitable for bidding on and he would surely bid five hearts.

West	North	East	South
—	—	—	1 ♡
1 ♠	2 ♡	4 ♠	5 ♡
Dble			

West holds:

♠ J 10 7 6 5 4   ♡ 7 6   ◇ K 7   ♣ A K 8

Here again, West's general high cards and doubleton heart suggest defending against five hearts, but his sixth spade, when his partner probably has five-card support, suggest bidding on. So he makes an 'Action' double. East may hold either of:

(c) ♠ A 9 8 2   (d) ♠ K Q 9 3 2
　　♡ 8 2　　　　　　 ♡ 8
　　♢ Q J 9 8 3 2　　 ♢ A 1 0 8 3 2
　　♣ 7　　　　　　　 ♣ 7 6

With hand (c), East would look at his doubleton heart, his singleton in an outside suit and his minimum spade length and would surely pass the double. With hand (d), on the other hand, he has much better prospects of making five spades and would surely bid it.

West	North	East	South
—	4♡	4♠	5♡
Dble			

West holds:

♠ K 7 2　♡ A 6　♢ K 1 0 6 5 4　♣ J 1 0 4

West has a problem with this hand – he doesn't know whether North/South are bidding five hearts to make when his partner was light for his four-spade bid, or if North/South are sacrificing. His double asks his partner to help him solve this problem. He might have either of the following two hands:

(e) ♠ A Q J 1 0 7 3   (f) ♠ A Q 1 0 6 5
　　♡ 7　　　　　　　　　 ♡ 7
　　♢ Q J 7 3　　　　　　 ♢ A J 3
　　♣ 7 4　　　　　　　　 ♣ Q 7 3 2

With hand (e), West's four spades was a very aggressive action, but he has good playing strength with little defence. He would surely choose to bid on to five spades, which is likely to be a good sacrifice. With hand (f), on the other hand, West's defensive prospects are much better and he would choose to defend.

Are there any other situations when these doubles might apply?
One very useful area is when one hand has pre-empted. One of
the fundamental rules of pre-emptive bidding is that the pre-
emptor should never bid again. That is all very well in theory,
but sometimes the pre-emptor has a much better hand in terms of
playing strength than his partner is ever going to expect; he has
chosen to pre-empt in the hope that this will silence his opponents
and he will be able to buy the hand. However, if he has failed to
silence his opponents, he may know that, provided his
opponents are going to make their contract, he could safely bid
on. His problem is that his partner might be able to defeat the
opponents' contract – for he will rarely double with trumps
alone. It is one thing to sacrifice over an opponent's making
contract, but it is frustrating to sacrifice when they were not
making their game. Hence the 'Action' double comes into being.

Could you give an example of such a bidding sequence?
Say we open four spades and the next hand overcalls five hearts,
which is passed back to us. Now a double would show some
defence – say one defensive trick – but an exceptionally suitable
hand for bidding on, for instance:

♠ K Q J 10 9 7 6
♡ —
♢ J 10 4 3
♣ A 6

If we were at favourable vulnerability, we would be unlikely to
go more than 500 down in a contract of five spades, but we can't
unilaterally bid five spades in case partner, with the help of our
ace of clubs, has five hearts beaten. Hence we double five hearts
and let partner make the final decision.

Does this mean that we can't play Lightner doubles any more?
We can't play Lightner doublers in all the same situations that

we did previously. However, it is not reasonable to pre-empt at one level and then, facing a silent partner, invite a bid at more than one level above that opened. Hence in the above example, a double of five hearts would be 'Action', but if the opponents reached *six* hearts, then a double would be Lightner as usual.

Here is an example where South would have been better advised to use an 'Action' double rather than his actual choice:

East/West Game. Dealer East.

West	North	East	South
		1 ♣	4 ♡
4 ♠	Pass	Pass	?

South holds:

♠ —   ♡ K Q 10 9 8 4 2   ◇ A 10 8 7 6   ♣ K

South, not unreasonably, felt that he wanted to bid again, and he chose to bid his five-card diamond suit. He was right in that he only went 300 down in his eventual contract of five hearts, but look at what would have happened to four spades:

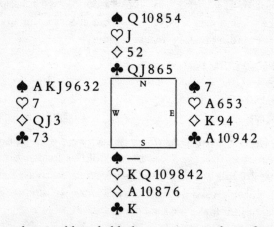

```
                ♠ Q 10 8 5 4
                ♡ J
                ◇ 5 2
                ♣ Q J 8 6 5
♠ A K J 9 6 3 2      N       ♠ 7
♡ 7                          ♡ A 6 5 3
◇ Q J 3      W       E       ◇ K 9 4
♣ 7 3                        ♣ A 10 9 4 2
                   S
                ♠ —
                ♡ K Q 10 9 8 4 2
                ◇ A 10 8 7 6
                ♣ K
```

Four spades would probably have gone two down for −500. Playing normal penalty doubles, North should have doubled four spades himself, to protect himself from South's taking further action. Playing 'Action' doubles, North would have been right to pass (as double would have suggested that South bid), but then South should have doubled four spades rather than bid five diamonds.

Some players take the use of this sort of double to an even greater extreme. The following was a problem set in one of the bidding panel features in a bridge magazine.

North/South Game. IMPs. Dealer East.

West	North	East	South
		1NT★	4♡
4♠	Pass	Pass	?

★ 12–14

South holds:

    ♠ K 7 4   ♡ K Q J 9 7 5 4 3 2   ◇ 10   ♣ —

A heavy majority of the panellists chose to go quietly, but the Canadian player Eric Kokish, who is generally acknowledged to be the world expert on this particular aspect of bidding, was prepared to double, even with a nine-card heart suit: 'Why not? Should we "transfer" them into four spades with this nine-bagger and go quietly? How wimpy! At least this way we can get a number (Lightner) *or* push on to five hearts.'

Love All. Pairs. Dealer North.

West	North	East	South
	1♡	Dble	Pass
4♠	5♣	Pass	Pass
?			

West holds:

    ♠ Q J 6 5 4 3 2   ♡ 5 4 3   ◇ K 10 5   ♣ —

The majority of the panel on this occasion chose to bid five spades and there were a couple who were prepared to go quietly. This time Kokish was on his own: 'A question of language. The sequence is not forcing on us, so if East had transferable values he would double (i .e. *not* purely penalty). If he had *pure* offence, he could bid five spades himself (given that four spades was descriptive, which is arguable). With an orientation toward *defence*, he had to pass, hoping that I would do the right thing (if there was a right thing). Double by me says only that I think it is right to act at all.'

The idea is that it is very unlikely to have a pure penalty double when everybody is bidding to a high level, so what an 'Action' double does show is a wish to do something. The corollary is that a *pass* may contain a hand which would have liked to make a penalty double, therefore the other hand now has to cater to that possibility.

Is it always necessary to have an agreed trump suit or a pre-emptive bid in order for an 'Action' double to apply?
Again it depends on our precise agreement with our partner, and it also depends on our opinion about the reliability of our opponents' bidding. Some pairs play that a double is always 'Action' if *either* side has pre-empted to game. Consider the following sequence:

West	North	East	South
—	1♡	1♠	4♡
?			

West holds:

♠ K J 6 ♡ A 7 5 ◇ K 10 6 5 4 ♣ 3 2

Again West would feel that it would be right to take some action, but he wouldn't have forced his partner to play game if the opponents hadn't forced him to such a high level, so why should he do so now? He can save himself from this guess by making an 'Action' double. His partner might hold either of the following hands:

(g) ♠ Q 10 7 5 4 3   (h) ♠ A 10 5 4 3
  ♡ 3   ♡ 3
  ◇ A 7   ◇ Q 7 3
  ♣ K Q 6 5   ♣ K J 6 5

With his good playing strength of hand (g) he would surely bid four spades, whereas with his minimum overcall and more defence than playing strength, he would pass with hand (h).

This is an example from play in the 1991 World Junior Championships.

Game All. Dealer East.

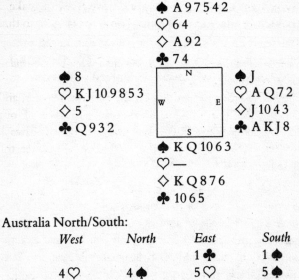

```
                    ♠ A 9 7 5 4 2
                    ♡ 6 4
                    ◇ A 9 2
                    ♣ 7 4
      ♠ 8                          ♠ J
      ♡ K J 10 9 8 5 3             ♡ A Q 7 2
      ◇ 5              N           ◇ J 10 4 3
      ♣ Q 9 3 2    W     E         ♣ A K J 8
                      S
                    ♠ K Q 10 6 3
                    ♡ —
                    ◇ K Q 8 7 6
                    ♣ 10 6 5
```

Australia North/South:

West	North	East	South
		1 ♣	1 ♠
4 ♡	4 ♠	5 ♡	5 ♠
All pass			

At this table East/West had to guess what to do over five spades and they guessed wrong. West felt that he had already expressed his hand and East had too much defence to bid six hearts. There is a widely quoted adage, which is usually sound

advice, that 'the five level belongs to the opponents'. East/West
were probably guided by this, but it was wrong in this instance.

USA North/South

West	North	East	South
		1 ◇	1 ♠
2 ♡	4 ♠	Dble	Pass
5 ♡	All Pass		

Here, where East opened one diamond instead of one club.
West was less suitable for an immediate bid of four hearts, so
instead he contented himself with a simple two hearts. When
North bid four spades, East now made an 'Action' double –
saying that he was suitable for bidding on if West thought so
too. Of course, with his shapely hand, West did indeed prefer
the idea of declaring and so bid five hearts. Now the spotlight
turned to North/South, who were undoubtedly deterred from
bidding higher in a denomination in which they had already
been doubled. However, North's hand is quite suitable for an
'Action' double, since it was unlikely to be right to defend when
he had six-card spade support. Had North or South bid on to
five spades, I wonder if East or West would have managed to bid
six hearts.

*I can see that this could help a lot on some high-level auctions but it does
seem as if there is a lot of scope for disaster.*

Indeed, it is very important to discuss with your partner exactly
when a double is 'Action' and when it is normal penalty. It is
better to define clearly when your partnership wants to employ
these doubles, perhaps missing out on some useful opportunities
to do so, than to be for ever in a fog of never knowing what
partner's double means.

Conclusion

In these pages I have tried to cover the majority of treatments of double that are in general use in tournament play at the time of writing. It must never be forgotten that the language of bridge is a living language and no doubt will change even more in future years.

In Chapter 6 we touched on the 'new-fangled' HUM systems, whereby a pass shows opening bid values and there is at least one bid that shows a very weak hand. It is yet to be seen whether this idea will enjoy widespread use. Those in authority who have the responsibility for legislating on and administering our game are often reluctant to see change and consequently such HUM methods are allowed to be played only in a very restricted number of events; so there has been little opportunity to investigate whether this idea is really an improvement on existing methods. Perhaps one day it will be more common than what we regard as 'normal' today. Each year sees a proliferation of new conventions, new ideas for the meaning of all sorts of different bids and no doubt we will see many new types of double.

Our predecessors would perhaps be surprised at how competitive bidding has changed, and no doubt we would be surprised at the developments which will surely take place in the next fifty years.